Leaving Me Behind

A Novel

Sigal Ehrlich

This book is a work of fiction. Names, characters, places and incidents are either the product of the author's imagination or are used fictitiously. Any resemblance to actual persons, living or dead, or to actual events or locales is entirely coincidental.

LEAVING ME BEHIND

Cover designed by Damon of www.Damonza.com
Cover Art:
Copyright © Shutterstock 57813955

Editing by Nicole Hornbaker Langston
Jenny Sims of www.editing4indies.com

Formatted by Polgarus Studio http://www.polgarusstudio.com/

Published by Author Sigal Ehrlich OÜ

Visit the author website:
http://www.sigalehrlich.com

ISBN: 978-0-9914007-6-8 (eBook)
ISBN: 978-0-9914007-7-5 (print)
Version 2015.06.05

For Tom, Bar and Daniel

"De ilusión también se vive."
A Spanish proverb.
(Also of hope and aspiration do we live)

Shut down, wait for the screen to blacken.

Grab purse, shove close to heart, necessary belongings.

Take one last sip of determination from the lukewarm coffee.

Stand up, straighten pose.

Walk out, close door.

Keep on walking, seal out noises, avoid eye contact.

Start car, direction: airport.

Drive. Stay focused on the target.

Buy ticket. Check-in. Board plane.

Get the hell away!

I heave a lengthened, full of missed potential sigh and resume putting together the last details of the kickass presentation for our new client. My escape plan, regretfully yet again, tucked away in my coward mental drawer – the one so packed it's about to burst.

The number of times and versions this same scenario has played out in my mind over the last couple of years would be somewhere in the comfortable zone of above a bazillion. Not today…

"Ready?" Saul's voice yanks me back from a brief "escape" lapse. I inch up to meet his eyes above my screen. Saul. Saul Cohen, my personal Yoda. Salt and pepper short do, trimmed goatee, red, wire rim glasses, pinstripe suit, as ever an embodiment of style with an old-school touch. Saul, who snatched me and tucked me under his wise wing right after I graduated from college and came to my first intimidating interview at corporate kingdom. From day one, he worked me to the bones, mercilessly. From day one, he started teaching me everything I know. From day one, I worshipped him.

Quickly, we became a team. He managed and I executed. He taught, and I drank every single word. We remained an inseparable team. Even when a larger firm lured Saul to work for them, he insisted that I be a part of the deal. The same company that a couple of years later was sold to an even larger corporation, leaving us, the employees, with more cushion in our bank accounts than we could have ever dreamed for. Yes, one of those Cinderella story companies. Let's just say that if I handle my finances wisely, which luckily is my field of expertise, I won't have to work another day in my life, *if I want*. Neither would Saul or anyone from the core team who were in the right place at the right cha-ching time.

"You're flying solo today," Saul says, seizing one of the granola bars on my desk.

"I better be." I pull out the memory stick from my PC, stand up, and redo my ponytail to make sure no loose ends are going wild.

"Took the chocolate one." His lips quirk up in a tease.

"Put that back this second! *No one* messes with my chocolate. Ever!" I feign a scowl, tucking my shirt, adjusting it inside my black, knee-length pencil skirt.

Saul chuckles lightly and gestures with his hand toward the door. We make our way to the boardroom to discuss the strategy we chose just before the show I'm about to put on to bait the new software wonder boy, gazillionaire to go for our financial consulting services.

Chapter 1
"Resolution"
Matt Corby

"Stop looking at me like I'm some gourmet dish."

"Gourmet dish?" I snort. "I'd say *maybe* the house specialty from a decent, greasy grill joint." He briefly chuckles and I continue watching Kai put the last items in his carry-on with a mildly heavy heart. His dirty blond strands fall forward to veil his forehead. He combs his fingers through the messy clusters, pushing them back. His gray eyes squint at the gigantic cameras waiting next to the almost packed suitcase. He pivots my way with raised eyebrows sensing my eyes still on him.

"How long will it be this time?" I ask.

"Missing me already, Scarlet?"

I send my eyes to the ceiling and kick my heels to the floor. They land on the bedside rug just below where I'm propped on Kai's bed.

"Scarlet, really? We're back to that? For the millionth time, I only wish I looked even a bit like her. The only resemblance between me and one of the hottest actresses out there is that we're both curvy. Only, she rocks it . . . and I don't." The last part comes out with a huff.

His lips pull at the corner into his trademark cocky smile. "Okay, don't bite my head off. So you look like her, only you're heavier." His eyes take a devilish glee.

"Fuck you, Kai."

"Oh, thank you." He grins. His smile melts into a thin line as he eyes me next. "You know I think you have a killer bod, right?"

I just twist my mouth in ridicule in place of a response. He twists his in frustration as if to say, "You're impossible."

"So, how long?" I ask again.

Slowly, cleaning one of the camera lenses with a special cloth, Kai answers, "Indefinitely." And the bastard has the audacity to smile at me with full-blown excitement. The new assignment, he tells me with way too much annoying zeal for my liking, is for an undefined period of time traveling across South America. This time, the magazine he works for as a freelance travel photographer is sending him to capture the "spirit of South America."

"I'm getting drinks," I say over my shoulder, striding into the kitchen.

I find Kai cleaning a different lens when I return with our drinks. He sets it aside as I hand him a cold beer.

"Indefinite sounds like a pretty long time to me," I say flatly, taking a long sip from my water. I tried hard, very hard, for my reply not to sound as dry and petty as it came out.

"That it is." He gulps from the brown bottle, tipping his head back, delight radiating from his features. His eyes with their tiny age signs scan me. "Hey, drop the excitement-killing face. I'm not dying. I'm just going away for a while."

I frown, thinking of how I hate it when he is on a shoot. Yep, I'm acting like some whiny girlfriend, which I'm definitely not. Not a whiner and not his girlfriend. I choose to stop nagging and instead just go with, "You jerk, you are sending me to the lion's pit alone?" Lion's pit, as in yet another engagement party we were both invited to. Another engagement party we are both less than inclined to go to. It takes him a moment to follow. His response comes as a mix between a snort and a laugh; he gazes at me amused.

"You can see it as payback for that disgustingly tacky one I had to go to *alone* when, you big shot, went to that 'geeks are us' convention."

"Geeks are us," I murmur, not letting it rub in. "Financial consulting *is* the new black." Instead of continuing our usual banter, I add, "Whatever." It's just not in me today. "You know, I just, well, do better when you're around."

He nods, sending me that stare he reserves especially for me. "Well, dear mine, life's a bitch and we're all getting screwed from time to time, so just loosen up and enjoy the ride."

I eye him for a long moment as he resumes cleaning his state of the art sacred photography equipment and shake my head.

I've known Kai forever.

When we first met, I was wearing a red corduroy overall, and he was wearing a *Star Wars* faded shirt and a map of scratches and wounds across his legs. I had puffy pigtails; he sported the wildest dirty blond mane. I was holding a Barbie, and he played with the wheel of a skateboard held tight to his chest.

It was when my mom brought the traditional welcome-coming-to-check-if-you-fit-our-standards pie when Kai's family moved to the pale green house next to ours that Kai took "big brother" custody over me. Though there are almost three years between us, throughout childhood and until this very moment we were, and still are, best friends. That is, of course, minus a couple of years in which I had the hugest crush on him and felt awkward every time he was around. When I finally gathered all the courage I had in me and told him how I felt, his playful dismissal slammed me, ending in the most humiliating pat in the history of humiliating pats on the head. It took me almost an additional year to get over that, or it might have just been me finally maturing.

It was years later, after Kai's beloved grandma passed away, that we pulled a soul-bearing all-nighter by the pier and discussed *that* incident among other emotional consuming subjects. More focused and cynical in our early twenties, we agreed to declare ourselves best friends with no benefits, none whatsoever, *ever*! So help us God and cold showers. And in the same breath made the ultimate opposite gender BFFs pack; that if, by the age of thirty-five, we were both still single, we'd marry each other. If our young souls only knew how we'd both feel by the time we reached our thirties, in terms of commitment and life, in general, they would have been horrified. Maybe even disinclined to grow up at all.

"Kai, I think it's time," I say to some indistinct point I'm fixated on.

"Time?" he asks, carefully putting his camera in its casing. The idea of Kai leaving for an extended period feels different this time. It spreads fuel inside of me, the fuel that quickly sets my courage and determination on fire. It's as if he just kicked my passive dream's ass to start moving.

"I think I'm finally going to do it." The registration flashes like lightning on his face. Kai reads me like no one else does. We don't need many words between us; we never did.

He stares at me for an assessing beat. "No offense, but I'll believe it when I see your ass on a plane."

I can literally feel it, together with the wild thud of my heart and the sudden edginess. I just know it. I'm going through with it. The plan couldn't be riper. In fact, it's so ripe it's about to decay. It had been building inside of me for the longest time. At first, the idea of giving up my comfortable life was terrifying. For ages, my dull-to-boredom existence has been revolving around my very rewarding job, and well, *just that*. Everything about my life on paper is just plain perfect, something to strive for, an object of envy. But it is all in great contrast to how I feel inside.

I am living the successful big city life. But it's all too much. And it's all too little.

The life I'm leading is a pale excuse for the one I really wish for myself. The little simple thing that is missing in my so-called impeccable reality is enjoyment. I've envisioned leaving it all countless times in my mind. The idea always felt like it would be taking a leap into a raging waterfall, not knowing where it would take me or how wild the ride would be. Thinking about it now, the fact that I wasn't complete, truly smiling from within, reached the surface by my twenties. This becoming an adult, doing the right thing suggested by society, the good-bye carefree-liberty era.

It was hard to ignore that for everyone around but me, the pieces of the adulthood puzzle had started to align. All my friends began to boast engagement rings with winning smiles and that spark in their eyes as if they'd successfully achieved their lifelong goal.

And me? I just couldn't relate to that; I didn't understand what the fuss was all about. I, hand on heart, didn't and still don't. Next were those over-the-top, ostentatious weddings, where doves were sent into the air while a string quartet played in celebration and, *ugh*, fireworks.

They all looked so happy; all I wanted to do was hurl.

And then those dreadful words, "ovulation, genetic tests, pregnancy," sneaked into my world, unwanted, unbidden, and most definitely uninvited. When those actual baby bumps showed up among my acquaintances, I was so freaked I just felt like putting on my running shoes and pulling a Forrest Gump until I was as far away as possible. Frankly, for me, a pet was too much to handle. Who am I kidding? Even a harmless cactus found its doomed death in my care. Somehow, it felt always as if it was me against society's expectations and life's natural course. Actually, truth be told, it wasn't just me; it was Kai and me.

It was always Kai and me.

And it's not a surprise that the actual wake-up call is subconsciously hollered from my partner in crime's mouth.

"I'm serious," I say in a more determined tone.

Kai keeps watching me for a short moment with knitted brows and the beer bottle's mouth next to his lips.

"Well, you know my opinion on the subject. Like I told you just about a gazillion times before, Liv, I think you should do it."

I nod and grab his laptop, starting to browse for properties to rent in this place I've been obsessively, secretly fantasizing about:

a tiny Spanish coastal town by the Mediterranean Sea. As I check out the first few houses, I think about how the idea just became an enlightenment, an illumination to the celestial of where *my life* should be heading. Now that it finally reached my recognition, I'm so pumped it feels like I can't spend any additional moment doing what I've been doing for a decade, and then some. The same thing that got me entirely withered.

The core of my burn: I want to wake up somewhere else, somewhere completely new. Explore new places, meet new people, experience life, and experience the joys of life rather than the daily comfortable and reliable, mundane routine. I just can't wait to get away and completely disconnect from all that's jadedly familiar.

"I am doing it!" I say, luminously grinning.

Kai returns my stare with a rare mixture of pride and skepticism. He touches his glass bottle to my plastic one.

"It's about time."

Chapter 2
"Wrap Your Troubles in Dreams"
69 Eyes

My eyes run over the sign on the heavy door before me. No matter how many times I've childishly snickered when I read this sign, it always has the same effect.

Dr. Schmurtaz.

Yeah, only I could have a shrink called Dr. Smartass.

Familiar rituals take place. His same ol' throat clearing, my same ol' fidgeting. The same small, cultivated argument about me not willing to dissect the one subject he's got the hots for . . . My mother.

I look out the window at the sky that lazily morphs into gray. The good head doc doesn't have to say much; his piercing eyes alone make me doubt myself and squirm in the luxurious sofa as he stares at my restless fingers molesting a little piece of paper I am ripping to smaller and smaller shreds. "I guess you think I'm running away, huh?" I say, my eyes still glued to my finger's hard labor, deliberately avoiding *the* stare I know I would be facing if I lift them an inch.

"Is that what you think you are doing, escaping?" I hate how he never really answers my questions but rather redirects my words my way, and in the most annoying, condescending manner.

"No, I'm just taking a break; a well-deserved one, if you ask me," I say while tightening my grip, maybe a tad too forcefully, around the pile of confetti I've crafted.

"A break," he says and types something in his black notebook. "In another country? For the foreseeable future? I can't see how this can be considered a break." His eyes lift above the thin framed, square glasses resting on his nose to observe me, his features as ever, placid.

"I am not running away," I almost scream at the plaid mustard and brown sweater in front of me, again, avoiding *the* look I'm sure as hell is waiting to trap me in.

Why can't I ever stay poised during our sessions? Maybe he is deliberately driving me crazy with his impassive tactic so I'll never stop treatment? So he can add a little sailboat to his lake house?

"That's the second time you've mentioned running away, and that is why I can't refrain from asking you, Liv. Is this what you feel you are doing?" Again, an aggravating, makes-you–want-to-jump-off-your-seat-and-slam-the-door-behind-you question.

When I stand up to throw my hand's contents into a leather, brown bin, I murmur, "No."

I don't think so, do I?

"I see." Low, calm, and pensive...and very much judging.

I never admitted the point he sought for me to admit, and he never really let it go, but somehow the hour ends with an agreement that even when abroad, we will continue our weekly sessions via Skype almighty. Before I actually leave the masculinity-emanating, wood scented office, he very uncharacteristically gives me a task.

"I suggest you write a journal of this journey you are taking to, ahem," he halts, coughs, and grazes his cheek's sparse growth, "To find yourself."

"I don't write; I am more of a numbers person," I say lazily, checking the time again.

"When reality is looking back at you in bold letters, it always makes more sense. It will help you better understand the path you choose and what lies beneath it."

"I'm not sure that's needed. If there's something about me, it's that I analyze, constantly, everything. This is how I am wired." That's why I am so goddamn good at my job.

"This is what I am suggesting," he mutters firmly, in that trait of his that leaves me complying, always. Sometimes I think he really is in it just for the money and if I weren't paying as much as I was, he would kick my round butt to the curb without as much as a blink.

"Since I suppose it's the last time we'll see each other face to face for a very long time, can I ask a question that you will actually answer?" I ask.

His brows unite above his rigid stare. He adjusts his glasses to the bridge of his nose and takes a bothered lungful, then nods. Seeming the far opposite of thrilled.

"Why do you never answer any of my questions?"

His planes as ever remain straight, but surprisingly, he rewards me with an answer.

"Explanations won't change the habits the brain has

established. *You* have to take on the job of changing your patterns *yourself*. An answer from *me* won't get you anywhere; it will just be a waste of your time."

Why did I even bother?

More surprising is the hint of warm expression he gifts me with before I close the door behind me.

"Two more to go," I say to myself, leaving Doc Smartass' place. "The Mentor, aka, boss, and the Firing Squad."

. . .

With Saul, I cut right to the chase. "I'm quitting, Saul." He raises his face above the screen before him, attentive although with a deep frown. "I'll be leaving the country in a couple of months. I'm finally going through with it." I observe him thoughtful as he takes off his trendy, red framed glasses.

He sets the glasses aside and gazes at me for a while. He scratches his head in an uncomfortable manner and quietly but firmly says, "I am not allowing this." He pauses long enough to make me squirm, a technique of his that I have grown to know and healthily dislike. I stare back at him quite perplexed.

"Don't you want the stars? 'Cause you'll be able to pick them in a couple of years."

I think for a long beat then shake my head. "No, I don't want them. I like them right where they are."

He sighs. "Here is my offer, Liv. Let's make a deal. I'm temporarily letting you go and will hire a replacement, but you won't officially quit and I won't officially fire you."

I start moving uneasily in my chair, removing nonexistent lint from my pants. I'm confused, trying to understand what he is getting at. Why would *he* of all people make it hard on me?

Noticing my troubled expression, he hones in on his point. "We will schedule a meeting for a few months from now, and then we'll discuss your situation. I can't promise you that your old position will be waiting for you. However, I can assure you that *a* position suitable for your expertise will be available if and when you decide the adventure has come to an end." Immediately, he adds, "You know what they say – every journey will eventually lead you back to the beginning."

His statement reverberates for an expanse of a moment in my head. I rise up to shake his hand. "It's a deal." In return, he gives me a fatherly hug and wishes me the best of luck.

"It takes courage to follow what you really want for yourself. I am proud of you, kiddo," he says with a sentimental tone.

I must admit that deep inside his offer makes me feel a little better and more confident. If this adventure ends up blowing up in my face, I would still have a place waiting for me to crawl back to.

I leave the familiar building, my second home for more than a decade, feeling as though I am taking the first step toward liberty. Waiting for a taxi, I contact a real estate broker in Spain and rent a two-bedroom beach house in a small and quiet beach town near Barcelona.

Nonetheless, what I believe will be an exhausting confrontation is yet to come, mockingly waiting for me. Time to face the shooting squad, or more precisely, my mother.

. . .

I open the rusty gate with its squeaking sound and a sweet scent greets me. I walk past the perfectly bloomed red roses, her pride and joy. This familiar smell always makes me think of that period in which spring overcomes winter. It's my favorite time of year here in my hometown, the place I am about to desert in favor of the unknown. I climb up the few stairs to the thick, wooden door that leads to my childhood memories.

"Mom, Dad?"

"In here, dear." My dad's bass voice echoes from the direction of the dining room.

I throw my purse in the kitchen and continue further into the house. My mom, clad in casual beige linen, pearl earrings, hair tight in a bun, ladylike straight, welcomes me. She holds her white wine, small drops trailing on the tall glass. My dad grasps a round and hefty crystal tumbler of scotch surrounding a pair of ice cubes. Looking my way, my dad smiles warmly and my mother scrutinizes blatantly.

"You look tired, dear," darling Mother says, wiping the corner of her mouth with a lilac cotton napkin, sitting way too straight to even look comfortable.

"Thanks . . . I work hard, you know." I start getting into my usual defensive mode when talking to her but quickly decide to hold it back before it gets too tense. Especially with what I am about to drop on her. "I am fine, Mom." I produce a thin smile, fighting the urge to roll my eyes.

"Wasn't this shirt a bit looser on you the last time you wore it? Oh well, maybe it's just me."

Although I'm supposed to be immune to it by now, I still wonder how each and every freaking time she comes up with another creative way of "subtly" asking me whether I've gained weight. She'd win the goddamn make-Liv-self-conscious

Olympics blindfolded and tied up. Me being the sole fruit of her size 6, Pilates loins, her greatest miss in life. I grew up making the most unfortunate mistake. I didn't become a perfect little version of her. The consequences of that — a lifetime of criticism and disappointed looks.

And holy mother of all greatest sins, I am a size twelve.

Kai gives my dear mother full credit for my weekly head doctor sessions. However, I believe Kai gives my mom too much credit. I know I've contributed plenty to my deep scars.

"You always look amazing, Livy; never let anybody tell you otherwise," my dad says with a wink. I reciprocate with a genuine loving beam. It's no secret that I've always been my dad's girl. I join them for a while, listening to them tell me about the week they've been having.

Him. "Can you believe the gas prices?"

Her. "I swear people in this country have lost the basics of proper etiquette. The other day…"

Inwardly sighing, I remind myself that these people have raised me and loved me for over thirty years. I repeat the same mantra I always chant in my head during family get-togethers, *keep calm and where's the damn alcohol.*

Next, they tell me about how excited they are for their upcoming trip to Prague; the one they had planned with the Bakers ages ago. Of course, my dad adds how he found the most "attractive" deal. So what if the hotel is under minor construction? It's just a place to rest your head, right? I nod, fighting my inner devil that's pulling the last cords of my patience.

I do my best to sit still and look interested, nodding and

reacting in all the right places while my message twitches on my lips, leaving me utterly restless. I play with the bun that's sitting on a small plate next to my dad's meal. As I eventually bring it to my mouth, my mom freezes, waiting for my next move. I take a bite and I know a piece of her soul just cracked. I take another bite and I can see out of the corner of my eye how she opens her mouth, words jittering on the tip of her tongue. I turn to send her a narrowed eyes stare. She snaps her mouth shut and grimaces.

I smile around my final bite. Prodigal Carbs Consuming Daughter, where did she go so wrong with me?

As moments pass by, I become more fidgety, having a hard time holding it in any longer. At a welcome pause, when they both realize there is still food on their plates getting cold, I seize the opportunity to barge in. "Listen, I've got something to tell you," I start. They trade somewhat hopeful glances. Oh for goodness' sake, it's not that; do not get your hopes up. Cupid's arrow hasn't stabbed my relatively large rear, yet.

"What is it, princess?" My dad is the first to speak, studying me affectionately. It makes me smile, thinking that even though I am thirty-three, he still calls me princess. I smile at him and can see my mom's concerned gaze out of the corner of my eye. I deliberately avoid allowing *her* stare to imprison me.

"What is it, darling, have you *finally* met someone?"

Here we go, again. Her grand wish for me, ranking even higher than me being skinny, is that I'd be *saved* – be coupled, be taken care of by marriage. It has always been a known fact; my mom's one true dream for me was that I'd settle down and start popping out descendants (while staying thin, of course). It was never enough that I took care of myself better than anybody could. It wasn't enough that by a fairly young age, I was financially secure and rocking a stellar career. The lack of a ring on my finger equaled failure in her book.

It was in one of my sessions with the good shrink that we discussed that the epitome of my resenting the idea of settling down started and ended with mother dearest.

"No, it is not related to that, *Mom*. I haven't," I say peeved. But for the sake of things to come, I add a fond smile, not willing to give the stage to any additional diversions.

"I've decided to make a change," I begin, watching their concerned yet curious expressions.

"Will you," my mom clears her throat, "start dating ladies now?"

"What?" God. "No. I'm not." Not that there's anything wrong with that, it's just not my gender of choice. Not taking into account that one drunken, exploratory moment in college, that is. Holding my voice unfazed, I resume. "I've decided to move to Spain." I pause again, letting my words sink in and take a needed breath of valor while organizing my next words and trying to serve them more palatable. My dad starts moving his drink from point A to B and back, while my mom straightens her posture, fiddling with the tablecloth on her lap. Both scan my face, trying to gather some better clarification of the explosive I've just dropped.

"That's the problem with young people that have more than they need these days. They don't know what to do anymore," my mom mutters, still fiddling with the napkin.

"You did *not* just tag me in *that* box. I can't believe you sometimes," I say, but quickly work to subordinate the temper tingling all over my skin. I should stick to the purpose I'm here to convey.

Having put my life on hold for more than ten years to work my ass off is not enough of a reason, I guess. It takes a lot of nerve, but I continue. "I have figured it all out. Well, there's not exactly much to figure out as I am plainly going to try and live my life there."

"What, as a long vacation?" my dad asks.

"Sort of. First, I plan to just travel around and get to know the country. In a way, have a break after more than a decade of nothing but work."

"I see. Are you planning to look for a job there?"

"Not at first, no."

My father's brows sink in together.

I go on about the house I have rented, quitting my job – trying to answer in advance all the questions I know full well are about to come.

"But-" my mom says, and I stop her, raising my hand. "Mom, please let me finish first." As expected, she disregards my request. Some things never change.

"But you have such a wonderful life. You have your great job, your lovely apartment, your old friends, and . . ." She takes a moment, clearly adding some dramatic padding to her next words. "And us." That last part, Oscar material. Like a pro, she ends it with an exaggerated, frustration-infused sigh.

I return her stare, trying to figure out the best route to continue without escalating to an argument, while getting annoyed quicker than I thought I would. After an extensive monologue in which I spread out my reasons, my dad steps in to help. As always.

"You do what's best for you, princess. You are a responsible, smart, accomplished adult. You should know what you are getting yourself into." He smiles warmly at me and turns to where his fazed wife is scrutinizing him with an eradicating gaze. "Jane, there are planes, phones, the internet; it's the twenty-first century. One big global village, you know." His eyes coax her down. "You are connected regardless of your whereabouts."

I mouth, "Thank you," to him. A surge of warmth, contentment, and admiration for this man twirls in my stomach. My stare softens to his smile.

"Will anything I say make you reconsider?" my mom asks as she wrinkles her nose in clear frustration, and yes, a sprinkle of scorn. Nevertheless, it is clear to us both that nothing she could possibly say would make me change my already made mind.

"No," I answer in a firm voice, trying to soften my answer with a thin smile. To emphasize just how unchangeable the situation is, I elaborate on how I've already made all the arrangements and about the fact that I've paid one year in advance for my new house.

They don't seem to fully understand why they were not involved in the decision-making process from the beginning, to which I reason with how I had to make the decision for myself to understand what I really wanted and that I didn't want anyone's opinion influencing me in any way.

"You should leave your apartment as is and not rent it out," my mom half orders. What she doesn't say out loud is evident to the three of us. It's her last try to make sure I don't completely cut off a connection to home.

"For the time being, I don't plan to, but Ma, I do intend to stay there at least for the full year I paid for." Confidence colors each uttered word with my attempt to convince us both, her and me.

I stay at my parents' a while, letting them repeatedly raise their questions and concerns. And just before I take the last step out the door, my dad says, "I really hope it will work for you as you plan, but if it doesn't, come back with your head held high. I will be waiting here with open arms."

A lump swells, thickening my throat as I hug him tightly, utterly touched by his supporting love.

Not more than a few weeks after this visit, at five a.m. sharp, I lock the door to my home of the past few years, the sanctuary I've made for myself. That simple, mundane task of locking the door has such a deep impact on me. I am closing the door on that part of my life.

Chapter 3
"This is the Beginning"
Boy

Sprawled on an antique bed, I study the room, moving my fingers across the dark mahogany-engraved wood. Still semi-skeptical as to whether the entire situation is indeed real.

I like this bed. I like this house. I like this place. *I can't freaking believe I'm here.*

I catalog every item as my eyes take a three hundred and sixty-degree tour of the room. My new home, at least for the next three hundred and sixty-four days. At the standing oval mirror, the tour stops, and for a beat, I carefully study myself. Everything about me is . . . undecided. My hair hasn't decided yet if it's straight or wavy. In the most untamed way, it's a combination of both. A few out of place waves amid strands of straight clusters of dark blond. My eyes – depends on the hour of the day, my mood, or what I'm wearing – sway between blue, to gray, to something close to the shade of raw asparagus. My mom once called it Laurel green. A color only her and her personal décor consultant would recognize.

Among all the undecidedness however, there is one thing very blatantly decided about my appearance. These, of course, would be my ever-present curves. I huff and dip my chin deeper onto the mattress.

This room, with its warm simplicity, induces a wine-in-one-hand-book-in-the-other, mellowing mood, but now it couldn't be more of a contrast to what my mind and heart are producing.

Did I make the right decision? Is this person reflected in the mirror across the room a coward, running away from something like the good doctor, so subtly, more than once implied? Or is she a confident, mature woman with a very determined plan?

Mature and confident, I decide. And uber excited.

My mind drifts to the day we hung out together, my friends (if you can call work colleagues that) at my place, each with a glass of something made of alcohol and a whole lot of fruity syrup. A group of crackling thirty-somethings, crammed up in my apartment, awaiting my big news. A smile threads to my lips as I conjure the way they were all looking at me as if I was about to validate their longtime premonitions. The keeps for herself blondie has finally lost it. All eyes were on me – a few over the rim of a glass, the rest above slightly dropped jaws.

"Well, I've never been as sure about something as I am about this. I have made my decision, and it is final. And this is an 'it was lovely working with you' soirée." I made sure to send Dorothy and Amy pointed, warning stares, knowing full well these two would be the first to speak their minds.

"Are you sure?" Chrissie eventually dared to ask, though it seemed the question just flew out of her gloss-coated mouth involuntarily. Chrissie, the quiet one among us, the one who never had an independent thought or ever bothered to speak up.

"Is that what you really want?" I just smiled dreamingly and nodded. Surprising herself and the rest of us, she blurted, "Oh, gosh, how many times have I wanted to just not come back home. Just turn the damn car around and disappear." She blushed, realizing she actually said it out loud. Albeit covertly, there were many silent consenting nods, more than anyone was willing to admit.

Peeling myself off the bed, I head to the shower, leaving my thoughts behind. While I let the warm water cascade warmly over me and wash away my concerns, I start to put together a small list in my head of the first things to do, and in the same breath, I order myself to stop. This is my thing. Lists, organizing, analyzing – the things that never really let my mind indulge in the beauty that is tranquility.

My life is nicely tacked into organized, methodical, unyielding neat lists. But the only list I actually allow myself to spend precious mental energy on right now is the list of my many strict rules I should start disobeying.

I stop the water and stand still for a few minutes, letting the last drops roll down to the floor till goosebumps start covering my skin. Wrapping a big, soft towel that smells soothingly fresh around me, I return to the inviting, vast bed. The tension gradually fades into the mattress as I drift into pre-sleep mode. And just before closing my eyes, I do what I do best, worry, *about everything.*

The unfamiliar, yet welcomed, sound of waves crashing to shore funnels through the shades and slowly brings me to resurface from my deep night's sleep. Excited like a little girl ready to accost her mother's make-up kit, I hurry out of bed.

Wrapping the thin bed sheet around my bare body, (sleeping naked, something new and liberating I explored last night) I nearly skip toward the window. I pull the sheer cream curtain aside, allowing the picturesque view in. The day is soft and bright, a perfect background to the ocean's palette of clear blues. My lips stretch in utter bliss.

I take a deep breath, closing my eyes, tilting my head back, and fill my lungs with the purest, fresh air. I slightly part the sheet covering me for the light breeze to caress my skin as I take in the magnificence revealed before me. A new sensation overwhelms me. Of adventure, tranquility, and excitement.

A glimpse of a movement in my peripheral view prompts my eyes to narrow sideways. As my mind registers the full picture, I find myself gaping at a smiling, handsome face that nods my way.

My eyes collect the visuals of the body of lean muscles in motion, running on the smooth sand. The details quickly set in place: tanned, tall, toned muscles alluringly gleaming with sweat, and the most significant ornament, one hell of a teasing, sexy smile.

He slows to a light jog and winks my way. When I realize that while I was too occupied gawking, I let go of the sheet covering me, I flinch and drop to my knees, *mortified.* Nevertheless, I still manage to catch a snippet of his lips stretching wider. Much wider. Oh, good Lord, I just flashed the guy.

Still mentally recuperating from the crime I've committed, innocent or not, there's still an exposure harassment tinting my records now. With nothing more to do about it, I turn to start the day. I shrug on a simple, navy cotton dress and my turquoise sandals. Having a mini, new-territory panic attack, I text Kai.

Me: Okay, I'm here. What the hell do I do now?

Kai: Chillax and start enjoying yourself. No overthinking is allowed, neurotic love o' mine.

Me: I love you!

Kai: I know.

I grab my bag, shove in the new spiral notebook that I've recently purchased for the purpose of putting to paper the journey I've begun, as instructed by Dr. Smartass, and lock the door behind me.

. . .

The old town seems like a great place to start. I stop my jaunt at a relatively busy, charming courtyard surrounded by a maze of narrow alleys with a white marble fountain as its center. A stone's throw from the old town square, I look for a café where I can burrow; somewhere I can come up with some sort of an unplanned plan. A slightly tattered, but charming sign draws my attention, *Café con Aroma* it reads. And really, what's better than coffee, especially one with an aroma?

The moment I set foot in the café, I feel at home. One of those welcoming, cluttered spaces in which the owner's tone emits even from the tiniest of items. A theme of books and everything antique dominates the cozy place with a dash of shabby chic décor. I take in the scent of roasted coffee, vanilla, cinnamon, and a whole lot of baked goodies with a soft smile. At lightning speed, I am hopelessly falling in love with the place.

I head straight to the counter to place an order for a large cup of café con leche. Startled, I flinch back when a flying towel hits the innocent surface mere inches from where I'm standing with a loud whipping thud. My eyes shoot up to deep cleavage and a wild mane of curls that breathes a curse. A very creative one. I have to give it to the composer.

"And eat?" The clipped question doesn't seem to be uttered to anyone in particular.

Seeing as I'm the only one waiting to be served, I offer an answer. "Ahem, not at the moment, thanks. Too early." I try to set my lips into a smile, fearing a second-wave attack. The lady turns her back to me while mumbling to herself. She continues doing so as she works the coffee machine. I can't help but gape at her, enthralled. She couldn't be more exasperated, and she has no reservations about letting the world know. She sets my order on a flower-decorated tray and slides it over to me. Her eyes are on me. However, her focus seems to be elsewhere. I murmur, "Thanks," and look for a place to sit.

A heavenly aroma indeed saturates the coffee, a roasted, semi-burned, earthy one. I take a sip and savor the taste, gazing at the mildly busy street with its buzz of people starting their day. There's a lady hanging her laundry up to dry in a second-floor window of an old gothic-style building. The florist in the shop next door to the café arranges a bundle of long-stemmed, vibrant yellow sunflowers in a bucket next to the shop's door, while people in business attire with phones stuck to their ears pass by local business owners opening their shops for the new day. I smile at the guy on the bicycle with the messenger bag who throws a bundle of newspapers tied with string to the pavement, and I turn to set my notebook before me. Opening it to the first page, I flatten the little gutter with the back of my hand. I fetch a pen and a pencil from my bag, as I haven't decided yet what'll work best for me.

Where do I even begin? A date? A date is always a good start. Telepathically, I send my beloved shrink a wish of misfortune for making me do this. Nonetheless, I still write today's date on the upper left side of the blank page. I tap the pen on the notebook and gaze outside. Nothing seems to come to my mind. I take another sip of coffee and turn to scratch off some dried grains stuck to the sugar holder. Focus, I need to focus. What on God's green Earth should I write about? I force myself to concentrate, but a disturbing, creepy feeling of someone watching me prevents that. Slowly, my eyes turn to scan the room.

My gaze doesn't just land on the person watching me; it literally slams flat on a pair of dark eyes that intensely bore into me. Instinctively, mine cast down, but there's something much more powerful that pulls them right back to the "dark source." The epitome of masculinity blatantly traces every curve and line of my face . . . and generous front. He doesn't tear his stare from me, watching me intently from across the space while waiting to be served. I shake the spell away and order myself to look the other way, anywhere.

I bite the pencil, doing my very best to focus my attention on the white sheet that now proudly holds a date. I twist my lips, absorbed with the blank page. I shift between my crossed legs and readjust to an upright position. I send my hands to my hair and rapidly twist it into a messy bun, securing it with my pen. Still sensing those dark eyes on me, I start to scribble nonsense on the page. I write *focus, dammit* in big, bold letters and retrace the lines repeatedly to thicken the words.

A shadow veiling me prompts me to tilt my head up, up to a wall of low jeans and a simple black button-down. Though, I promise you this — *nothing* about the total look is even the slightest bit simple. I trail my eyes higher, right to a hint of a teasing smile on lips that just scream festivities. He smiles with a spark and my eyes melt at the dimple sinking into his semi-shaven, mocha cheek. He looks familiar, but I can't place him. Although, how can anyone look familiar when my seniority in this town hasn't even passed the forty-eight hours mark?

Feeling less at ease with every passing second of intense staring, I murmur a tentative, "Umm . . . Hey." A glee of amusement that seems to be a product of my discomfort touches his stare. Involuntarily, my eyes take a short, detailed tour of his face. Frankly, what is a girl to do when a whole lot of attractiveness showcases before her to admire? Her only choice is to appreciate the goods, right? Anyway, any other action would be disrespectful and ungrateful to the gods of supreme male creation. And the last thing I'd ever do is mess with anything that's holy. So, drink him up I do. He is beyond handsome, in an embodiment of virility kind of way.

There's nothing refined about him. He's all rough, sharp, and dripping of sin. Tan skin. His eyes warm; luring pools of dusky brown framed by thick, black lashes. It's more than evident his nose was broken. Nonetheless, it just adds the necessary touch of roughness. And . . . hand on heart, who doesn't really healthily appreciate roughness? His dark hair seals the heart speeding deal with a crew-cut style.

"Hola," he finally answers after giving me a much more blatant scanning, a bit on the molesting side. The tip of his tongue reaches to stroke the edge of his front tooth. His look makes me think he might have been in a serious fight, one that has left him imperfectly, perfect.

"May I?" His hand tentatively inches toward me.

Ah? I gape at his hand frozen in mid-air, aiming toward my . . . hair? At this point, I literally squirm, my eyebrows melding into one, and I bite my cheek. Slowly my head tilts sideways in question. In place of an answer to my wordless muddle, he moves his hand to the pen holding my hair and gently pulls it out. A warm tremor trickles up my spine as I study him watching my golden strands as they cascade down my shoulders. I blink, more than once, and swallow hard as his eyes caress the sight of me, sluggishly trailing back to my eyes. I gaze back at him, entranced. Gone is my breath. Present is a tidal current in my stomach.

"I like it better this way," a thick, somewhat strained voice ringing with a delicious Spanish accent explains. While I'm struggling to remember what comes first, the inhale or the exhale part and how to get damn air back to my lungs, he reaches for a cluster of my now loose hair, making my attempt at breathing even more of a challenge. He plays with the lock, threading it between his fingers, watching the action attentively. If I wasn't in a seductively heated stupor, I might have pushed his hand away, or at least done something, anything. He is a complete stranger, after all. Hair or not, alluring as he is, I don't let complete strangers touch me, ever.

"See you around," he says next, letting the little bundle of hair drop back. I watch him motionless as he retraces his steps back to the counter, gives the lady at the register a heart-melting grin as he grabs his paper cup, and heads to the door. He sends me a glance over his shoulder and steps out to the street.

I absently take another sip of my coffee, this time a tad too generous, resulting in a first-degree burn of my tongue. Shit.

Did *that* just hit on me?

And I can easily crystallize my doubt by going back to the fundamentals of my so-called relationships throughout my "dating life." The prototype of the guys I usually saw/dated/was in a relationship with were, as painful as it is to admit, hotness challenged. Smart? Yes, all of them. Cute? Yep, some less, some more. Attractive? You can say that, mainly in the geeky-chic spectrum. Heart racing virile? Sadly enough, *never*.

All of my relationships, starting from my first boyfriend in junior high to the last one I broke up with merely a few months ago were always too serious, happened too fast but, yet banal and painfully so, lacked passion. Better described as some sort of an out of convenience and lack of energy from both sides consensually coupling. Life was too demanding to even have the time or will to be picky. For a very long time, I wasn't "looking for something," I was more into "settling on someone." Most of my men were always about my age, and all had the same interests as me. I usually met them through work, and it was always just too ordinary. I think I can count on one hand the number of times I had sex with the light on.

"I apologize for before." The towel whipper lodges herself into the chair opposite mine. Surprised, still reeling from the hot-stuff typhoon, I send a questioning look her way. "For being a loud mess before." She waves her hands dismissively. There is only one word to describe the spectacle opposite me. *Exuberant.* And that's putting it mildly.

"Don't worry about it," I return with a thin smile, still assessing her, and her choice to sit next to me out of the many vacant tables. My stare gets caught by her smile. With the shortest of peeks, it transferred so much. Her smile is a smile from within. By this smile and this smile alone, I know she is truly content.

"Oh, embrace it. I don't usually do apologizing," she adds; her accent vividly tints each and every word. She raises an eyebrow and lightly laughs.

Something about her makes my lips pull up on their own accord.

"C'mon, I'm a woman, aren't we always right?" She winks and my smile broadens. "Vivian." She extends her hand to me. I shake it while studying her vibrant features. She has an untamed halo of black curls, big, almond-shaped hazel eyes, and one of those sexy moles just inches below her left eye.

"Liv." I return the gesture.

"So, did you sign up for my cooking lessons yet?"

I find myself momentarily searching my brain, questioning if I was supposed to do so, if there was anything I missed.

"No?" I ask tentatively.

"So you must! Now. It's even in English . . . sometimes. You can start tonight."

Something about this person makes it hard to say no. She just pulls you in. Scratch that, hoovers you in. And before I manage to let out a single word, she adds, "It's Catalan food, muy deliscioso!"

And who can really argue with very delicious? Obviously I can't, hence my size twelve. Yep, momma's "concerns" are deeply entrenched.

"Well, I can't say no to that." My smile gets wider. I like her. A lot.

"Excelente! So, when did you move here?" she asks next, rearranging the salt and pepper shakers, and the little white vase that holds a single red chrysanthemum.

"What makes you think I'm not a tourist?"

"Tourists around here smile like the sun radiates from their throats. You, querida, have some sort of a lost Bambi air about you."

"Thanks, I guess . . ."

She laughs it off. "I like you, Liv." She glances at me and pivots to tell the girl currently working the register, "Estrellas," raising two fingers, and in a place of a thank-you, she winks.

The Estrellas, which I quickly learn are local beer, don't take long to arrive. I can't help but think she didn't even bother asking if I'm into alcohol at eleven freaking thirty in the morning. Well . . . when in Rome, *drink* as the Romans do. Vivian produces a bottle opener from a pocket in her apron. "Cheers." She winks again. I nod and take a sip.

"So, you were telling me your story." She narrows lit eyes at me.

I smile and take another substantial mouthful. Uncharacteristically, I tell her but just the highlights. When I arrived and the overall reason, more precisely, the official one I choose to publicize. Mainly, a vague, "I'm on a sabbatical, looking to improve my Spanish and to get to know this beautiful country." She eyes me for a lengthened moment, making zero effort to look even remotely convinced.

"We'll get there," she says idly and puts her bottle on the table. I don't answer and instead overtly turn to look at my notebook. "I'll let you get back to whatever I stopped you from doing." She gestures with her chin to the notebook. "So, tonight the cooking lesson, you join us!"

"I think, I will," I answer, returning her stare.

"It starts at seven, come at six thirty. That's when we start drinking." She gives me a crafty smile before heading to the back of the café. I watch her as she sways away and can't help my thoughts from drifting back to the short encounter I had before she joined me. A bulb lights up in my head. *Oh shit*, of course. Dark Intense was familiar, and it's no surprise that he acted borderline creepy. I. Flashed. Him. Earlier.

. . .

It takes me a while to convince myself to join the cooking class. Eventually, the part of me arguing against embracing old habits, meaning indulging in a comfy bed and TV, wins but only by the minimal required votes. A few hours later, I end up showing up at the café a bit after six thirty.

"She's here," Vivian's vibrant voice throws everyone's attention my way.

I wave, rather self-conscious. "Hi."

Five pairs of scrutiny-embedded eyes give me a thorough once-over. The youngest of the group, a freckled, sweet looking redhead, sends me a warm smile.

"I'm Embar," she says, inching my way for a handshake.

"Dominique Bouchon." An elegant, absurdly thin, blonde half smiles.

"Alma-Maria," says a woman with a bouncy, stylish, shoulder length 'do who seems to be my age. She eyes me with a "new female to assess" look.

"Stephania . . . Stephy," says a fleshy, sweetly smiling beautiful lady. I return the same welcoming gesture.

"I'm Liv; nice to meet you all." I smile at all the sets of eyes that look my way.

"Bon, now dzat we got formalities out of dze way, what are you drinking?" asks Mrs. Elegance, the refined blonde, in a somewhat conceited French accent. I blink, still cataloging each of them in my head.

Embar: The girl next door, with a tang of ginger spice.

Dominique: An elegant blonde, the one who should probably come with a hazard warning, not sure yet against which disasters.

Alma-Maria: Fun. Style and sass.

Stephy: A thick waist embodiment of sweetness.

"Um…" I make a quick visual survey of what the majority have in their glasses. "White wine, thanks." Vivian sashays my way, handing me a half-full glass and a wholehearted smile. She gestures for me to follow her, as do the rest of the ladies.

We all cram around a long white table in the country-style kitchen at the back of the café. Vivian ties a crisply ironed white apron around her sensually padded waist.

"So, it's going to be . . ." And she starts shooting out names of many delicious sounding dishes, ending with something "pimientos." And with no further ado, she starts puttering about on the working area all *by herself*.

Slightly confused, I look around. Just as I'm about to ask what are *we* supposed to be doing, Stephy, the epitome of sweetness, explains with an undercurrent of mirth. "We don't exactly *do* the learning how to cook thing; it's mainly Vivian doing the job. We just drink, talk, and eat fantastic food." She lightly chuckles and the rest of the ladies mirror her. "You can call us a bunch of happily heady guinea pigs."

"Oh, sounds perfect," I say. "Good food without lifting a finger. Of course, I'm in." Vivian sends me a joyful smile over her shoulder.

"I'm going to start," says Alma, the lady, and the sass. She is wearing what looks like a colorful map for a dress, one that could perfectly serve as a throw pillow fabric. That in my book would be a gigantic no-no, but strangely, she absolutely owns it.

"Say, do any of you ever feel like your sex life is a bit dull, you know, with everyone online bragging about extraordinary kinky stuff?" Alma sends us a flit, flushed glance and turns to observe her bitten fingernails. I gape at her first, and then join the rest of the ladies as we trade stares back and forth between us. That is until, abruptly, Vivian yanks our attention toward the kitchen work area.

"Oh, I have had enough with this thing!" Vivian turns, frantically cleaning her hands on her white apron, her eyes a manifest of aggravation. "I blame the media for that, and everyone who thinks they have to follow new trends," she says, her tone more livid; "trends" comes out with a spike of disgust. "Come on, if you are not trussed up like a roasted turkey, have someone calling you slut in bed, treating you like his sex toy, or better yet, slave! It's not good enough? Sex needs to involve pain

36

now, eh? Spanking, *spanking*, really? What in the name of God . . ." She stops for a minute, murmuring, "Forgive me Dios mio for dragging you into this one but higher powers are needed these days to bring back logic to some women's brains." She huffs. "What in the hell has happened to enjoying plain ol' sweet romance, loving gestures, and oh, the dreadful missionary?" Her hands fly to the ceiling at the latter part of her words. She eyes us all as if we were the founders of the Kinky-Sex Without-Borders Organization. "It seems like women's sexual expectations have been pumped up to an absurd degree. *Poor men,* I say, poor men! If you don't end up in intensive care after sex, it's not thrilling enough, eh?"

The silence in the room is so blatant we can hear the sound of the yeast dissolving in the water. I think everyone's afraid to speak. I know I am.

Dominique tsks twice and says in an airy French lilt, "Bon, I think spicing up your bedroom is *extraordinaire*." Of course, it had to be her to respond. There's a collective feminine laughter following her words.

"I guess those who need it will find it helpful." We are all floored, including said Frenchie, to hear Stephy of all people say that. We watch her for a stunned beat. Her face blends with the crimson tablecloth. Though her bust is too large, her waist disproportionally thick, and she's, sort of, too tall, it all blends into an out bursting prettiness. Flushed prettiness.

By my fourth sip, and the third declaration coming from the elated group of women, I know that I've found some new friends.

The wine and the merriment flow while the indeed mouth-watering, otherworldly dishes start to pile up on the table. All through the evening, Vivian adds more plates together with her own hilarious pearls of wisdom.

"Alors, Liv, what made you come here?" asks Dominique. She twists her lips; it's quite evident she's doing her best to appear a touch bitchy.

Wine-happy and headily much more liberated, I say, "Would you think I was insane if I told you that I chose this place because I *really* liked the name of the town?"

"Ehm, well . . . Oui!" Dominique's lips curve into a side smile.

"I'd say you even made me like you more," says Vivian as she gestures for me to scoot over with a slight shove of her rear against me. We exchange a bond-starting glance.

"Bueno, now." She claps her hands. "Alma, are you ready for the big engagement party?"

Alma-Maria cracks an expressive smile accentuated with a quick nod. I learn next that there's a big engagement party coming in a few days to which practically everyone in town is invited. Or as Vivian explains, "Of course, everyone is coming! It's such a small place; if you sneeze at one corner, then the entire town calls 'salud' in stereo."

As we say our good-byes, I'm held at gunpoint in the form of a very persuasive group of women who coax me to join them at a club on Friday in a neighboring town. Quickly enough, I learn that I should just give in, as any refusal on my part would not be accepted. So, I do.

Chapter 4
"Playing with the Boys"
Kenny Loggins

Snuggled on the porch's wooden white swing, with my legs tucked under me, my hands caging a warm cup of coffee, I breathe in the morning. Watching a flock of birds wheel and swoop in perfect synchronization crossing the cloudless powder-blue sky, I beam with a pleasant sigh. This place is the essence of tranquillity. Too rudely, I'm shaken off the momentary bliss. No, I shouldn't go there. God, I might have flushed my career down the toilet. I set the cup aside. All too soon, those qualms that I tried to keep locked at the very back of my mind march in, with drums and all.

I storm back inside the house and start what I always do when it begins. When I start to beat myself up mentally by second-guessing every decision I've ever made, I clean.

By the time the kitchen is literally gleaming, smelling of lemon and bleach, I stop and take a deep breath. Maybe now would be the time to start that journal I've been ordered to write.

And like magic, letters populate the pages quicker than I can say therapy. My phone pings me off my writing trance a quarter of an hour later with an incoming message.

Kai: How's my one and only doing?

Me: Better than she thought she would be. Met new people, going clubbing later. ME clubbing, yep sir.

Kai: Who are you and what did you do with my Scarlet?

Me: Tied her up, gagged her, and left her in the closet.

Kai: So you became a party animal and a felon in less than a week. You make me proud to no end.

Me: Doing my best. I have a Dr. Smartass session in a few days, wonder what he'll have to say...

Kai: Tell the charlatan to skip jacking off and go for drugs. I miss you.

Me: I miss you crazily! How're things going?

Kai: Great, as always. Send me your address, I got you something.

Me: What is it?

Kai: Surprise, something to help with your future.

Me:?

Kai: *evilly laughing*

Me: Can't wait.

. . .

Plight at hand – what to wear. A dilemma of a person who for far too long, or maybe not far enough depending on how you look at it, hasn't visited a club. The last time, as far as I can remember, was somewhere near my mid-twenties when Kai managed to persuade me to go dancing with him. When the evening came to an end, I was sweaty, sticky, and my patience had been pushed beyond its limit. When Kai announced he was going home with a Swedish flight attendant, I declared a much determined "not happening again." If I recall correctly, my mini-tirade was about how these places seemed to be nothing other than people drinking and dry humping each other under the pretense of dancing.

Kai's answer, of course, was a joyful "exactly," which he followed with the widest smirk.

What can I say? I'm more of a book-in-hand, talk-show-in-bed kind of gal.

My red wrap dress should do the job. The same one that artfully showcases my assets in an hourglass kind of way. Make-up: light. Mascara and blush, the universal code for, "I'm not trying too hard, but hey, c'mon, I am still a woman." Hair: as I'm about to tie it up, a certain dimple owner crosses my mind, and I leave it loose. Why? For the life of me, I have no clue. Maybe it's something in the air, or maybe I'm officially starting to lose it. Which would actually explain so many things I've done lately.

. . .

"I'm buying; what's everyone drinking?" I ask, working on acclimating my eyes to the thick layer of artificial smoke and my ears to the loud music. Truth be told, I haven't missed this much.

"Whatever is good with me." Alma-Maria smiles at me, gesturing toward a small sitting area where they'll be waiting. As it turns out, the gang this evening is the younger ladies of the group and me. My mood bumped a notch higher when I learned that Dominique would not be joining us. Yeah, I know I shouldn't be judging people on first impression but something about her brings my guards to full alert. My menace female radar, to be more precise.

Miraculously, by the time I reach the girls, all four glasses still have enough liquid in them.

"Oh, me like." Stephy licks her lips.

"It's my favorite," I say and take a sip. "Bee's Knees."

"Lame-ass name for a cocktail." Stephy giggles above the rim of her glass.

I nod, mirroring her smile. True.

"Okay, I don't know about you ladies, but I'm here to shake my lovely butt." She sets the cocktail onto a side table and saunters toward the busy dance floor.

Alma-Maria and I fall into conversation about her upcoming engagement party. When she concludes a short but heated rant about how her soon-to-be in-laws drive her crazy with the decision making on the catering and number of guests (and everything in between), with how she's one argument shy of strangling one of them or both, I laugh at the determination in her voice, slightly tilting my head back. As I meet her stare again, I catch a glimpse of someone's eyes piercing into mine. Instantly, my eyes respond, darting back to the source. Something stirs inside of me. Something that takes the liberty of controlling my blood's temperature. I slightly blush at the force of that look and the familiar person. I can't help but curiously return for more.

Sexy dimple guy is slouched on a sofa across the room, blinking lights playing a game of colors and shadows on his sharp features. He is sporting a well-worn tour shirt that stretches around his cut biceps. Okay, sporting would be putting to shame what he does to that shirt; it's more akin to royally rocking the look. Jeans and black work boots add the final hot but in a not caring much, touch. He tilts a bottle my way in greeting before bringing it to his mouth for a long swig, eyes still on mine. I send him a half trapped between my teeth smile and am momentarily struck as he crooks his finger in a nonverbal invitation. It's like having an Armani Jeans ad materialize before my eyes, and for the model to crook a finger invitingly and say, "Hop in, baby." That's how surreally attractive this guy is, and how even more surreal this entire situation is.

I shake my head with a cheeky beam, meaning: ain't going to happen, sir, I'm but a couple of drinks short from following my hormones rather than my brain. He shrugs, but his captivating stare doesn't waver.

"Liv. Earth to Liv!"

I tear my gaze back to Alma's. She looks over her shoulder, trying to figure out what caught my attention. She shrugs and asks, "Coming to dance?"

"I'll be there in a sec." I bring the glass to my lips and take a generous back-to-focus sip. I steal a fleeting glance to the cause of my short lapse only to find his eyes still boring into me. I inch up in confidence, empty the remains in my glass in one throw, and head to join my friends. Those dark and intense eyes now taking hold of the greater part of my thoughts.

The beat of the music that drums through my skin and the flickering lights induce a vibe of liberation, elation, and a pinch of control loss. I close my eyes and sway my curves in sync with the hammering rhythm, enjoying the slight buzz of the drink. I blink my eyes open to a tap on my shoulder. The girls smile at me, and Stephy says loudly next to my ear, "We are going to the upper level, there's techno music."

Now, if there's something I can't stand, it's techno music. I'm actually very much enjoying the 80's throwback they have on this level.

"I'm going to stay here for a while. I'll come look for you guys later." I strain my voice to be heard above the music. They nod and head toward the spiral staircase.

The song dissolves into another, a less hectic rhythm but still in the energetic realm. I dance, closing my eyes and letting myself get lost in the music. As my back bumps into a hard body, I pivot my head just a bit, not enough to grace the fender-bender suspect with a full scan, and murmur, "Sorry."

"*I'm not.* Please, do it again," says a voice with a hint of a tease close to my ear, close enough for me to feel his warmth hovering across my back. I peek over my shoulder and have to trail my eyes further up to meet his. When they do, a small current sparks in the center of my chest. It's *him*. It's the runner; the hair releasing, dimple owner, ad materializing guy. He gifts me with a small pull of his lips. With a tilt of his head, he asks my permission to get closer behind me.

My heart gets noticeably racier as in place of an answer I take half a step back to nearly lean on him while still holding his stare over my shoulder. Sooner than I can decide if I should let a stranger – well not exactly a stranger, yes a stranger – grind against me, he is in my personal space. Deep inside my personal space. As in, we're about to fuse into one body, close. Whether it's the music, alcohol, or my aim to disobey my letting-loose-is-not-part-of-my-game rules, I can't say, but suddenly I find myself leaning against him, dancing. His moves sync with mine, and he squats just enough for my rear to fit with his groin. His hands reach my shoulders and one of them slides down for his fingers to thread with mine. He lightly lifts our joined hands to wrap mine around his neck. His other hand sprawls on my hipbone, setting my skin on fire under its touch.

Another song comes, carrying a steamier beat to which our joined moves become searing. His spread hand pulls me closer to his broad chest, sending vibes of exhilaration to my core from where it rests. His lips hover next to my ear, touching, not touching. My nerves? Hanging in the balance. A hint of his scent reaches me. I close my eyes and breathe it in. He smells seductively overpowering, a swirl of masculinity, warm boy, and sweet. Under the liberating high of alcohol and hormones, I let myself indulge in the feeling of every firm ridge that defines his hard body. And hard, he is. *Everywhere.*

Slowly, we shift into our own rhythm, leisurely and much more passionate than the played tune or the crowd around us. I let my head fall to rest on his chest, sensing his breath through my hair. A wave of heat washes over me, spreading from deep inside to every hidden part. A wave that comes to life with the move of his hand to rest mere inches below my navel.

All too soon, something stops this thing, this new thrilling zone I've been so easily seduced into. I turn my head to look at my dance companion. My hand still draped around his neck. I catch only a glimpse of his jaw and of someone talking to him. He curtly nods and his body stiffens a notch. I take it as a cue to slide my hand down, back to my side. As we reluctantly detach and I turn to face him, our eyes lock with a potent intensity that leaves me ill at ease. Holding my stare firmly captivated, he leans in, slowly descending toward my lips. I watch him with my breath held back. He inches some more and leaves a soft kiss on my lips, turns on his heels, and follows the guy who just interrupted whatever we were doing on the dance floor.

Stunned, I watch him leave toward the entrance. Dazed, I make a mental assessment of what I've just been a part of. Random words and phrases run through my head. *What came over me* and *cheap* are the ones to conclude the race. And that kiss? With an urgent need to cool down, literally and figuratively, I start toward the bar.

"Water with ice, *plenty of ice*, please," I request from the slender, brunette bartender with the distinctively red lips. She smiles at me, taking her time as she runs a cloth over the wooden surface that's separating us. She seems to enjoy some inner joke. My eyebrows pull in as I wait. Her grin doesn't fade while she reaches for a wide glass.

She sinks the glass into a chopped ice tub and says, as though to herself, "Yeah, that's what happens when you dance with *him*." My eyes squint to hone in my stare at her, creases now decorating my forehead.

"Excuse me?"

She doesn't answer, just hands me the cold glass.

"You're new around here, huh?" Her smile turns into a calmer line, an annoying one. I nod. She gives me a quick once-over and turns to the buffed guy, sporting a buzz cut next to me.

"Yes, handsome, what can I get you?"

Bothered, I empty the contents of my glass in two long swigs. Deciding I've had enough adventures by myself, I go look for my friends.

. . .

Slowly, Alma-Maria brings the car to a halt next to my house. My hand clasps around the handle, but I stay a few minutes more with the girls in the car. We laugh hard, exchanging last witticisms that can only be as funny when alcohol, fatigue, and elation are involved.

"Good night, Liv," they chorus through the rolled down windows as they finally drive away.

I get ready for bed on autopilot. My brain is working on getting back to neutral territory, fighting weariness and the last remnants of adrenaline while conjuring snippets and the scent of *his* body, and how it felt against mine. God. I roll my eyes at my reflection in the mirror and resume brushing my teeth. We were practically outcoursing in public. His hand was one short movement from touching my . . . actually *touching* me. I spit into the sink, rinse my toothbrush, and put it in a cup. A stranger, in a mother-loving club!

I splash cold water on my cheeks and observe my damp face with hard eyes. I'm not so sure how well I'll survive this new "liberated me" thing I'm trying. Though the first taste, I must admit, was way too good.

As I finally sink my slightly throbbing head onto the plump pillow, my ears are still ringing. A teasing dimple packs my mind, decorated by handsome roughness – or the other way around, who cares, really.

It feels like someone is pounding my head when I jolt at the sound of my phone hollering from the pile of clothes I deserted on the bedside bench. It's rather late, very late, for anyone to be calling. I answer and my lips curve into a warm smile to Kai's low voice.

"It's late, Kai. *Really* late."

"You want me to call some other time?" he asks, his voice softening. I purr something that sounds close to "nuh."

"Where are you these days, anyway?" He's been traveling around South America; it's hard to keep track.

"In this small city bordering Chile and Peru. Miss me?"

"You should rent the house next to mine as your new hub. That's how much I miss you." I close my eyes, burrowing deeper under the covers.

He snorts. "What have ya been up to?"

"Are you sitting?"

"More like lying, in the dirt."

"That'll do. Wait, you're doing what?"

"Waiting for this fucking turtle to move."

A short laugh erupts from my lips. "Since when do *you* take photos of reptiles?"

"I'm doing this as a favor for this guy; his wife should be in labor any day now. So, yeah, I'm lying on the fucking ground waiting for the damn turtle to move his ass."

"Thrilling. So, I've started a cooking class."

"Did you release a public service announcement to the good people of Spain with the new hazard?"

We chuckle in tandem. The combination of preparing food and me usually ends up in catastrophe, to put it mildly. My last attempt led to a representative from the fire department visiting Kai's apartment. Needless to say, I might never hear the end of that one. To my defense, I do *sublime* ordering in.

"Honestly, there's not much learning going on. We just sit around, talk, and taste amazing dishes cooked by a not less amazing person."

He hums a brief confirmation.

"They are a pretty great bunch. We've connected quite quickly. Well, most of them."

"So there's someone you don't like. Already?" he asks, and I hear clicking sounds coming from his end. Must be the damn reptile finally moving his ass.

"Well, there's this Frenchie, Dominique. I don't know her story yet, and I know I shouldn't be so judgmental, but she has malice written all over her face. I got the vibe she might not be all that crazy about me, either."

"Then, tell her to fuck off," he murmurs through additional clicks in the background.

"Oh, you'd definitely want to tell her that yourself. She's so your type."

"Starting to sound interesting."

I hear him light a cigarette. One thing about Kai that I could really live without.

"Older and beautiful in a cold kind of way," I continue.

"Intriguing."

There's a soft whistle like sound of a puff.

"Okay, my dear, it's late and I'm tired. Here's the deal; you should quit playing with turtles and come visit me. You'd love this place."

He chuckles. "I'll see about that. Go to sleep."

Chapter 5
"Seduce Me Tonight"
Cycle V.

Ten hours of deep sleep and a hangover-ish later, I'm trying to get up and take control of the mess that's me. *Thank you alcohol, once again*. You never fail to abuse me. I'm not the most skilled alcohol consumer – never have been and possibly never will be. A single glass is enough to get me buzzed in a "looking at the world in brighter, comical colors" kind of way. Pathetic, really.

I almost hug the inanimate machine that works hard to brew my coffee. Sacred device. Running a short checklist in my head, I remind myself that in a few days I'll have my first cyber Dr. Smartass session. For a brief moment, I dread what I'll tell him when he asks what I have been up to so far. It would probably be something along the lines of, "So, doc, I'm here, been doing next to nothing of importance, and haven't written much. But hey, I got myself a bit obsessed over a sex phantom who keeps appearing out of thin air and disappearing just the same way." I can't seem to get young Sir Phantom out of my mind or what's commonly known as "I'm pretty horny and he's undoubtedly got the goods." Apparently, he opened up an appetite in me last night. Maybe he is not exactly all that. Maybe it's just my dry spell attacking my mind, turning him into something I'd have a great time fantasizing about. Though, to his defense, I must admit he does seem to possess the potential.

I settle on the porch swing, my bent legs serving as a docking surface for my notebook. I take a long appreciative sigh, observing my surroundings before bringing the steaming cup to my lips. The whitewash railing that surrounds the porch blends seamlessly with the house. It's a perfect relaxing den in a form of a beautiful beach terrace. I sink deeper into the large, white crochet pillow seat and watch the blue sea in front of me. Perfection.

A failed attempt at writing and a teacup later, I head back inside. I pull on a pair of ankle crop jeans, loose fit, ivory draped top, and electric blue flip-flops with the thought of visiting my new friend, the lovely café owner, and running some getting settled errands while I'm at it.

First stop is a too-long-due-to-excessive-bureaucracy stop at the post office to get whatever it is that Kai sent me. Twenty-friggin'-five minutes that I would never get back later, a brown package tied up with string in hand, I make my way to Vivian's. Curious, I shake the content in my hands, which doesn't give any clue to what it might be. Feels like some solid, heavy object. Kai mentioned something about helping my future. I shrug and push open the shabby, turquoise door of the café, sending the door's bell to announce my arrival.

Vivian's face above the register brightens as she spots me. I acknowledge her with a thin smile as I make my way toward the counter. Vivian, in a floral embroidery pattern dress, hands a skeletal, pale lady a takeout bag and her change. With a gentle glee, she sends the lady on her way while I wait, watching their exchange.

"You." She turns to me as soon as her customer leaves. "I have a huge favor to ask." No preface, no hello. A favor. Okay . . .

"Good morning." I grin at her. She casually gives the clock above the main door a short, pointed peek.

"Noon to some of us," she deadpans, turning her back to me and places a white ceramic mug under the coffee machine's spout.

"Shoot, ma'am."

"Are you busy tonight?" she asks with her back to me, still fussing with the coffee machine.

"Nooo . . ." I answer tentatively, stretching the one-syllable word.

"Good, 'cause I'd like to ask you to . . ." Her words are swallowed by the evaporating noise the steam nozzle produces. Finally, she turns back to me with a cup of coffee. She sprinkles cinnamon on top and slides the warm beverage my way. One that I didn't ask for, yet is so welcomed.

"Well?"

It takes me a moment or two to gather that she expects me to answer a question. My eyes narrow at her as I take the cup of telepathically ordered coffee into my possession.

"I didn't hear your question with all the noise," I clarify the part she'd apparently missed.

As we make our way to sit in what has become my regular spot, if two and a half times can be considered habitual, she says, "Any chance you'd be willing to cover for me for a couple of hours at closing time?" She gazes at me for a brief beat and goes on. "Everyone I know *and trust* will be at the engagement party, and I understood from Alma that you are not coming."

I nod, appreciative that Alma understands that I wouldn't feel comfortable coming to such a big event where everyone has known each other for forever, and the few people I know are going with a date.

"Sure, I don't see any reason why not," I say over the rim of my delicious cup. "Is there anything special I should know or do?"

"Not really. I don't expect many people to come in since all the locals will be at the event. I'll teach you the basics of the coffee machine and register. Anyway, really, it should be a quiet evening."

I nod.

She takes a deep breath, biting her lips, her eyebrows furrow and she freezes for a long, contemplative moment. "Oh, I'm waiting for a couple of wine bottles to be dropped off. I guess you'll just have to wait till the guy comes in and then close up. Pity you're not coming to the party, though."

I shrug.

"What's that?" She points her chin at the brown-paper wrapped box next to me. I'd almost forgotten about the package.

"Something Kai, the photographer friend I told you about, sent me," I say, unwrapping the object in subject. Vivian observes me while blabbering about her outfit for tonight and about how her husband refuses to wear a tux. *Oh, good God, KAI!*

I wouldn't be surprised if Vivian's laughing outburst is heard all the way to Peru or wherever this "gift" came from. My own laughter shortly tops hers as I read the note it came with.

My one and only,

For best results, rub three times a day. Perhaps HE will bring dear mommy the craved grandchild. K.

P.S. It's an ancient fertility god, in case you didn't know.

As our hoots subside, I explain to Vivian my mom's obsession with me getting a ring on my finger, the accompanied family thing that usually comes with it, and Kai's love of ridiculing that same desire. I shake my head at the wooden sculpture of an ancient creature holding his massive, erect pride and joy. At the same breath, I try to wrap the salacious, glorious art piece back up with the brown paper it came in.

"Ooh, I like him," Vivian says through a wide grin.

"Each to his own, not judging." I twist my mouth with mischief.

"Your friend . . . the wooden trinket with the wood doesn't do it for me, sorry." She laughs, nudging my arm.

"He's the best. I adore him," I say smiling, yet missing Kai deeply.

Though Vivian made operating the café's appliances and register sound easy, she had understated what was involved. We spend the next hour going over the highlights of running the place. Being the nitpicky, anal creature that I am, I bombard her with questions as I take notes, which she dismisses with a hand wave and something about, "Once you try it, you'll see how easy it is." When she finally acknowledges the concern I radiate, she just pats my arm, covertly rolling her eyes, which is not subtle enough, as I do notice it and respond with a frown.

"Don't sweat it, Liv. Honestly. If *I* can operate this thing, anyone can. Anyhow, like I told you, it'll be quiet." Her eyes take a devilish glee. "Just like me during my first time."

I raise an eyebrow, and she winks at me.

"Silent and bored."

. . .

I take a last look at myself in the mirror, making a mental note to buy new clothes. Most of the current clothes I own are composed of conservative black, white, and some "daring" gray corporate attire. I'm in desperate need of casual, vacation-esque appropriate apparel. I add a thin, braided black belt to the soft granite maxi dress I went with. Slipping into my leopard flats, I grab the set of keys Vivian gave me earlier and start toward the café.

Vivian apparently knew what she was talking about. Besides a smiling, charmingly wrinkled grandma with a purple bob who took her time drinking a glass of Cognac while watching the quiet streets, no patrons came in.

I polish every available surface to an almost blinding shine. I refill every paired set of condiments and end with an ardent sweeping of the floors. Bored to soon plucking my eyelashes out one by one just for fun, I decide to play kitchen and make the one (and only) dish I'm capable of cooking. A cake I baked in the past that actually got a few compliments, and better yet, no one rushed to the hospital after tasting it. In my book, that's a winner. I head to the kitchen, trusting that the doorbell would warn me of any customers or the delivery guy I'm waiting for.

Quickly, I mount the two squeaking stairs to the back kitchen and start with the cupboards, assembling all ingredients needed for my job at hand. I pour some flour into a measuring cup and slowly stir it in with the ingredients already swimming in a large silver bowl. Done, I turn to put the flour back onto a high shelf, only for the bag to slip from my hands and land with a thud while puffing a white cloud that ends up on the counter, my face, and my neck. *Shit.*

A light layer of white dust covers everything in my near radius from the fallout. Cussing seven ways to Sunday, cleaning the little mess I've just produced, I flinch at the sound of the front doorbell. I grab a towel and quickly work to clean my hands. To the sound of heavy steps nearing me, I call out, "I'm in the back kitchen, be there in a sec." I try to clear the last flour remnants from my fingers and throw the cloth to the counter. To the sound coming from the crackling stairs, I turn my stare to the swinging half-door and my next breath is sucked right out of me. Our words collide as they meet in a stuttered staccato.

"Oh . . . it's . . . *you.*" Him.

"It's . . . um . . . *you.*" Me.

The corner of his mouth slightly inches, and like the times we met before, he shamelessly drinks me head to leopard flats. His semblance of a smile stretches enough for his dimple to make an appearance as he takes time passing over my healthy chest. I fidget, not able to take my eyes off him. The thought of how it felt to press against *his* chest at the club jumps to my head, adding to my unexpected discomfort and light warmness, everywhere.

We both freeze for a lengthy beat, with our stares quickly morphing from a collision into an active blast furnace. To an involuntary fierce heatwave, I break the connection, but as if enchanted, my eyes go back at their own volition. His return the stare and run across my face, becoming alight.

He side smiles at me and says, "I'll just put these away," gesturing at the bottles of wine in his hands. I nod and follow him with my gaze. Fitted gray tee, loose, low-riding jeans, and black boots all perfectly wrap his impeccable tall and lean body. This guy. *This guy* I had not so long ago grinding against me is beyond sizzling, and *young*! I take a deep get-your-act-together-now breath and resume whisking the batter. *I better focus on whisking rather than on grinding.*

Hearing the patter of his footsteps return from the pantry, I make a production that would pass even Spielberg's deft eye of concentrating on the concoction before me. Mr. Scorching Dimple halts at the counter a few steps from where I labor over the bowl. He takes the deserted kitchen towel and steps closer. My heart jumps in double pace as he gets even nearer. Just like the times before, creamy dark eyes leisurely trail over me. For a stolen moment, I glance at his lush lips as he moistens them by running his tongue slowly over them. Oh, the slow, sensual motion. *Self-composure, Liv.* I inwardly scold myself to focus on the gooey mix instead.

Reaching my personal space again, close enough to send my body into a frenzy, he says, "You have some . . ." and his hand that's holding the cloth stretches to remove something from my cheek.

Oh, shit, the flour!

It slowly, very slowly, as if he's in the process of seducing that part of me, descends down to where my cleavage starts and sweeps ever so lightly, *there*. His eyes stream from the hem of my dress to my lips as he says, "There." His lips tug at the edge. "You're clean." I need to swallow over the drought that is my mouth. Yep, but first I need to close my parted lips. Reflexively, I bring my hand to my now burning collarbone to the spot he'd just so adeptly cleaned. A true talent.

I don't make a sound, nor an additional move for that matter, as he observes me, seeming undecided.

"Now I'll need to clean you again. Did it deliberately, didn't you?" His dimple appears in tandem to a low, brief chuckle.

It takes me more than it should take a relatively intelligent person to realize what he means. When my sensually overloaded mind finally acknowledges that I littered my chest again with flour with my semi-clean hand, I mumble way too quickly, "Oh . . . no, no. Thank you . . . no! I will do that. *Thank you*."

The dimple deepens, and his eyes amusedly read my ridiculous agitation. We stay still: him boring into me, as if calculating a pounce. Me: bothered, and flustered, and well, let's face it, feeling dumb.

"I'll leave you to get back to your . . ." He motions with a tilt of his chin at the bowl. He adds something under his breath that's too low for me to catch. He gives me one last thorough gaze, shoves his hands into his jeans pockets, shrugs, and makes his way to the door. I gape at his toned, ridged, and exquisitely tanned forearms. He sends me a stare over his shoulder, that contemplating air still decorating his eyes.

"Adios."

"Good-bye," I say, stunned, troubled, and mostly disappointed that he just left.

For the life of me, I can't figure out where this disappointment is coming from, but it's here and it's annoying to a degree that overwhelms me. Irritated, I take a pause and prop my hands, holding each side of the bowl, and let my head fall. I inhale deeply, attempting to push out whatever it is that's seizing my head…and body. I take another lengthy breath and a spark of realization makes me straighten with a start. *The doorbell didn't go off.* Instinctively, my eyes fly to the kitchen's swinging door and crash into his, watching me. Words are beyond me. I tilt my head in question, a question mixed with much surprise and a dash of excitement.

For some ticking moments, we hold a feral charged stare down. I eventually break eye contact due to a wave of heat that covers my cheeks that I try to conceal by looking at the bowl below me, only to notice that I've accidently sunk my fingers into the batter. Great, just great. I find myself ill at ease waiting, not sure for what. His next steps are the only sound in the expectant silence surrounding us. It's clear he is making his way toward me; alas, I cannot face him due to my more than evident edgy-basket-case condition.

My chest tightens as the notion of him standing close behind me registers. There must be but a sliver of space separating us now, as I can clearly feel the heat his body radiates and hear a hint of him breathing next to my ear. A warm shiver trails from the very top of my arms all the way to my toes as his hands gently move to hold my shoulders. Slowly, they trail down, rising my skin in their wake. My breath is held and everything inside me springs tight when his body presses just enough for mine to absorb his warmth and to feel the firmness that I recently learned is part of him. He brushes my hair over my shoulder with his chin. A tidal wave of heat spirals below my waist once his warm, minty breath hovers closely, and his bristled cheek softly grazes my flushed one.

He halts for a long moment.

"What are you doing?" I croakily breathe.

"Waiting for you to stop me." His voice is rasp and low and reaches to every single part of my alert body.

My heart and mind speed at a hazardous velocity while I struggle for my next move. The last thing I want is for him to stop. I don't say a word but blatantly press back against him, resting my head on his drumming chest. It's less of a spoken consent and more of a silent agreement. Whatever is starting between us is happening nonetheless, with my undeniable blessing. His hands reach mine and gently pull them away from the bowl I'm still holding on to. One of his hands leaves mine for the towel. I feel his hard chest and ridges move against my back as he works to clean any remnants of the batter from my hands. He then tosses the towel aside and moves his hand across my stomach to curl around my waist. In one fluid move, he turns me; my rear meets the counter and I'm facing him. My eyes drop to the floor. His hands grab my hips from both sides and lift me to sit on the space I've just worked on. I lightly jerk, landing on the counter, and my lips reflexively part. He inches closer, parting my thighs and making my dress lift up as his hips settle between them. A spot of heat spreads by the touch of his finger beneath my chin as it tilts my head to meet his gaze. I blink into his feral browns.

"I wouldn't do anything you don't want me to do."

My mind is saying: "You can do anything you want to me . . . please do, *everything*, now!" But my lips don't move. I am just staring at him, boiling up inside, my cheeks and my entire body feels as though a ring of fire surrounds me. With my continued silence, he slightly crouches, twisting his face a little. Ever so slowly, his lips brush mine. His mouth hovers there, waiting. Pulled into his force field and into the lustful moment, I move my lips closer; close enough for the tip of my tongue to stroke his upper lip. In less than a breath, his hand threads into the hair at the back of my head while the other cradles my rear and both push me into him. Our mouths crash and his tongue coaxes my lips to gape. I part them and close my eyes, drunk on his taste as his tongue sensually traces mine. His taste streams most divinely from my enthralled tongue down my throat to the rest of me; velvety, warm, and deliciously smooth, just like savoring a sharp, sweet liquor. His hand at the back of my neck eases me deeper into our kiss that's on fire while the one holding my rear slides under me, teasingly grazing, and almost driving me to the edge as his fingers press against my sensitized skin. Red-hot desire is taking over me and my legs wrap around his firm ass, pressing him closer to me. Every sensible thought flies out of my head as I devour his mouth, indulging in his touch. Our tongues unite in haste, vigorously.

Too abruptly, both his hands move to my shoulders in tandem to his mouth gradually disengaging from mine. He leans his forehead to mine, his breath as my own, heavier. He takes a deep mending breath and says to my lips, "How about we take this somewhere else?"

He tips back to look at me, waiting for my reply. The only motion I am able make at this stage is a small nod of consent.

It takes less than a few hasty moments for us to lock up and leave the café. Once the night's breeze hits me, my courage takes a step back and I start processing what has just happened. Reason kicks in now that he is not between my legs. Many questions and warning signs parade through my mind, but before I'm able to speak up and call off whatever I've just agreed to, he hands me a black, shiny helmet. The promise in the gleam of his eyes makes me overrule any objection my mind has just raised.

"I've got only one; you put it on."

I do as told and peek at the beast that firmly stands on two wide wheels before us, gleaming in metallic black under the streetlight. I take a second look at the blown out of proportion metal bulldog, and my stare bounces to my dress; these two don't exactly harmonize. There's a low chuckle from right beside me. I lift my eyes to meet his, crinkled at the edges. He motions for me to climb the vehicle that any minute now will force me to spread my legs wider than I've spread them while I had its owner between them not so long ago. I frown and consider the best tactic to mount the bike elegantly. There's a mumble behind me, and before I know it, I find myself being plopped onto the leather seat. As gracefully as possible, I lift my leg to straddle the bike, somehow adjusting the crumpled heap of fabric that is my dress between my now exposed legs.

"Your place?"

I bob my head under the helmet. He tips my visor down with a tap of his finger and gifts me with a light smile before mounting the bike. Fascinated, I watch his butt as he settles in front of me and kill the urge to grab a fistful of that alluring firmness. As it comes to butts, the mister here seems to possess a perfect one. Or at least it appears that way from the tight fit of his jeans.

The engine roars as he squeezes the throttle, and my heart jumps at the escalating sound. He takes my hands at each side of his waist and tugs them to wrap around him.

"Hold on tight," he orders and takes off.

Hold on tight. He couldn't have said it better. When it comes to him, I have no problem obeying that command. In fact, I'd probably obey just about anything he said at this point. Seems like he could easily sweep me far away from my safe shore. Heck, he already has.

Adrenaline is rushing through me together with desire, excitement, and anxiety. I close my eyes, pushing away the red alarms flashing in all shapes and sizes in my head, and focus on the cool wind brushing against my bare legs and the wide, firm body I embrace tightly. At the next red light, he reaches his hand to caress my exposed knee, sending an electrical current that's been steadily buzzing within me to intensify. The ride, luckily, is short enough for my courage not to fade away completely.

His hand burns the small of my back as we silently make our way to my doorstep. It slides to hold my hip, not exactly helping my wobbly attempt at unlocking the door. The beat of my heart hastily develops as we stand in my living room facing each other. I can almost hear the air crackling with the carnal charge looping between our bodies. All of a sudden, it feels like the place is too illuminated and the bed far, too far inside. He inches closer and my breath hitches.

"So, what would you like to do?" I croak out the dumbest question to have ever been asked. In my defense, I might be freaking out a tiny bit. It's not like every day I have a younger, hotter than I'm not sure even what guy in my house for the sole purpose of carnal knowledge. Talk about a one-night stand baptism of fire.

His lips wickedly crack up at the side, and his eyes meld into mine.

"Which version of what I want to do would you like?" The question on my face prompts him to elaborate. "A cultivated answer or the one on the tip of my tongue?" Thinking about the many possibilities that the tip of his tongue holds, I swallow hard.

"Tip of your tongue," I say softly, looking at him from under my lashes.

"Well…" He licks his lips and I follow the simple motion, captivated. "I want to taste you so I can finally put to rest my recent obsession with how you taste."

Flames erupt from my insides out. I feel them pour out of my cheeks, neck, and chest. Dumbstruck, I just lift one finger and squeak, "Excuse me." And bolt to the bathroom. Holy. Momma. Of. God.

I hold the sink, more accurately grip the sink, white knuckles and all, from both sides. I drop my head down. What have I gotten myself into? If there's something I don't do, it's these kind of "adventures." Hell, I've never gotten into bed with anyone before knowing him, or at least having some basic background about him. Good. Lord. At least known his friggin' name! Yeah, I know, I know, my grand plan is to stop being . . . me. Too calculated, always doing the sensible thing me, but in my book of basic morals, this doesn't translate to converting into a slut.

Holy shitness, he has an obsession with the way I taste?

Just the mere thought of him saying that brings my nipples and the organ on the menu to full attention. Truth be told, I've never been much of a lingual mining in my cave kind of gal. Never worked for me and always made me feel uneasy, unnecessarily stressed when I obviously needed to be relaxed, and sadly enough, it not even once brought home *the* gem. Yet, I must admit, it's a nice, natural creative way to "oil the wheels," alas, that's it. I raise my head to look at myself in the mirror. Flushed would be a compliment to the display echoing from the reflective surface.

My eyes roam south and a frown settles on my face as I give my stomach area a hostile glare. If I go through with the "tasting" and whatever else is on the Carte du Jour of the forthcoming degustation feast, I'll have to be naked next to *him*. If I recall correctly, and boy, *do I*, he has a perfect, swimmer kind of bod. Tanned, lean muscles, everything in place in the right sizes and shapes. Self-conscious doesn't begin to cover how I feel right now.

Sadly, *very sadly*, I start looking for a good enough excuse to give Mr. Professional Taster to call the whole thing off. There are too many doubts outweighing the let-loose, get naked, and ride that man like you've never rode anything before sizzling desire within me. And just before I'm able to come up with something better than, "excuse me but I'm a complete moron and I'm about to pass on *you* . . ." a knock on the door jerks me back from my white-flagging thoughts.

"Can I come in?" his voice funnels from behind the door,

coated with determination.

Unfortunately, I am a grown-up woman who cannot just close her eyes tight and pretend that whatever's making her uncomfortable might just go away. Instead of an answer, I just unlock the door.

"Are you okay?" His eyes run over me somewhat concerned. I downcast mine and my stare lands on his wrist. And what a wrist it is, wide and bronze, and perfectly virile. The metal watch wrapping it gives it an extra masculine look. Even his wrist is goddamn attractive. He takes a step toward me and ducks just enough to level our eyes. Okay, how on Earth do I answer that . . . am I okay? Certainly one of those must-lie situations.

"Um . . . I was planning to take a quick shower."

He doesn't waver his stare from mine as he extends his arm to turn the shower on. I watch him static as he checks the water and sink my teeth into my cheek when he gestures for me with a small tilt of his head and a swift eyebrow raise to get in. The way he looks at me alone has the power to chase my sanity away. Sensing my discomfort, he leans toward me, slightly tips his head, and ever so slowly, his lips meet mine. After the second jaunt on my lips, his tongue urges entrance and with the parting of mine delectably reaches in. His hand moves to cup the hollow below my chin while his other slowly makes its way from my collarbone to the side of my breast. My nipple hardens, sending a calling of want in the direction of my thighs with the soar of his hand, just a hint of a touch, over the swell. I let out a soft breathy sound as his thumb moves to graze the edged peak.

His hands slide toward the hem of my dress at my thighs. His fingers gently graze my skin as he slowly lifts the fabric up over my waist, my chest, and above my head. I stare up at him with my lips agape, part in desire and part in enchanted daze. He tips back and gazes at me as I stand before him in my lavender lacy underwear. The earlier self-conscious feeling is now overpowered by how bothered and hot for him I am. A feeling that intensifies as he relishes the sight of me with unmistakable heat. He bends to leave a soft kiss on my bare shoulder and gestures for me to step into the shower.

I stare at him and my brows squint. I swallow hard and ask, "Um, are you staying . . . hemm, joining?" The latter part of my question comes out mildly raspy. A hint of amusement touches his eyes. He slowly shakes his head and his lips join, crooking up at one side.

"I'm watching."

I'm not sure what takes over me, but whatever it is, it's burning and exciting and new. He leans his hand on the mirror behind me, and in an expanse of a blink, his lips taste the skin right below my ear. A tiny bite makes me flinch and for my middle to simultaneously tighten. I close my eyes and let my head fall back. *Everything* inside me aches for his touch. Somewhere along the trail of kisses and bites he leaves while advancing toward my shoulder, he manages to unclasp my bra. He sends his hands to the straps that now lay loose on my shoulders. With the tips of his fingers, he grazes my skin, dragging the straps to fall down. He crouches and treats my panties the same way, sliding them down, leaving faint marks on my skin. He inches up, his eyes re-meeting my glazed ones. He offers me his hand and I take it with mine. It's barely a step away, but he still leads me to the open shower that has thickened the air around us with humid warmth. There isn't even a steam-covered glass or any barrier for that matter to hide behind; I'm completely and tensely exposed to him. I take a step back with my eyes glued to his. I can't seem to be able to break the intense lock he has on mine.

He leans with his shoulder to the wall, raptly watching me as the water cascades down my body. I close my eyes and tilt my head back for the warm stream to wash over me. As I flutter my eyes into his, my lips part in response to what's spoken through them. He sends his hand toward me and with the pad of his finger he slowly follows over the routes the descending water drops leave between my breasts. My skin rises, electrified by his touch, the water and this entire scenario webbing me in. I hold my breath while warm waves tidal from my core to the rest of me. I watch him, burning, and my mouth turns dry as he absorbedly retraces the trail of the droplets on my skin.

It's almost inhuman how I crave for this man's touch to cover me, *all over* and *now*. He takes a step in and stands under the water with me, fully dressed. Without any warning, his hands reach to hold my face and his lips urgently cover mine. He pulls me into the connection of our mouths, leaving tenderness aside. He pins me to the tiles and brings his leg between mine, covering me completely with his firm body as the water keeps pouring above us. The rasp of his warm fabric clad body teases my skin and a soft moan floats from my lips. His damp shirt whispers teasingly on my oversensitive nipples, the warmth of his hands hovering my flesh. I'm breathless and he hasn't even really touched me yet. His thigh presses against my middle and I gust out another strained moan.

He doesn't kiss me next; his mouth raids mine, frantically, feverishly, keenly. I counter him as eagerly, my fingers lace into his wet strands and tug him into me. Pants entwined with carnal hums waft through our searing connection. My heart is racing, that warmness in my lower body expanding, reaching deeper, making me heady with desire. He sucks my bottom lip between his, still holding my face near. Gradually, he leans back, breaking our mutual trance. The grasp of his teeth slightly pulls my lip back. He releases my lip, inclines back to brush my mouth with his again, and drops to his knees. My eyes fall after him. Water flows over his face, enhancing his masculine, hard features. Droplets cling to the long dark lashes fencing his raw-brown stare that's holding mine with irresistible intent. With his eyes still boring into mine, he sends his palm to cover me and for his thumb to slowly sink between my folds. I almost lose my balance as a surge of heat runs down my spine to where he touches me. Still gazing at me with a stare that takes over the control of my breathing, he starts caressing ever so slowly up and down my cleft with the pad of his thumb. I close my eyes and a breathy, "Oh, God," rips off my mouth as his tongue takes the place of where his thumb just marked. God, it feels so good. So. Good. Electrical streams play at my spine. *I guess it's all about the miner after all . . .*

I shiver all over, *all over*. Shiver and pant. Heatwave after heatwave wash over every inch of my skin. My legs lose the ability to hold me, and I grab the shower arm for support. His tongue spreads flat and firmly presses slowly over me, and over again, and again. Up and down, and slow and heavenly. And inside and out, and, "*Oh, God . . .*" I whimper as he sucks my clit into his warm, fleshy lips and the aroused spot responds in an overpowering spasm. I let out an uncontrollable moan followed by hurried pants as his strokes and suckles become even more profound and precise. He grabs my leg behind my knee and drapes it over his shoulder, spreading me wider for him while helping with my balance that has become a great challenge. At the verge of torture, the sweet ache is too much to bear. I let out wild cries, no longer in control of myself as his tongue works harder and deeper each time over my burning flesh. I peep at him with hooded eyes and parted lips, watching his mouth against me and it's almost my undoing. As his finger joins and the pressure grows, I feel myself build up, on fire.

When a second finger fills me in steady slides and his tongue moves to circle the very point that delightfully throbs with my desire for him, my orgasm doesn't reach me, it crashes upon me, strong and hard. I'm shattering into a million heavenly pieces.

Spiraling in ecstasy, I lose my ability to stand on my own two feet, but I don't have to as he helps me straddle him on the damp floor. I let the waves of my after bliss wash over me, resting my head on his hammering chest as warm water caresses us both, steadily dropping from above. When I finally come back to the present, secured in his embrace, I realize just how surreal the situation is. I am naked. Sitting astride a complete stranger, who's probably much younger than I am. Still recovering from the ultimate orgasm he just gave me . . . and *he is fully dressed.*

There's a tense strangers-post-coital ambiance between us or at least on my part. Before facing him again, I try to think even how to start any sort of communication.

From hardly ever having sex with the light on, to: "Oh hi,

71

thanks for the mother of all orgasms. What was your name again?" *Oh, my parents would be so proud.*

When I finally collect some courage and inwardly whisper: "Oh hell, here goes," I lift my eyes to meet his and learn that there isn't any discomfort on his side, quite the contrary. Together with that, I also learn that there's a very evident bulge, almost tearing the seams of his jeans, between us. His hooded eyes fall to my lips that reflexively part and his mouth follows suit. He starts with soft fluttering over them, tenderly. He then licks my bottom lip, sucking it into his mouth. His fingers comb into my wet hair and tug it back for him to reach deeper inside my mouth.

Water trickles between our engaged lips, adding a moister, steamier sensation to our fervent tasting of each other. I fist his shirt and he leans back, helping me rip it off him. My hands dart to his firm, defined chest, a mass of slabs covered in divinely taut and warm skin. Both my hands leisurely graze south to the set of six ridges decorating his flat stomach. His hand cradles my rear; he squeezes it, pulling me closer till his jeans-clad swell is between my parted legs, instigating a new spark of want. It's as though the orgasm he just gave me had only opened up an appetite for more. I want, *need*, more of him. Much more. Hastily, I reach between us to unbutton his pants. He sends a hand to the back of his jeans, producing his wet wallet. Behind my back, he fiddles with his wallet then throws it to the side. He lifts his hips and so do I, allowing him to better maneuver in pushing off his pants. His impressive, thick, and alluring erection makes its début between us. Oh, *good Lord, he goes commando!* Search no more, I've found the very epitome of sexy.

His thickness brushes me as I hover above him, my breasts in tandem become swollen and tender, again. I shamelessly watch his hand sliding a condom over his slick length, utterly burning for him. He grabs me by my waist next.

"I need inside you now," he rasps in a low, warm delicious accent wrapped voice. And not long after his last word is uttered, I'm placed right above him. He moves his hands to prop himself below me, waiting for me to take the lead. Flushed, hot for him like I've never been for anyone in my entire life, I. Slide. Over. Him. *Oh, God.* I gasp.

"Fuck." He shuts his eyes and drops his head back. I move to adjust, to absorb his wide length. It takes a few slides for the hunger woven aching, burning delight to replace the discomfort. And he pulls me closer to him. My breasts graze against the light hair on his chest. I seek his mouth, desperate to slide my tongue against his. Our mouths unite feverishly. His hands cup my breasts between us, and he firmly massages them. I let out a cry into his mouth. He circles my nipples with his fingers, teasing me. His mouth follows to suckle ardently, giving each of my nipples enough attention to drive me almost over the top for him. I let my head fall backward and he grabs my waist, positioning me to arch back from where we join. This new angle allows him deeper, much deeper, and I moan loud, with him filling me completely. I bite my lips and mumble incoherent sounds of pleasure. His right hand stays holding my waist while his left cups my cheek and his thumb slides between my lips. I lick the pad of his thumb, sucking it into my mouth. His thrusts become more fervent, and so are my counters to absorb him better. The deeper he reaches, the more forceful his strokes grow. My sensitized swell delectably spasms. And he pushes into me. And his grip becomes painfully pleasant. And I rub against him. And we move fanatically. And our moans come out stuttered. And in unison, we drop our eyes to watch our connection. And we pant heavily. And his last thrust sends us both to gasp and shudder.

For a long serene moment, only our heavy breaths color the silence as we come down from the mind-blowing experience we've just given each other. My head rests on his shoulder while our heartbeats calm. As the moment of landing back to reality arrives, he kisses my lips briefly and helps me up. He turns back to get rid of the condom and I quickly grab a towel to cover myself, my well-entrenched self-conscious reemerging from a lengthened slumber.

When he turns back to face me I say, "I don't have a dryer."

Glancing at the pile of soaked garments, I'm suddenly conscious of what I just said. Applause please. Best opening line after the rawest of sex, no?

His lips twitch at the corner and he shrugs, "I'll just put them out to dry." *That means . . . he's staying? Oh, shit.* He grabs a towel from the counter and secures it around his hips, all afterglow and nonchalance. The very opposite of me, minus the afterglow, of course.

"I'll come out shortly," I say, subtly asking for some privacy. He nods and heads out with his wet clothes huddled in his hands. I watch as this perfection of a man walks out and closes the door behind him. I take a deep breath and turn to look at myself in the mirror. There's a lot to be said about sex, and one of them is how *I* never knew it could be so . . . mesmerizing? Phenomenal?

Fucking electrifying? Yeah, fucking apparently *is* electrifying.

My eyes gleam and my cheeks radiate a soft pink. I'm delightfully, wearingly, and utterly spent. I shake my head thinking that I still don't even know his name, but then again, maybe it's just better this way. I'm pretty sure this otherworldly encounter of the fleshes was a one-time occasion. Sad but true. Sad but the exact way it should go.

I step inside the shower, again, closing my eyes and letting the water drop on me, warm and relaxing. I take the longest shower in the history of mankind, trying to put off the moment in which I'll have to step out and face him again. What do I even say?

"Hey, so you are like a pro in the oral art department . . . eh? How about tea?" I snort, take a reassuring breath that does shit to actually soothe anything, and open the door. It's time to face the musician.

A smile creeps to my lips when my eyes land on him. He's fallen asleep at the base of my bed. His upper body rests on the mattress while his legs are still planted on the floor. It's quite obvious that he didn't intend to actually take a nap. I take a step toward him, hug my waist, and gaze at him. His arm drapes over his face, and his long lashes caressing his hard, defined cheekbones. A light stubble exquisitely adorns his square jaw. His chest rhythmically rises and falls. I swallow hard, watching the dark, soft trail leading to the hem of the towel still secured around his waist. The thought about how some images represent an era pops into my mind. The *We Can Do It* lady representing the World War II effort. Madonna wearing the Gaultier bra – signifying sultry is epic. Miss Lewinski's blue dress – manifesting adultery is the shit. Well, this guy like that, in my bed, represents sex is better than any legal, or illegal, rush.

The exquisite visual journey I take wakens the appetite I've blissfully sedated less than a long shower ago. And what a shower it was. This one skyrockets to the first place in the history of divine showers. Heat takes greater momentum as snippets from the "cleansing" in subject flash before my eyes. Hungrily, I watch the person who labored exquisitely *hard* to make me "shine." An inner debate starts between my head and the rest of my instigated body. Wake him up and beg for more vs. control myself. The verdict rendered is based on the logic of probably never having this opportunity ever again. Enjoy it while it lasts. In other words: have that candy, life's too short.

Shutting the mental door on my manners, suppressing desires, mature behavior, and oh, self-respect, I slowly inch toward the bed. Contemplating how to approach the waking process, I decide to, ahem, return a favor, as they say. Slowly, I sit on the bed next to his handsome, serene self and reach ever so gently to remove the towel hugging his loins, allowing myself better access to wake him *up*. Having a fist full of the towel in my grip, with my head tilted toward my target, I hear a soft, embarrassingly petrifying chuckle. I'm not sure what occurs first, the eruption of flames that cover my face or the jump my eyes take to meet a very sexy, amused gaze. I must look like the girl caught with her hand about to violate the cookie jar. *Oh Lord, the road to ultimate self-humiliation never ends.*

The grin he sends me next, after I timidly smile at him, might have just disintegrated the stiches of my skimpy panties. His eyes turn to bore on me in tandem to his tongue playing with the edge of his front teeth. My heart starts to beat in double pace as the notion of what's coming next registers. My lips gape and the center of my body burns as, with my eyes still glued to his, I slowly lean in toward him. Abruptly, he breaks our promising eyes connection to look out the window.

"Mierda!" He jolts to sit. "Shit, shit." He jumps from the bed, his towel dropping to the floor, leaving him all bare and glorious before me. I try not to, but end up staring, of course. Who can really blame me? Some things were artfully crafted to be stared at.

"I'm going to miss my flight," he murmurs, his fingers push through his hair as he looks around the room on edge. "Where are my clothes?" He finally addresses me, bringing me back from my momentary fixation on him. I shake my stalking off.

"Um, just a sec," I say and head to get his clothes that are hung on the ropes on the back balcony. Not a second passes from the time he snatches the semi-wet pile from my hands till he starts shrugging them on, ridiculously hurried. Between buttoning his fly and shrugging on his shirt while almost losing his balance, he sends his thick metal watch a peep that results in a string of impressive swear words in Spanish. Something clicks in my head and I take a step back, fold my arms, and watch him. I have an urge to start clapping for the performance he is giving me. Best. Flitting-a-one-night-stand-excuse. Ever. The guy should quit his day job and pursue an acting career.

Buckling his belt, he finally lifts his mesmerizing dark eyes to acknowledge me. He takes a wide step to reach me, and before I realize what's going on, his hand cups the back of my neck and pulls me into one hell of a kiss. I gasp, and his mouth presses harder. I get sunk into the kiss until his lips gently release me, his hand still holding my neck. His breath mixes with mine as he says, "I'll be traveling on business for the next three days. I want to see you when I get back." Another kiss and I watch the door as it closes after him.

Wow, *he is good. He is really good.* Not only has he managed to sneak away with no awkward, "Good-bye, hope to never see you again," but he actually made it somehow look promising. Not to me, anyway – maybe it would have worked on some pathetic airhead. *It's not going to happen.* He didn't even bother to ask for my number. I roll my eyes; a smile laced with scorn forms on my lips as I head to rip the sheets he slept on off my bed and throw them in the washing machine. I can't even cross this one off my bucket list because I couldn't have even allowed myself to imagine what he just did to me or even to imagine just . . . *him.* Even if I tried hard, really hard . . . still a solid no.

And what the hell is a delivery boy doing going on a business trip anyway. God, what a player. But who really cares. I've started experiencing the goods this new country has to offer, which, after all, was the crux of my grand plan.

Chapter 6
"The Morning After"
Meg Myers

Sluggish doesn't even come close to describing my morning. If I took it a tad easier, someone might need to check for my pulse. Literally and figuratively, I indulge in every moment as it passes, from drinking the extra froth, extra espresso shot, and extra cinnamon coffee, to the extra jam with my roasted butter scented croissant. Alas, this serene mode is plagued when I check my phone. There are more than ten missed calls and one message screaming in bold letters from the screen. A sense of alarm enfolds me before I check the message. My worries direct in two separate paths – one leading to my parents and the other to Kai. It's quite sad, come to think about it, that I actually worry about three people on the entire planet. Oh, Dr. Smartass would have a field day with this one. When I check the number and the text that follows, any worry I might have had diminishes.

Vivian: are you alive?

I cinch my light, white cotton robe at the waist and melt onto the porch swing, returning Vivian's not at all exaggerated number of calls. Before I manage to add "morning" to my "good," missiles of words assault my ear, "worried" being the most popular one.

"I'm fine, Vivian, really!" I say, still trying to understand what lies behind this sudden concern for my wellbeing.

"Well, you sure left enough evidence for me to imagine all the horrible scenarios possible."

I try to think about last night and what "evidence" we might have left. Oh, heavens. I'd be mortified if there are any clues related to me molesting a younger stranger.

Feigning casualness, I say, "I'm not sure I follow."

"Not that I mind, it's really only about you being fine. But you left quite a mess in the kitchen."

Oh. I think fast for the best excuse to be given in place of: "I left in quite a hurry because I was practically about to be banged on your precious kitchen's counter. See, the thing is, someone had to taste me."

"Oh that, I'm so sorry. I had such a terrible stomach ache and couldn't wait to be home and rest." The ease at which lies have recently flown out of my mouth is beginning to scare me. The qualities I've been enriching myself with since setting foot in this place are overwhelming. I'm turning into a liar and a slut, in record time. Just splendid.

"How do you feel?" The concern laced to her question just makes me feel even worse about lying.

"I'm better, thanks. I guess it was just something I ate."

"Well, as long as you're okay," she says, thankfully not as stressed as a moment ago. "Then come over, I need a coffee companion."

I smile and assure her that I'll be there soon.

. . .

"Ice coffee?" Vivian asks, not really waiting for a response as she's already starting to fix said beverage. I just shrug with a thin smile.

"You look good," she says before turning to the blender. She pours the coffee, milk, and ice into the container.

"Thanks," I say, having a little mental debate of "to eat or not to eat, that is the question" while surveying the display of baked goodies separating Vivian and me. The noise of the blender crushing the ice cubes and amalgamating the brown and white liquids into a marvelous mocha hue fills the café.

"So . . ." Vivian asks and her next words are swallowed as she flings the little button for one last quick whisk. "Came last night?" She turns to me, holding the container in one hand. "I saw the bottles in the pantry."

Came last night? Bottles? THE DELIVERY GUY! Oh yeah, he came last night. He *came* hard, with me. I also came, no less hard, twice. I really hope not everything that buzzes inside of me reflects to my new friend. And shit, I missed his name, she just said his name! Snaps of visions from last night burn before my eyes, visions to which my body responds in a heated wave.

"Um, yeah . . . the delivery guy dropped by." I play casual as if I were auditioning for the role of my life.

"Delivery guy?" Her brows join. She hands me a cold, tall glass filled with her iced production. "He is the owner of the vineyard. Okay, more like runs his family's vineyard. You must taste their wine; it's heavenly. I'll get you a bottle so you can try it."

And hence the business trip. So, he wasn't lying after all? I'm not sure I like the way my insides react to the notion. Though I mentally beg Vivian to shed further info on the still nameless best sex I've ever had, she changes the subject while gesturing for me to follow her.

We take our seats at one of the little tables just outside Vivian's café, blending with the sound and ambiance of the lively street. After she tells me a bit about her night at the engagement party, including what each of my new friends was wearing, I ask her, "So what's everyone's story. Better yet, what's Dominique's story?"

Vivian's dark curls turn my way. That beauty mole below her eye lifts with the rise of her cheekbones. Her hazel eyes smile as she says, "She's quite a character that one, eh?" We trade an agreeing smile.

"Well, she's the bored wife who has been left behind. She's a diplomat's wife, the French ambassador."

I gaze at Vivian as she tells me Dominique's story.

"She wanted to become a diplomat herself. She actually worked very hard to get to that point. But she gave it all up when she fell in love with one. She dropped everything for Gérard and became the ultimate helpmate. After ten years of playing second fiddle, she started to get bored and frustrated. A hazardous combination for any woman who spends many hours alone while her husband shines. Especially doing what she had dreamed of doing for years." Vivian sighs. "When he got the position of the French ambassador in Spain, Dominique decided she'd play wifey only part time. He lives in Madrid, she lives here, and only on really special occasions does she accompany him to events. He visits her every other weekend, and that's kind of it. I guess they lost each other along the way."

"Sad," I comment, fiddling with the straw in my glass.

"And your story, will you tell me the real version?" Vivian's eyes challenge mine.

I take a sip of my cold drink, slouch back onto the wicker chair, and with my eyes trained ahead, I say, "Well, I came here since *I* didn't want to lose myself along the way." I turn to her. "Let's just say I wanted to take a breather from my career and from everything familiar. I looked for the one place that seemed to be a piece of tranquility and, funny enough, came across Serenidad. So, here I am, and that's basically my story in a nutshell."

"You're not young," she states and my eyes fling to hers.

"Gee, thanks!"

She laughs it off. "No boyfriend or husband left back home?"

I shake my head. She presses her lips together and eyes me suspiciously.

"Well, you came to the right place; nothing better than Spanish men." She grins at me.

So, I've noticed.

"Not looking for that, either. I'm here to enjoy your beautiful country."

Now her lips turn into a deriding arch. "Everyone's looking for that, consciously or not. Everyone. *That* makes people happy."

"I still believe that true contentment comes from deep inside of you."

She huffs. "Maybe when someone is deep inside of you." We both chuckle in unison, and chuckle some more after she tells me the story of how she met her man. That one goes on for an hour.

An hour of recounting a tireless pursuit that spanned over half a decade, which led to a long, solid marriage and two children. Just before I leave, Vivian stops me and goes to fetch the wine she told me about before; the wine the alleged delivery guy brought.

After taking the longer stroll back via the beach, I get home right in time for my first cyber session with my shrink. I settle in front of the screen, camera aimed at my face, and reluctantly press the video call button. Of course, he is there waiting with his trademark diamonds pattern, mustard sweater, and hair slicked to the side.

"Liv." Curtly.

"Dr. Schmertaz," I say, getting accustomed to the screen interaction.

"How have you been so far?"

I trace the rim of the wide ceramic mug resting on the desk before me, contemplating what I want to tell him.

"Well, I must say that the acclimation part went smoother than I even hoped for."

He nods.

"I met some new people. And my new place already feels like home."

He types something into his black notebook.

"That's good," he says, his attention back to me.

"I did a couple of things that are out of my comfort zone." I take a sip of my coffee and meet his eyes on the screen. Sir Poker Face actually seems intrigued. "I went out clubbing. And quite quickly connected with some new friends." My lips rise involuntary. He keeps looking back at me, static. "Nothing extraordinary, besides," I comment flatly. Um, unless you count having a complete stranger in my house going down on me in broad daylight in a steaming shower. I squirm in my chair just thinking about it.

"How did you leave things with the people back home?" he asks solemnly, getting right to the crux.

"Most of them I said good-bye to in person, like we discussed."

He nods, not a twitch of a muscle.

"How did you feel about saying good-bye?"

I inhale and reach for a piece of deserted paper left next to the keyboard. Distractedly, I fold it in half, then fold it again, and start tearing it apart piece by piece. A cough from the monitor yanks me from my absorbed assault of the innocent paper. I fist the white ruins and send my eyes to the open window saying, "Nothing." I return my stare back to my therapist. "Nothing. No emotions, positive nor negative, while saying good-bye to everyone."

His expression demands me to go on.

"It felt fake, the hugs, the pretense of somehow feeling anything."

He adjusts his glasses and leans back into his brown, leather armchair.

"I was even unaffected saying good-bye to my mom and Saul."

"And your father?"

I contemplate his question for a long pause.

"I guess I could say there was something. I can't exactly describe it, but there was definitely something there."

He nods again and types some more on his notebook. I can

just imagine the title of his notes: Cold Hearted Bitch Strikes Again. We've been through this virtue of mine so many times before. I'm surprised he might still think anything would change. No matter how many diplomas he has decorating his brown plaid walls, he is still a brain therapist not a Voodooist.

"How about your friend?"

I follow his eyes as they search his notes.

"The photographer, Kai?"

That's an easy one. "It's different with Kai. I'm used to not having him around all the time. In a way, it's like we never really say good-bye."

"Right." Deep breath from the stoic authoritative figure on the screen. "Have you written in your journal?"

I bob my head and a soft, "Yes," floats from my mouth on an exhilarated note.

"About parting from people?"

I shake my head. "Not on that subject, I didn't."

"Can you try to for our next session?"

"I can give it a try . . . but I'm not sure I have it in me." His head rises and his stare penetrates my shield, even from behind the monitor. "We've discussed it so many times before. I just don't feel this attachment to people. I can move on in a blink of an eye; I move on in less than that."

"Experiencing as many changes in environments and detachments from people as you've experienced growing up could cause an emotional trauma. Of course, it's not trauma per se, but many repeated situations in which you face contradictory emotions at times leads us to hide behind what's commonly known as emotional guard. You've developed a mechanism that deters you from letting yourself get attached to people so when you eventually have to leave, you won't be faced with the dejected emotions."

"I'm really screwed up, huh?"

"Liv, a normal rationalization is that good-byes are an unpleasant experience and escaping it is good. There's nothing wrong with feeling this way. But you need to understand that not every relationship ends, and you need to let people in even with the risk of eventually letting them go."

Once we end the call, I remain seated and gaze outside at the spectacular blend of pink and gray that is the evening sky. I stare at the day as it darkens into early evening, thinking about the good doctor's last words. Beside Kai, who's always had a constant part in my life, I haven't really let anyone in. Not even Aden or Kevin, both men with whom I had the longest relationships of my adult life.

I bring my eyes back to the room and they land on the wine bottle Vivian made sure I took with me; the bottle the "delivery guy" brought. The bottle the guy who's been starring in every nocturnal thought I've been indulging in lately. I decide to have a taste of it. If it's anything like its owner, I'm in for one hell of a tasting experience.

Twenty minutes later, I still let the dark liquid deliciously flow through my mouth as I swallow the last of my glass. I'm not a wine person, but without a doubt, I can declare it was more than good. And it just brought back that night I spent with Nameless Guy full force to my head. Every twitch of lips, every motion of a muscle, every intent stare, every breathy pant, every shiver – every part of complete ecstasy.

Chapter 7
"You Can't Always Get What You Want"
The Rolling Stones

I'd be shamelessly lying if I said I wasn't giddy all through day three, post "I'll be traveling on business for the next three days. I want to see you when I get back." I'd also be boldly uttering lies if I said I hadn't thought about that night, or him, for a substantial amount of my waking and not so waking hours over the past three days. Thoughts that stormed into my mind, vividly, and pulse rising. Snippets of him on his knees below me. Of his handsome features covered by trails of water. Of his mouth on me. Of those magnetic, heated dark eyes piercing into me.

The biggest lie of them all would be if I said I hadn't touched myself every night since, thinking of him. The truth would be though, that it didn't even come *close* to the real deal. Seeing that I can't get him off my mind, and maybe since I couldn't really get off, the thought of him somehow reaching for me hasn't left me. Not on day three post *him*, not on day four, and ridiculously so, not even on days five, six, and seven.

Albeit, on early evening of day seven as I'm making my way

to Vivian's, I decide to finally ax this mini-obsession I've been nursing throughout the week. It was what it was. A. One-night. Stand. The best one in the pantheon of one-night stands that shall now be declared the night my O had a hangover. And as such, be nicely filed away as a momentous event in my sexual history, and as of now, be put to rest in peace. Amen.

I push open the door to Café con Aroma flinging the bell to ring. One of Vivian's employees, a slim, smiley redhead, grins at me and tilts her head in a gesture toward the back kitchen. I nod at her with a soft beam and head to meet the ladies, aka my new friends, for another "cooking lesson."

Before I even make it to sit at the table next to Alma, Dominique is passing a glass of white wine my way. I smile at her and at the rest of the ladies crammed around the table that's already packed with an assortment of mouth-watering dishes.

Stephy, the embodiment of sweetness, in a Pakistan-esque brown and turquoise embroidered dress wears the naughtiest grin. She takes a dramatic sip of her glass and lifts her eyes to look at us. "Let's all take a respective moment of silence and mourn the latest rumors about recalling millions of 'pocket-missiles' following the discovery of a faulty part," she says, ending her comment with a charming snort-laugh. "I can just imagine how frustrated the customers are with their battery-operated boyfriends failing to function during action."

"Poor ladies, now not only can dzey not trust men to do the job, the machines fail them, too. Ooh là là . . . C'est pas jolie, my friends," says Domonique flatly.

Vivian's laughter comes from the kitchen working area. She turns to us and humoredly shakes her head.

"So Liv, what have you been up to?" Embar asks, nudging me with her elbow.

"Not much, yet. Just taking it easy. I guess I've been acclimatizing." *Possessed by erotic thoughts, you know your usual humdrum.*

"So, I was arguing with Gustavo the other day . . ." says Alma, drawing all of our attention her way.

"Already arguing?" Vivian asks with a wide smile. "I'm still licking the frosting off my lips from that delicious cake I baked for your engagement party."

Alma's response is a thin smile. "I was reading this article the other day about Beta man."

"Hold up, what's *beta man?*" I interfere.

"I guess the best way to describe it would be men who prefer for the women to be in charge of basically everything."

My brows sink in. Just one sentence and she's summed up all of my past relationships.

"You mean pussies," Dominique deadpans, and we all snort.

"Anyhow, when I told Gustavo that I'd be more than okay with him being at home while I take care of the providing part, he told me that I was crazy. And what kind of a man did I think he was. He actually got offended."

"C'mon, he is Spanish," Vivian admonishes in a fruity tone, untying her apron. "Our men don't cry when they first meet the world, they bang on their chests and roar."

A collective feminine chuckle rolls around the table.

"I think it's endearing that some men would do that; let their woman be dominant. It shows they have a softer side," counters Alma.

"Pfft. You never want your man soft," Dominique chides and our grins grow.

"Right there, ladies, a life lesson for you," Vivian says, beaming.

Another round of chuckles follows.

"I'm with Alma." Stephy nods and her shiny, heavy fall of dark hair bobs with the motion. "I think these beta men possess quiet confidence over cockiness, and what's more important, they see their woman as an equal, or the boss."

"Color me chauvinist," I state, taking a quick swig of my sweaty glass. "But I need some alpha in my man. Tried the other option and it's like drinking an instant coffee. It's nice, does the job, but not wakening. Not fierce or strong."

"I couldn't agree more with Liv," says Embar in freckled seriousness. "I had a couple of dates with this guy who I was very attracted to and couldn't wait to have him . . . make me call for the divine."

We all side smile at her. I bring another spoon full of exquisite seafood paella to my mouth and pat my lips with a napkin. "Well, let me tell you, *alpha*, he wasn't. After he made me barely call for the altar boy, he started talking about emotions and shit, telling me how he felt closer to me now that we made love. And he wanted to cuddle! So, you know what? Thank you, but no thank you. Give me an alpha, who'll throw me on the bed and do a better job communicating with my clit than talking about goddamn emotions. Now, pass the olives!" Her nostrils flare as she commands Dominique to slide over the little plate.

"Amen to dzat!" Dominique declares while executing the order with the widest of grins. It's a bobbing head dog display around the table as we all take part in nonverbally agreeing with Embar's sermon.

. . .

It's a breezy warm evening. A dark blanket already covers the skies, and the air smells of sea, tranquility, and bliss, so I decide to walk home. Work off the glass of alcohol I had, let the delicious food absorb better, and enjoy this beautiful, *beautiful* Serenidad night. The saying 'you can lose yourself in a wonderful place' comes to my mind as I marvel at the beauty before me. Because, hands down, this place is a slice of paradise.

I choose to enjoy the longer path home, the one via the beach. Taking off my sandals, I let the chilled, white sand cover my bare skin. Taking a content lungful, I let out a giggle reminiscing about the topics of tonight's gathering. I think about how comfortable I feel around these ladies, and how my new home truly feels like home. This little town – with its wealth of charm, beautiful seaside, alleys, and narrow passages – is like a passageway to uniqueness. So different from the busy and diverse city I used to call home.

Funny enough, the only thing I miss, the only person I really miss, is the same one I missed when I was in my real home – Kai. I miss Kai. Truly miss him. But then again, I always do because he is always away. Along these pleasant thoughts, I work hard to push away those of a certain guy who has put me under a spell. The one I've pledged to exorcise from my mind earlier this evening. My nameless one-night stand.

As I turn toward the illuminated path that leads to my home and a few neighboring houses, both my eyes and my heart take a plunge upwards. My heart at the direction of my throat and my eyes to the four stairs leading to my door. Someone is sitting on my stairs. I narrow my eyes, trying to get a better view of whom it might be. It's a guy given the broad figure. I can clearly see a dark suit over a white button-down and a tie. My heart begins to drum in my chest with an undercurrent of anxiety in a "there's a serial killer at my door" kind of distress. But as I take the next cautious steps that gets me closer, the drumming turns to a loud, unsteady hammering timbre. All of a sudden, my steps feel wobbly, and I start playing with my hands, lacing my fingers together to attempt to stop the nervous current.

The high light at my porch's roof falls in a soft halo around the guy who's apparently waiting for me. He sits on the last step, his legs bent, slightly gaped, resting his feet in the sand. His elbows are on his thighs and he leans slightly forward, tilting his head to square our stares. He studies me for a span of a moment as my eyes meld into his dark liquid ones. My stomach is in a twisted string as I wait for him to speak.

He doesn't.

He just gazes at me. Intently.

With an urge to kill the intensity of his stare I blurt out, "Um, hey. We meet . . . once more. Um, what was your name again?"

He inches to stand, towering above me. The light becomes weaker as it hides behind his wide frame. Eyes so deep into mine, I can nearly feel their weight.

"I never told you my name," he says in a low, hoarse voice. He grins next, and I want to die. The small, wicked twitch still adorns his lips as I gape at him, mortified. The look in his eyes makes me think of his head moving between my legs and I consider dialing the fire department to put out the flames covering my face. He easily takes the last step to stand beside me. Almost popping the bubble of restless vibe that is my personal space. He extends his hand, takes my dazed one in his, and covers it with his other. Holding my palm between his, he dips his chin to captivate my eyes.

Misty silence lining with a soft sound of easy waves and the sporadic hum of the light blinking over the porch surrounds us before he breaks the stillness.

"It's Sebastian Noé Balle," he answers my question. Low voice with an edge of husk covered by a mouth-watering Spanish lilt that reverberates all the way through me. "My friends call me Seb. My family calls me Tian." His hold of my hand becomes more palpable. "*You* can call me whatever you want as long as you'll let me touch you again."

If I repeat what he just said in my head, with the way he said it, how his accent caressed each word, I would never again have to use lube. As long as I shall live, so help me God.

"That's the part where you tell me your name." A smile plays on his lips.

I blink at him and blink again. I force my lips to shut and swallow over the little drool puddle in my mouth.

"I'm Liv . . . Sebastian Noé Balle." Really? From all the names in the entire universe, *his* has to sound like foreplay?

His lips tip higher. "Liv." He rolls my name on his tongue.

"Um." I swallow again. "Would you like to come in?"

He pivots his head to glance at the door and returns his attention to me.

"No."

"No?" escapes my mouth in surprise. *So, why are you here?*

His lips lift even higher. "Later," he says and takes my hand in his again. "Let's go for a walk. Talk for a while."

Here goes. I knew there had to be something wrong with him. That's it; he is going to murder me on this picturesque piece of paradise.

We lie on the sand down the beach from my house, both propped on our bent elbows, legs sprawled straight ahead, mere inches separating us, gazing at the dark, lazy sea.

"So what would you like to talk about, now that we've got the name thing out of the way?" It's my turn to break the silence. He gives me a look that says, "Really?" A small curve almost seemingly plays at the corner of his mouth.

"Let's start with basic things. For example, what brought you over here?"

"What do you want?" I snap. Noticing his cringe, I realize I might have surprised him with my bluntness, just as I did myself.

"Whoa, talk about right to the point, eh?"

"What can I say, something about this . . ." I gesture with the palm of my hand from me to him and back, "just doesn't add up for me."

"Why's that?" He gazes at me with furrowed brows.

"Really?" My eyes roll to the murky sky. "What do you want with me?"

"What do *you* want with *me?*" He serves me back my question with a hint of an edge to his voice.

"I wasn't the one waiting for you at your door."

"No, you weren't, unfortunately. But you were the one following me here." Dark eyes challenge my greenish ones. He has a point. Okay, here goes. Let's go with honesty; well, honesty without the "I've been fantasizing about you naked for a week" part. What he doesn't know can't hurt me.

"To be honest, not much. I'm not looking for anything. You kind of crashed on me full-on, and I'm still absorbing the impact," I say, looking ahead at the cycle the small waves make as they reach the shore and retreat. "I didn't expect to see you again," I add and meet his narrowed gaze with my own. He runs his eyes across my face for a beat, one that's long enough to make me squirm some. He clears his throat.

"Tell you how I see it. I met this attractive lady with the sexiest smile and wanted to get to know her."

I roll my eyes overtly this time, and he side smiles.

"What?" His question comes through a chuckle.

"Come on, if there's anything happening here, whatever it is, this mutually beneficial nonverbal agreement, can we please make it a bullshit-free zone?"

He tips his head back laughing. I can't help but utterly enjoy his bass, hoarse laughter. It's a beautiful mixture of virile and elating.

"I can do that," he affirms, still clearly amused. I motion for him with my hand to elaborate, a smile tugging on my lips.

"This incredibly sexy lady flashed me." He chuckles at my immediate flush. "Fortunately, I kept bumping into her. She kept occupying my thoughts, so much so that I had to make her come for me, so I went after her."

Why did I have to ask? I smile timidly, my gaze glued to the misty horizon.

"Hey." He cleans his hands, patting them on his jeans, and then cups my cheek, bringing our stares to align.

"I'm not looking to get involved with anyone," I say in a quiet, somewhat croaky voice.

"Don't worry; you will not fall in love with me. I will not let you." He winks and his tongue moves to caress his front teeth. "You are safe with me. Trust me. Let's just enjoy each other's company." He grins at me; his smile is so contagious I can't help but mirror him.

"Enjoy each other's company." I taste the words as I contemplate them.

"So what are you doing in this charming hole?" he asks, amused by his own question. I beam and recite the same reason I've been using so far. The sabbatical, break, enjoy a new place. He cocks an eyebrow.

"Didn't we just declare a BS-free zone?" he asks with unconcealed doubt. "You sounded even less convinced than I am."

I take a deep breath, not sure why I'm sharing this with him, but it just feels . . . okay.

"I needed a break . . . from everything. Quit my job, rented a house somewhere quiet, intriguing, and faraway." I bite my cheek; it sounds even crazier saying it out loud. Something settles in his eyes, something I can't translate. He opens his mouth to speak, but what he was about to say remains unspoken when he presses his lips together.

"So, Sebastian Noé Balle, what's *your* story besides going after women you find attractive?" I shake my head as I utter the last part. A gorgeous dimple hides inside his bristled cheek in response.

"I've been living here for a few years now, but I'm originally from Barcelona. My family still lives there. I got my degree abroad, in the States, and came back to start at the bottom of the chain of our family business, which I'm now running. Sort of, as my father finally starts to let go." His forehead creases, his stare bores ahead into the dark sea. A whole moment he seems wrapped up in his own thoughts. A whole moment in which I study his profile, admiring his handsome masculinity. His pouty parted lips, strong jaw, the rich mocha color of his skin. And those dark, absorbed eyes. He shakes his head and rises to stand. "Let's get inside? Yes?" he asks, and I need to gather all possible control not to respond to the oh-so-asking pun. He pats his hand on his jeans to clear the sand off and takes my hand, helping me up. The pull jerks me to crash into his chest. His eyes descend into mine, and he tilts his head to feather a kiss on my lips. Something pulls at my stomach, a little flutter that comes as a big surprise. He smiles next. There's a message inscribed between the lines that smile sends, it's like *the* biblical apple, it powerfully lures you in and you know you can't resist, but oh, the troubles it will bring.

"Before we go that way, again… are you involved with anyone? Infidelity is a hard limit for me," he says. There are so many reasons I like his question, it seeds a sweet notion in me.

"The only relationship I'm in is with my coffee machine."

He nods with a hint of a smile and tugs me after him. I follow, willing whatever stirred my insides to disappear just as it appeared. I catch a glimpse of how the jeans encase his ass so delectably and beam. I must admit though, it's not only this part of him, but his entire encasement that is beyond delectable.

Delectable and young . . . younger than me, for sure. I decide to decipher the riddle.

"Um, Sebastian, how old are you, anyway?"

His eyes crinkle at the sides as he sends me a short side-glance. His lips slant a bit higher when he says, "I think you're just a bit too late to be asking me that after you took my innocence and all."

Oh, God. He grins impishly, and I feign a frown.

"Come to think of it, it was you who took anything related to innocence away from me!" He chuckles and squeezes my hand, pulling me after him en route to where there is no doubt further innocence is about to be taken away.

"I'm twenty-eight."

"Oh, God."

He turns to look at me, and his features crunch in question. "Is there a problem?"

"No, no problem, just excuse me while I tie a rock around my neck and walk toward the deep waters."

He chuckles briefly. "And why would you do that?"

"Because it's better than doing time for statutory rape."

The next rolls of laughter coming from his side are louder. He shakes his head at me, amused. "How old are you?" he asks, still somewhat elated.

"Older."

He twists his mouth, in a "come on." Or maybe more akin to a "come on, I went down on you fully dressed in a shower and now you're holding back?"

"As in almost five years your senior."

He shrugs and just pulls me to follow him faster.

Chapter 8
"The Way it Seems to Go"
Rachael Yamagata

I'm a bit thrown aback by the immediate charge that suffuses my living room as soon as we close the door behind us. It's as if the pull we share outgrows the confined space.

"So how did you like our wine?" Sebastian gestures with a hint of a knowing glee to the half-empty evidence on my coffee table.

"Vivian suggested I try it," I blabber. "Umm, it was good."

He cocks an eyebrow.

"Frankly, I'm not much of a wine person; I'm more of a sweet cocktail kind of gal. It was very good though, but I couldn't elaborate on the taste or anything else as *you experts* would."

"I see," he says somewhat pensive. He motions for me to take a seat at the low coffee table and settles himself on the sofa in front of me. His slightly parted legs almost touch mine. He takes the bottle and deftly removes the cork.

"Let's try to do it together, shall we," he says, his voice a degree huskier. "You need to use your senses to evaluate wine, scent, taste . . .sight." He gives me a soft, yet bluntly suggestive look. "Sight," he says as he brings the bottle to his mouth, wraps his lips around the narrow opening, and takes a slow sip. I swallow hard, following the motion of his Adam's apple under bristled, tanned skin. He then inclines his head toward me and cups the nape of my neck. He slightly tilts my head back and touches his mouth to mine. With the parting of my lips, his tongue reaches in, filling my mouth with warmness, wine, and an intoxicating breath. His tongue commences to stroke mine through the rich moistness; a combined sensual flesh on flesh electrifying sensation hovered by the tingling of the aromatic liquid. It skims around my tongue, letting the luscious liquid reach every part of my greedy mouth. I suck hard on his tongue, tasting the wine and him; my desire grows, and grows with every erotic stroke of his.

"Taste," he says low as he pulls back, lightly biting my bottom lip causing a sting that crawls all the way between my legs. "Keep your eyes closed, Liv. I'm going to do that again. I want you to suck on it, swirl it in your mouth, and try to think what flavors come to your mind." And he does, with one hand at the nape of my neck and the other sliding to curl around my knee. Everything inside me tightens, everything around me melts, and everything about me arouses. It's a sensory overload.

"Open them . . . now, tell me if it's balanced." He kisses my lips gently. "Complex." Another kiss. "Evolved." A more profound one.

Tastes like an orgasm? I close my eyes and lick my slightly pulsing lips. His hand trails slowly under the hem of my dress, holding my thigh with mild force. I lick my lips again, distracted by the touch of his hand.

"It tastes warm and rich."

"Mmmhmm." His hand sprawls, making my skin burn at the spot.

"Fruity and sexy," I add quietly, my eyes still closed, the edge of my lips slightly curved.

"Keep going." His other hand cups my cheek, and his thumb grazes my lips.

"It tastes like something I want in my mouth again." My eyelids slowly lift and my eyes meld into his with everything that rages inside of me.

"Sold," he says gruffly, with a hint of a heated smile. "Oh, and there's the scent," he adds next, nuzzling the area just below my ear. His hand on my thigh under my dress advances till the tips of his fingers whisper over the delicate fabric of my panties. I strangle a moan while his lips sear the skin of my neck. He murmurs, "Divine."

My eyes remain closed as I savor the taste of his mouth, his tongue, and his sweet, musky scent wafting around me. God, he smells like warm, rich, spicy chocolate. He smells like molten chocolate with a sprinkle of chili.

"Take your dress off for me, Liv." His voice reaches me, and we slowly flicker our eyes into a scorching, locked stare. He speaks to my mouth next, though it feels like he speaks to the spot between my legs as it insentiently starts pulsing in heat. "Undress for me. Stand up and slowly take your dress off."

Our lips hover next to each other, our breaths mixing before I rise up to stand. As I do, his hand trails from my neck, grazing over my skin till it stops on my hip.

He tips his face up and croaks, "Take it off."

With my breath hitched and every part of me tense with

excitement, I bring my hands to the hem of my dress and pull it up slowly. He slouches back to lean onto the sofa, further parting his legs. His eyes slowly trace over my naked, heated body. He brings his finger to the knot of his tie and pushes it in, releasing it by a small jerk to each side.

"Your bra," he orders quietly but firm. With my eyes trained on his, I do as ordered. As I release the satin, champagne garment to fall to the floor, he breathes gruffly, "Beautiful." His tongue slowly skims his bottom lip, his stare even deeper on me. I feel my already swollen breasts become heavier and the sting of my nipples as they harden in need.

"Panties."

And I do, slowly, feeling his stare caress over every part of me.

"Straddle me," he commands and the short demand comes out with a thick accent. I take a step toward him, plant one knee next to his thigh, and slowly spread to plant the other on the other side, all under his scorching gaze. His eyes lift to mine, and his lips part. He brings his palm to cup me, and I shiver and let out a breathy moan. Two fingers scrape between my folds accompanied by a throaty, "Fuck," that leaves his lips. His stare darkens as he brings his hand between us, watching the light gleam on his fingers indicating just how much I want him. He slowly brings it to his lips and closes them around his fingers. Watching him do that causes the heat where his fingers have just marked me to increase drastically.

"Undress me, beautiful," he says next as he positions me with a less than gentle hold of my hips to spread over the bulge in his pants. I narrow my eyes at him and before sending my hand to his shirt's buttons, I slightly graze over him. A unified sensual breath parts our mouths, feeling each other through the rough fabric. I release button after button of his crisp, white shirt under his gaze. Before attending to his tie, I spread the fabric to the sides after ripping it from inside his slacks to reveal a tanned, defined chest. He leans forward to shrug off his jacket and shirt at once. Wordlessly, I move to his belt, unbutton his fly, and lean in to leave hot, moist kisses on his honeyed collarbone.

His fingers move to comb into my hair, and with a light tug that instigates a spark in my groin, he tilts my head back. Still holding my hair in a rough hold that hitches my breath, he leans me even further back. His eyes leave a trail of flames as they trace from my eyes to my lips and then to my neck where he stops and dips his head to bite my skin. That bite will surely leave a mark. It's a bite that sends electrifying current to whisper all over my skin. As his head tips back for our eyes to level, he grabs me again by my hips and rises to stand with me.

I blink at him as he lets his pants drop to the floor, revealing his vein ridged, thick, smooth erection. He kicks his shoes off and sends his hand to spin me around so I'm with my back to his firm chest. With me held firmly in a caged embrace, he walks us a step back to the sofa. He settles on the wide cushion, positioning me atop him. His hands slowly caress my skin till they cup each of my breasts and gently pull me back into his chest. His fingers find both my nipples and start delicately rolling them in mild force. I drop my head back to his shoulder and pant as the sweet torture heightens to the verge of pain. Gone is my stable breathing. Gone is any barrier I might have had before. Gone is any desire for what he's doing to me to ever stop.

"Straddle me," he rasps. "Backward." His words trickle down my spine and cause for a greater heat to resonate over me. I part my legs to lift one over his thigh and then do the same with the other. Once my rear plants on his crotch, he shifts some to position himself just below me. His mouth finds its way to my shoulder and starts sprinkling warm kisses toward my neck, leaving heated skin in his wake. When he nuzzles my neck below my jaw, I drop my head to the nook of his neck and close my eyes.

He slides his warm hand under mine and whispers in my ear, "Take my hand and show me how to please you."

My breath catches before I respond, "You are doing a great job by yourself."

"Show me." He laces his fingers with mine and starts grazing our way toward my thighs. With an accelerated heart, I take over the control of our linked hands and slowly caress my skin till together we stroke inside my thigh. "Liv, show me," Sebastian rasps behind me, his throaty words reverberate through his chest into my back. I close my eyes and my lips part as I slide his palm to cover my heat. I hold his fingers in mine and glide them slowly between my folds, in a lingered motion, back and forth slowly. He groans, nibbling my jaw. I continue to stroke myself with his hand while his other moves to squeeze my swelled breast. I sink his fingers into me, clutching around him, nearly desperate.

Once I slightly lift my pelvis to better graze against his hand, a curt curse leaves his mouth against my skin. I move his thumb to circle around my clit as I push his fingers deeper into me, repeatedly, anxiously, fast, scraping harder. I pant and moan and move against his warm hand. Anxious, all inhabitations dissolving as I work my high with his hand. I pant and push him deeper. I pant and bite my lip, clutching around him tighter and tighter till I fall apart with a cry.

As I'm still reeling from my orgasm, Sebastian hands me a condom. With my vision in a haze, I fulfill his silent command. He shifts me up next to position himself under me, and in one slow push helps me glide around him. A unified groan leaves our mouths at the contact. Slow moans follow when he leisurely starts thrusting into me. His hold on my waist tightens as he helps me dance over him. Sebastian's lunges grow with force as he engulfs his hand around my belly and pulls me back against him. One hand is holding me tight while the other moves to stroke my clit. This guy is killing me, softly, gently, and almost impossibly shattering. We move against each other, him under me, me above him. The air around us thickens with our scents, sex, and raw, sensual hums. His breath kisses my skin accompanied by a low groan. I come around him again, melting into his hold. My eyes roll back as he holds me tight against him still moving with force in and out of me. A strained call of my name gusts out of his lips with his last slam. He drops back still holding me to his chest, and we calm our erratic breath in a quiet, sated daze.

"What are you doing?" Sebastian tugs at the throw I'm trying to wrap around my blissfully content, naked body. My brows sink in when I pivot to look at him over my shoulder.

"Pardon?"

"Why are you hiding your sexy body from me?" My already warm cheeks color a shade darker. If there's a subject I'm not comfortable discussing with him, or anyone for that matter, it's my body. Even though he's seen me naked, touched every inch of my nakedness, I'm still less than inclined to parade full-frontal around him. My round belly, round thighs, and basically, round everything is not something that makes me too enthusiastic to put all out for display. Although, the "everything round" package excludes the girls, those I have no problems with. Au contraire, I wear them most proudly.

"Ah, I . . . I'm . . ." I just drop it. I'm not about to explain a few decades of entrenched body image issues or, as I like to call it, my "skinny challenged matter of contention."

"You're too uptight, Liv," he states. I snatch the fabric he's still holding from his hand and tuck it tight around me.

"You're kidding, right?" I fold my arms over my chest.

He shakes his head. "I let you inside my house before I knew your name. I practically let you dry hump me after we exchanged less than three sentences. After everything we've done, you think I'm uptight?" I frown at him, and my frown deepens at the hint of a smile that plays at the edge of his lips. "After what we've just done?" I murmur under my lips.

His lips stretch, and he tips his head for our eyes to square. "Hey, come over, ven aqui." He gestures for me to sit next to him. Still with furrowed brows, I take a step and sit on the sofa, leaving a substantial "I need some space, you're starting to piss me off" gap between us.

His hand rests on my knee while his eyes penetrate deeper into mine. I can't help but bite my lip at the exquisiteness that is Sebastian post sex – tanned pecs, bare and glorious, toned, curved arms, unruly "you just messed my hair like crazy" mane, swollen lips, and glistening eyes. Do I want to nip this conversation in the bud and help him back inside of me right now? Oh, yes, I do. Will I do it? No, because it's not what I do. I'll never jump him just because I feel like it. Or it could be that I'm just uptight, but that's for me to know and for him to never repeat. His lips stretch even wider with a knowing glee to his eyes.

"Yes, beautiful, you're uptight."

Jerk. "I can't believe you. Honestly. Well, do educate me, what makes you believe I might be . . . less adventurous?"

A small chuckle leaves his lips.

"Well, you run and cover yourself the minute you stop panting. Second, whenever you're naked, you turn your back to me. The first time you let me in here, you locked yourself behind a door. After you came twice for me, you didn't have the nerve to face me, or to even ask whatever you wanted to ask me . . ." Humor lines his dark eyes.

"Why would you assume there was something I wanted to ask?"

"You wanted to know my name," he states, and I inwardly cringe. "Since everything that happened between us freaked you out, excited you, but freaked you out. And you thought if you at least knew my name, in a way you could tell yourself you knew me."

Okay, I officially hate him. I officially hate him and he reminds me of a certain diamond pattern, mustard sweater, hair slicked to the side doctor. I glare at him and the jerk has the audacity to grin wider. He winks at me next and says, "Don't worry; we'll work on it together."

I ball my fists and scoot back. "Why do you even care if I'm uptight?" There's a harder tone to my voice.

"Well, we haven't known each other for long, but the part I got to meet, well, I like it. *A lot.*"

My fisted palms relax and my lip starts to pull up at the side, but I trap it with my teeth. He doesn't deserve a smile given his previous statement.

"And there's an abundance of *knowing you* I'd be more than happy to explore, And it will work better if you loosen up a little."

"Which kind of exploring are we talking about? Should I be concerned?" I narrow my eyes at him.

His palm travels from my knee, under the fabric wrapping me, to the very spot where my thighs connect. "You decide. If my fulfilling every fantasy I have of you should be a matter of concern, then you should be."

Not breaking our stares, he inches to stand and drops to his knees before me. His hands slide under the throw and clutch my thighs. He tugs me forward, spreading me wider. I slide forward, my head lower on the back of the sofa and my lower body exposed; my legs on either side of Sebastian's waist. I lick my lips; eyes focused on this handsome man between my thighs, and untie the fabric from around me, dropping it to my sides. With a strained growl, Sebastian grabs my legs and drapes them on each of his shoulders before leaning in.

. . .

Two orgasms later when Sebastian tucks his shirt inside his slacks and buckles his belt, his eyes lift to mine. I quickly shift my eyes to the window, trying to appear as if I wasn't ogling him while he was getting dressed.

"Come with me to dinner," he says, futilely trying to comb his hair into submission. I walk to the dining room to collect his jacket from the back of a chair. I hand him his jacket and shake my head.

"Let's keep our 'enjoying each other's company' an indoor activity, okay?"

"No, not okay. I'm starving and you should be, too. Let's go grab something together."

I shake my head again, smile at him, and inch up on my toes to plant a small kiss next to his lips. I then rest my palms on his chest and lightly push him backward. His eyes drop to my hands as he takes a step back.

"Are you kicking me out?" he asks in a confused yet somewhat humored air. "If it's some sort of reverse psychology thing you're trying, don't worry, you don't have to do that. I want back in, more than you can imagine."

I beam at him and take another step, shifting around him to open the door. My hands return to his chest; I add a little more pressure, and with a final soft push, he's out the door.

"Hold on," he says through a soft chuckle. "Can I at least get your number?"

I say the first digits as he hurries to fetch his phone from his pocket. "Let me just," he slides the screen to light. Not waiting for him to add the numbers, I just continue with the last four digits. He cocks his head.

"Try to remember it." I send him a side smile. "If you really want to fulfill every fantasy with me, you'll remember."

He repeats the numbers I just gave him with dancing eyes.

Dimple full-on. I slowly start to close the door after blowing him a kiss and a small wave. Not a moment passes before I hear an incoming message from my phone that's on the dining table. My lips widely stretch as I read the message.

Unknown: To be continued...

A gigantic grin plasters over my face as I save the new number to my contacts under The End of Me. A giggle escapes my mouth moments later as I make my way to the kitchen, thinking about how I've just pushed him out.

I push him out of my house five more times after he comes, every following night, and makes me come. *Every night. More than once.*

. . .

I drop the piece of rustic, sliced perfection of bread, topped with freshly chopped tomatoes and aromatic olive oil, to the plate. My eyes widen as I listen to the small exchange between Embar and Dominique.

"How do you feel about men showing emotions?" Stephy asks no one in particular. Clad in black, she pervades a sweet with a touch of sexy, curvy appearance. We are all having a late lunch at the back kitchen of Vivian's café. Vivian in a deep red cotton dress brings a pot of soup over and settles at the head of the table.

"Define 'show emotions,'" says Alma, while filling her glass with the water jug, looking stylish in an asymmetric blue and bottle green V-neck dress, her bouncy 'do complementing the look.

"I don't know, cry for example," Stephy answers with a shrug, pulling her heavy, auburn mass of hair up in a band.

"Oh, dzose. Dzey have a name," Dominique deadpans with her nasal French accent. A vision of cold chic, in a Boho blouse and designer jeans, her silky blond clusters drop over her back.

"Is that so?" Stephy frowns at Dominique, who pats her lips with a white, paper napkin.

Dominique throws the napkin aside and squares her stare with Stephy's. "Mais oui, dzey are called gay."

"Dios mio," Vivian breathes.

"That's such bigotry," Alma chides. Dominique just rolls her eyes in a blatant "whatever" way, which I've learned is a theme with her.

"I think that it's very individual and should be judged on a case by case basis," I say. "I must admit that I'm not so much into bawling men. However, there are extenuating circumstances. Sometimes a small tear or glossy eyes could even strike the right chord. Seeing one of my friends' husbands hold their newborn in his arms, looking at his son with watery eyes, well, I've never seen anything sexier."

Silence enfolds us as we all ponder my last words. Our brief, quiet moment is broken by the bell declaring the front door has been opened. Vivian stands up to take a few steps to peek inside the café. Her lips stretch into a welcoming grin, "We're back here, Amor."

A quick taste of delicious jambon later, a deep voice greets us. A voice that trickles through my skin and down my spine.

"Hola, lovely ladies," Sebastian says to everyone in the room but his eyes dart to mine, holding them with powerful pull. There's a collective feminine crackle in the form of responding greetings. My face lightly warms up, and I hope it's an inner heatwave, not a visible one to my companions.

"I'll get you your order," says Vivian, walking toward him. She embraces him with one hand, a semi-hug, before leaving toward the pantry. "Take a seat," she calls back.

Sebastian grabs something from where Vivian had been cooking before and pops it into his mouth. He turns to lean his hip to the counter and faces us. I turn to look out the window when his stare burns into me. The way he looks still plays before my eyes as I gaze at the clear sky. Dark gray slacks, soft pink button-down, patterned gray and navy tie, neatly shaved, dark crew cut in a disarrayed order. Sebastian in his business-esque version. Business-esque-uber-fine version.

"So, Sebastian Noé Balle, who's dze current lucky fuck-du-jour?" pitches a French accent. Involuntarily, my attention shifts to Dominique and Sebastian. She stretches her lips at him with a sex dripping, predatory smile. Immediately, a verdict is rendered, as of this moment and forever Dominique is to be referred to as the French bitch. Sebastian doesn't even grace her with a semblance of attention. Instead, his eyes pierce mine.

Never wavering in his gaze, he asks, "Who is your new beautiful friend, ladies?"

My cheeks feel warm when everyone in the room shifts to stare at me.

Alma couldn't sound more eager to share when she answers, "The beautiful Liv."

The actor of the year, followed by everyone's eyes, walks

slowly my way, takes my hand, and kisses it lengthily. "Pleasure to meet you, beautiful Liv." I counter him with a pointed stare of my own, only mine says, "What the hell are you doing?"

"Nice to meet you . . ." I tilt my head up to him. "Umm, what was your name again?" I sweetly smile and Sebastian's eyes take a mischievous tone.

"I never told you my name." His thumb starts circling soft patterns inside my palm, where no one else can see. "It's Sebastian." He winks at me and I nod, subduing my smile by a clench of my teeth.

"Here you go." Vivian returns with two square polystyrene containers in her hands. Sebastian turns to make his way toward her. They start a short, easy exchange in Spanish that ends with Sebastian leaning in to kiss each of Vivian's cheeks friendly.

"Don't work too hard." She pats his back.

Sebastian returns to face us. "Ladies." He nods and a string of good-bye and nice to see you echoes from my friends' mouths. I nod at him with a soft smile, and he reciprocates with a stare that tells me how our next encounter will play out; a stare that sends heatwaves between my thighs.

I almost choke on the next sip from my glass and start coughing.

"If he were a god, I'd turn into a nun and dedicatedly worship him till my last day," Stephy says once Sebastian leaves the room, and then snorts a light chuckle.

"Coffee anyone?" Vivian asks.

"I'll get it. Cortado?" I say, needing a moment to myself. Vivian's small nod is followed by a few hums of affirmation from the rest of the ladies. I leave them to fix our drinks, my new favorite coffee – a shot of espresso with a drop of warm, frothy milk, just the right amount to reduce the acidity. I press a button for the coffee machine to come alive and hover my nose above the aromatic steam. A short chime of my phone while filling the first cup distracts me. I set the clear glass aside and bring my phone from my pocket. My first thought when I check the message is thank God I didn't leave the device on the table. The second thought brings my body to attention.

The End of Me: Beautiful Liv, I need you sitting on my face tonight.

This guy is indeed going to be the end of me.

Not even a beat passes before my thoughts are flung to the little dirty world inside my head that's dominated by Sebastian, where every moment of our "encounters" is safely cataloged. I chance a glance to where my friends are deeply engaged in a conversation and type a response.

Me: I'd be more than happy to collaborate with that.

The End of Me: Come over later.

Now, that won't happen. Just as I've politely rejected his previous invites, I'll do it once more. I'd rather keep our affair casual and discreet. Since that's obviously what it is, an affair, I'm not inclined to publicize it in any way or take any actions that would imply it's anything but supreme, mind-blowing sex. I'm not willing to let our coitus activities take place in any other location but my home, where I can keep it as shallow and discreet as possible.

Me: My house.

The End of Me: I have a thing I need to attend later; my place would be more convenient.

Me: My house.

The End of Me: You're impossible.

Me: There's always a rain check . . .

The End of Me: Your place.

Am I grinning now? Glowing would be more precise.

. . .

"Oh, Gawwwd Sebastian, God, Sebastian, yes." We haven't even made it past my closed door, Sebastian holds me suspended with one hand, pinned to the wall, withering and panting. His other hand holds my hair in a grip, tugging my head backward for his mouth to better mesh with mine. It's a rough hold, somewhat primal, and it just adds the last wonderful bit to his almost savage, heavenly attack.

"You're so damn gorgeous," he growls and thrusts harder into me, skillfully having his pelvis rub against my clit. Flashes of my forthcoming ecstasy start to show their delightful signs. I moan and bite his lip, hard, clenching around him.

"Yeah. Dios, Liv." He accelerates his pace, harder, forceful, rocking me against the wall, and I cry in incoherent bliss. His hand moves to cradle and secure the back of my head while each of his slams bounces me back against the hard concrete. He grinds into me in tight, close rotations, touching, grazing against each of my oversensitive spots. I come so hard that black spots appear before my eyes while achingly supreme currents run under my skin, inside my belly, twirling around my groin. My weak, boneless body drops to rest on his chest while he pumps in me in hurried, lingered hard slams.

. . .

"I have a business dinner in thirty; come with me," Sebastian says, toweling himself off after the steamy shower we took together. I watch him, resting my hip against the vanity counter, already snuggled in a thick powdery-blue robe.

"It's a business meeting," I say.

"He's bringing his wife," he argues.

"No. We don't do that," I say next, handing him his soft pink button-down, raptly watching him adjust himself in his dark slacks. I'm not sure I'll ever get over the going commando thing. He sends me a bothered glance and drops his eyes to the lower button of his shirt.

"Says who?" he says to his shirt, working on the second button. "Us?"

Another sharp look is darted my way, sharper than its predecessor. "What's the problem?"

"I love this thing we've got going on, you showing me all the goodies your people have to offer. Why complicate it, jeopardize it? Why not leave it what it is."

Sebastian is fully clothed by the time I end my sentence. His brows sink together and the twist of his mouth doesn't hold any joy.

"Are you kidding me? You think that if you joined me for dinner it would change anything? Four adults having dinner together isn't that momentous, Liv. Lots of people have done it before and survived. Come on, we can have dinner together. We are friends."

"Well, it will change the activities we usually engage in together, which I'm perfectly happy with as they currently are. We are . . . Friends?" A quality of doubt enfolds my voice.

He shakes his head and fetches his phone from his pocket. He starts working his thumbs on the screen. It's my turn to look at him curiously.

"What are you doing?"

He lifts his eyes to mine for a flit peep and bounces them back to the device in his hand. He clears his throat and starts, "So, the definition for the word friend is, 'a person with whom one has a bond of mutual affection.'"

"Let me see that," I add, taking possession of the device. "Ehm, funny. You've missed this interesting part, *typically one exclusive of sexual or family relations.*"

"I see," he says next, expression blank but that jaw of his working under his skin. He swipes his finger over the phone's screen and brings it next to his ear, crouching down to tie his shoe. "Hey Lola, what's up? So, I have this business dinner in thirty, want to join me?" I gape at him while he listens to this Lola person, whoever she may be. "You're the best, sweets. I'll pick you up in ten."

He shoves his phone back to his pocket and pivots to face me. With a mildly irate stare, he sends his hand to my waist and swifts me into one hell of a raw kiss that lightly shakes the ground below me.

"Have a great evening, Liv." And he is out the door.

I blink at the door a couple of times, muddled.

Did that sting? Oh, yes, it did, royally.

Have I brought it upon myself? Oh, *yes*, I did, definitely.

Chapter 9
"Can We Figure it Out"
Ana Graceman

"I want us to revisit your last relationship, Liv," says Dr. Smartass as soon as he learns about my new no-strings-attached, ongoing-hookups "relationship."

I grimace and huff loudly. As ever, the good doc disregards my conveyed resentment. "Let's go over the breaking point." He adjusts his square glasses up on his nose.

I push my head back onto the comfy sofa with a bothered sigh and let that last time we hung out together, before I kicked Aden's ass to the curb, play vividly before my shut eyes. It was a few months ago, a morning after he slept over, which didn't happen too frequently. I was having my first cup of coffee of the day, the one no one who cares for his dear life should attempt to interfere with by either speaking . . . or breathing next to me.

Aden lumbered into the kitchen, wearing loose, worn-out boxers, a button-down, socks, and glasses. Not exactly the walking aphrodisiac.

The moment he stepped in, in all his morning glory, two things ran in parallel through my semi-functioning, daybreak hours mind. The fact that yet again last night's orgasm was my doing, and that he does not, for one frigging moment, shut the ever-loving fuck up.

"Where are my corduroys?" he asks going to the cupboard. "You're out of green tea." He turns around to face the sink. "Where's the paper? Oh, I forgot to tell you, I got us tickets for The Vagina Monologues.*" He moves toward the coffeemaker and pours himself a cup. Finally, he turns to meet my irritated, silent gaze. "Where's the half and half?" He cracks a smile. "Last night was great, huh?"*

Urgh!

I try to meditate, mute him out, and drift into my waking up place where the entire human race is banned from visiting. But what he's about to do breaks my bubble in the most terrifying manner. Please, not again.

Aden is about to perform one of his "morning rituals." The same one that, time after time, provokes each and every one of my nerves to spike, and prompts me each time to mentally run to the toilet and retch. I am looking at him while chanting in my head, "don't do that, don't do that, for the love of . . . don't."

And he does.

Just like every freaking time before, I watch, as though in slow motion, appalled. He bends to take a long sip from the running tap, no glass, gargles twice, loudly mind you, and spits his mouth's contents flat-out onto my sink full of dishes. My dishes, *the ones I eat from.*

"Besides his, ahem," coughs my shrink from the direction of the screen, "varied idiosyncrasies, what made you decide to end the affair?"

"Many things," I muse for a short pause. "I guess I wasn't ready to share my apartment with anyone, my private time, my space, *my life.* There was nothing actually wrong with Aden. He was smart, kind, and genteel. A decent guy. But nothing about him excited me. In a way, he just fit well with my hectic schedule and

my reluctance to actually make an effort to start dating again."
How sad does that sound? And to think I spent a good part of a
year on that relationship. "I don't believe he essentially did
anything wrong."

"And yet you were in a serious, monogamous relationship
with him for several months. Did you, at any point, see any
potential in this affair, a future with him?"

I shake my head. My therapist just stares.

"Right from the beginning, I knew it would never evolve into
anything meaningful. I think I didn't want to disqualify him with
no special reason. On paper, he was . . . a good guy. I wanted to
give him a chance." The doctor nods and I know he knows
where, subconsciously or not, I'm going with this.

"I was afraid I'd be acting like her," I say and stop, shifting my
eyes to the window.

"Our time is up," he declares, and I let out a relieved sigh.
"Next time, we'll resume from here."

Of course, he'd never pass on an opportunity to analyze my
"special" relationship with my mother. A tireless relationship
grounded on a tug-of-war over who's right and who's wrong.
Where, of course, I'm the one who presumably doesn't know
what's right for herself, ever. Our precious way of coexisting is
mainly settling even the smallest of discussions in a battle.

It takes me a while to get into a calm zone post the weekly
session. Everything we discussed seemed to be stuck in my mind,
raising questions I've already asked myself a million times in the
past. Questions that have always come back empty. With a great
need for a positive distraction, and some longing for a faraway
friend, I fetch my phone and close the door behind me.

A few porch lights softly illuminate the beach; the sky is dark, but clear, and the salty air lightly caresses my face. I start toward the shallow water, where light, lukewarm waves kiss my ankles. I indulge in the tranquility that the evening induces for a long moment and dial Kai's number.

"Hey you, busy?" I greet Kai, more than glad to hear his voice.

"Not for you."

"Just finished a call with Dr. Smartass."

"Did he manage to fix you yet?"

"I'm unfixable, but you already knew that."

Kai's response is a snort.

"How about you; what are you doing?" Not a beat passes before a feminine laughter fills his side of the line.

"Making friends with the locals."

"Gross, please tell me you're at least decent."

"I'm never decent, but you already knew that. Hold up, let me step out to the balcony." I can literally hear him shrug his pants on and I shake my head. A flicker sounds, followed by an audible heave, telling me that Kai has lit a cigarette.

"So how's fulfilling your dream been treating you?" The last of his words comes out on a prolonged puff.

"I don't know . . . it's been great so far, but I feel like I'm wasting my time doing practically next to nothing."

"Having a great time doesn't sound like a waste of time to me, Liv. That's what you wanted forever. Stop being so neurotic and enjoy it to its fullest. Stop giving yourself a hard time."

"You're right."

"So, what constitutes *great time?*"

"For starters, this place is everything I thought it would be, different, exciting, and gorgeous. Oh, my God, Kai, don't even let me start on the food. It's like a culinary heaven."

"Sounds great."

I close my eyes and lift my face up for the light breeze to tickle my neck, "And I sort of have a . . . lover."

"Say what?"

"I guess you can say I'm having an affair. No strings attached, just a sex kind of thing."

"Are you sure you're up for something like that?" The severity his voice takes as he asks his question makes me stop short. "I'd be the last one to preach against casual sex, but . . ."

"I can handle it, Kai. In fact, I'm handling it perfectly well."

"In that case, I'm happy for you. It's about time."

I let out a light chuckle.

More than twenty minutes pass of Kai telling me about all the places he's been to before we say good-bye. With a soft smile on my lips, I retrace my steps back to my lovely new house, more than ready to spend the rest of this evening with a book and my cozy porch swing.

Chapter 10
"This Probably Won't End Well"
The Order of Things

"Oh, no. We're going to dinner this time," Sebastian says to my lips, pinning me against the wall while his hands do an amazing job at tracing my breasts. I shake my head, lightly whimpering as he scrapes his teeth next to my collarbone. He leans back, and I immediately miss his touch. I flicker my eyes open to a mildly peeved brown gaze.

"This is ridiculous, Liv. I'm starving, it's been a long day at work, and I want to eat."

Sometimes there are situations in which you need to consider slightly bending the line you have drawn. When you know you've pushed it to the point where it's about to turn absurd. The last time I didn't budge on my stubbornness, he ended up leaving to have dinner with someone else, which was followed by three days of an MIA Sebastian.

"Umm, maybe we can just order in?"

Sebastian inhales through his nose. He gives me another look that clearly transmits he is losing his patience with me. "Let me just grab my purse," I say and wiggle out of his touch, stepping toward my sandals.

. . .

"I still can't seem to figure you out," Sebastian says, pouring a second serving of red wine into our glasses. My eyes jerk up in question to meet his.

"What's that supposed to mean?"

He wipes his mouth with a napkin and tosses it aside. He gives me a brief, silent assessment and says, "Your insistence on keeping this distance between us though it's very clear you don't really want to."

"Excuse me?"

"There are many things you can easily fake, Liv. Attraction is not one of them."

I hide my lack of a valid argument with a generous sip of my drink.

"What are you so afraid of?"

"The decision I made to move to a new place, by myself, was so I could focus on me. I'm not looking for a relationship, or anything for that matter, that will take too much of my time or attention."

His expression turns pensive. "I've never mentioned a relationship. Just having a good time together in and *out* of bed."

I sigh over the rim of my half-drunk glass. "As long as we're on the same page."

"What's got you so reserved?"

My brows meet in response.

"Did someone hurt you?"

I shake my head. "No. All of my relationships were straightforward, black and white, nothing too complicated. No drama." I shrug. "Simple."

"My relationship with my nurse after I had my vasectomy was steamier than what you just described."

Lucky nurse...

My eyes grow wide. "Vasectomy?"

"Appendicitis," he snorts. "God, the look on your face was priceless."

Banter or not, funny or not, this conversation is leading down a path I don't want to follow. I'm not willing to analyze my past relationships, nor myself, with . . . him. Light as we keep it, our conversations always seem to leak into topics of intimate levels I'm not inclined to reach with him. A distraction is in order. I take a small crouton from my salad and bring it to my mouth.

"So, you were a fireman?" I casually ask.

His eyes bound by surprise dart to mine. "What?" comes out on a breathy chuckle.

"In my head you were." I produce a sexy smile. "Just go with it."

Another low chuckle. "Honestly, it was an incredibly rewarding job. I even got a medal once."

I love how quickly he plays along. "Oh, you did?" I mirror his suggestive grin.

"Yeah, for saving a couple of pussies." His tongue comes out to play with his front teeth.

"Aww, you saved kittens. You did it shirtless, of course, right? And I bet you had coal marks on your forehead and pecs. Did you have to use your hose?" I blink at him.

Sebastian eyes me with amusement.

"No, but I'd be more than happy to rescue you. . . with the

help of my hose." He catches the waitress's attention and signals for the check. I beam at the knowledge we're leaving, probably to further explore the subject of extinguishing hazardous, needy fires.

A signed bill and a generous tip later, Sebastian rises to stand and holds out his hand for me. "Let's go practice the two in, two out rule and proper hose handling."

A few steps into the night, Sebastian ducks, allowing his low voice to reach my ear. "You know that you'll have to open up to me eventually?"

. . .

"Who's this?" Sebastian halts mid-fly zip. I lean in to fish my dress left midway between the living room rug and my breakfast bar. Right at the very spot of my first orgasm. I turn my eyes to the direction his are zeroed in on.

"That's Kai," I say, trying to no avail to smooth my wrinkled dress. Sebastian's stare doesn't waver from the photo of Kai and me on a sandy beach, lips locked with goofy expressions. A kiss that meant nothing more than us fooling around for the camera.

I am taken aback by the lack of amusement, or better yet, the gravity in Sebastian's expression as he turns my way.

"And what is this Kai person to you?"

"My best friend." Is it me, or did he just scowl at me?

"Is he gay?"

"Pardon? Not that it's any of your business, but he is heterosexual." My eyes follow every notion revealed on his face that simply screams absurd. The little head shake, the wince, the twitch of irritation at his ticking jaw.

"There's no such thing as opposite sex best friends." He air quotes the last part he utters with pure disdain.

"Oh c'mon, don't. Let's not start one of these ridiculous arguments."

"I'm not arguing with you. I'm just suggesting you stop diluting yourself. If a man is straight, healthy, and at the minimum mentally stable requirement, he is never actually your friend. There's always something out there, an ulterior motive that usually begins and ends in your panties."

I roll my eyes. "Believe me, there's none of that when it comes to Kai and me. We're immune to each other's 'heat scents.'"

Somewhat snappy, he quickly resumes buckling his belt and sends a hand to his abandoned shirt on one of the high chairs. "I'm telling you, it'll come, sooner or later."

"What makes you think you're right?"

His stare turns from dark brown to pissed. "I know so."

"Okay then, let's agree to disagree. Shall we?" I say, heading to freshen up. I find Sebastian dressed, shoving his wallet into his pocket and grabbing the bike keys when I return to the living room.

"Come for dinner tomorrow," he says.

I'm about to argue, but his stare tells me that I might want to let it go this time.

"Okay. Good nigh…" This time I don't get to push him out, as he is out the door before I'm even able to finish my sentence.

As I turn to get ready for bed, satiated like only Sebastian can make me feel, there's a little itch of annoyance floating in my stomach. It takes a few minutes, during which I brush my teeth and set the lotion back on the counter, to realize the little argument we just had apparently has left its mark. I'm equally annoyed about his presumption of Kai and me, and the fact that we actually had an argument about it. Ultimately, I am left with the most troubling thought of all - why does it bother me when all I want from him is sex?

Still absorbed in my thoughts, I make my way to the bedroom after shutting the windows and locking the front door. I stop short when my eyes encounter the mantel. My brows furrow at the framed photo of Kai and me lying face down. *No, he didn't . . . did he?*

Chapter 11
"First crack"
Stephanie Schneiderman

"I went on another date last night," Stephy says, ending her words with a dramatic sigh.

"That sigh tells me this date is about to turn into one of those fast Vegas weddings, eh?" Vivian sends Stephy half a smile while bringing a small plate of butter cookies to our table. We both nod in appreciation at the munch.

"I'm telling you; modern dating is exhausting. There's so much involved besides two people getting to know each other or having fun together. To begin with, whenever you go on a date these days, you already know everything there is to know about him or at least what he publicizes to the cyber world." Both Vivian and I wait for Stephy to go on. "You Google the heck out of them before." I nod into my steamy cup. "The adventurous, witty, good-looking guy you've stalked online turns into a non-airbrushed version of average."

"Sad," I murmur and take another sip of my coffee. "That's why I've decided not to date for a while. I'm so done with average, in every aspect of my life."

"Speaking of you not dating and things way above average, Sebastian Balle asked about you the other day." It takes twenty-six muscles to smile; I need to work them all to do the exact opposite.

"Sebastian was the wine guy, right?" I go with blunt nonchalance. "Um, what was it that he wanted to know?"

Vivian shrugs. "You know, just asking in general." She eyes me next, carefully studying my reaction. And as much as I want to grab her by her shoulders, shake her, and make her elaborate, I continue my cool stance. "I told him I think someone should crack your shell."

I almost spit out my next sip. If there's anyone who's doing a good job of "cracking my shell". . .

"Oh, he is the finest breed," Stephy swoons.

That he is. God probably dropped mass man production when it came to him. He went with delicate handiwork instead.

"But isn't he in a relationship with that Lola person? They used to be inseparable." Stephy asks. That pinch in my stomach? I choose to disregard it.

Vivian shakes her head, her eyes glued to a point ahead of us. "Not as far as I know." Words are burning on the tip of my tongue and I press my lips to prevent their escape. Who the hell *is* this Lola person? That pinch turns into to a tight knot as I recall Sebastian asking a certain Lola to join him for that business dinner after I refused to go with him.

"You might want to get to know him, Liv." Vivian pulls me back from my musing. "He is a great guy." I nod at Vivian. With that, I can't argue. And so much more.

"Hola, ladies." The ring of the bell above the door comes in

132

stereo with Alma's greeting.

"Good afternoon, lady." I smile at her, loving her overall look of sass and sweet. She is a cool vision in a jacket of assorted fabrics with a theme of beautiful embroidered red roses.

"I need coffee, like yesterday." Her stare shifts to the register and she mouths, "Coffee," to the girl behind the cakes display. "To go."

"So, what are you all gossiping about?" she asks us, snatching a cookie from the table.

"A whole lot of nothing," I reply.

"Where are you off to?" Stephy asks Alma.

"Wedding stuff. We're meeting with the wedding planner downtown. Speaking of planning, don't go too crazy with the bachelorette party. I'm marrying a hot-blooded Spanish guy, after all. No strippers and keep the smut at jealously friendly level. I don't need a duel before the wedding day."

"Gotcha," Stephy replies.

Alma's eyes slowly scan my delicate lined lace cami, black midi skirt, and T-bar kitten heels. "You look lovely. Big plans tonight?"

My eyes rise her way and continue to the other two ladies who are watching me now, intrigued.

"Thanks. Nothing too special, just dinner with a new friend." Vague truth.

"Which new friend?" Vivian's eyes narrow.

"Is he cute?" Stephy grins.

"Just someone I met, and yes, he is sort of, um, easy on the eyes." Right there, the mother of all understatements. Before they manage to thread another question, I send a glance to the grandfather clock next to the bookshelves. "In fact, lovelies, I really need to get going. I don't want to be late." I quickly stand up and set my chair back in place. "Chau." Three sets of eyes follow me as I scurry toward the door.

. . .

I'm frozen at Sebastian's threshold, staring at the vision before me. Sebastian, light stubble, tanned bare chest, black, perfectly fitted slacks, barefoot, drying his hands with a dishtowel.

"Hola, you." He takes a step to press an utterly welcomed kiss on my semi-parted mouth.

"Hi." I lick my lips of delicious Sebastian taste. He steps back to let me in. I chance a quick glance at the surroundings. His home is designed to instill a sense of clean elegance and coziness. Dark wood tones, large TV, brown leather sofas, hardwood floor. An upscale bachelor pad that manifests masculinity.

"It's nice having you here," he says, sending his hand to my waist while sending my heart to twitter, as he leads me inside.

"Which part of me?"

He turns my way, his eyebrow cocked. "The whole package. Your smart mouth, incredible body, and sweet, sweet pus . . ."

"I got you," I stop him mid-sentence, gaining a naughty, dimple-coated smile in return. Biting my own smile, I follow him to a small yet well-equipped, rustic kitchen adjacent to the living room. Setting the tone is a massive butcher-block island with a couple of high chairs by its side. I give the space an appreciative scan, ending it with much more appreciation as I gaze at Sebastian's bare chest.

"So, now that you've got me here, what's on the menu?" I ask, leaning my hip against the substantial island. Sebastian sends me a flirtatious glance over his shoulder. He returns to pour wine into two tall glasses from a carafe. He brings a glass to his nose for a long inhale before turning to me.

"Salud." He hands me a glass, resting his hip next to me on the island. I take a taste of the wine and stare at him from under my lashes. Sebastian leans forward and tastes the wine from my lips. "So, you wanted to know what's on the menu? Let's see, tapas and wine for you. And you, for me."

"Sounds mouthwatering, the entire . . . um, set of choices," I say before bringing the glass to my mouth for another sip. "Tapas, the exquisiteness of simplicity."

Sebastian sets his own glass on the granite countertop and turns my way. I lock my eyes with his as he takes a step to face me. Soon, his hands reach for my waist and he lifts me to sit on the textured, cold surface. His fingers graze my skin from my knees to the hem of my skirt. They continue their path, scraping my skin, pushing the fabric up my thighs.

Trailing down to halt mid-thigh, Sebastian slides his hand between my legs and helps them further gap. He takes another step and plants himself between them. I drink him in, absorbing the light hot wave he instigates under my skin with his motions, gaze, and scent. I set my glass aside and send my hand to the nape of his neck, pulling him to my lips. I raid his mouth once it connects with mine. My fingers skim his skin and I push my chest against his. A groan bubbles from Sebastian's throat when my teeth sink into his bottom lip. Sebastian slowly eases backward, gradually extinguishing the energetic festivity we've begun.

"I need to feed you first," he says, rubbing my lips with his thumb.

"Why's that?" I breathe, utterly hot and bothered and very hungry, definitely not for food.

"We have a very long night ahead of us."

"Sounds promising." My voice still comes out shaky.

"There's an expression in Spanish, 'el amor entra por la cocina,' love comes through the kitchen." He smirks at my blatant eye roll and mocking smile. "Now, you drink your wine and keep me company while I make you dinner."

I put on a mock pout, not the greatest fan of him leaving me right now.

I watch him raptly as he starts cutting fine slices of ham and sets olives bathed in a reddish oil into a small dish. Roasted peppers follow, and a hand full of small cauliflower heads coated with shiny, dark balsamic glaze. My eyes run over the small portions of alluring food and Sebastian's hands as he labors. Tanned, masculine fingers brush some crumbs away after cutting fat chunks of rustic bread.

"Penny for your thoughts," Sebastian bursts my momentary porno reverie of him and food. We bring our eyes to meet in unison. "Ten euros if they're dirty." Our lips twitch on cue. "Twenty if they include me."

"Now, that would be telling." I lick my lips; following his eyes as they trail the slow trip that my tongue has taken.

"Whatever they are, show me later."

"I plan to."

The chime of his phone breaks our little promising flirtation.

"Mamá," Sebastian answers and tilts his head to hold the phone with his shoulder. He listens while arranging the bread on a plate.

I hop down from the counter, prompting him to look my way. "I'm going to freshen up," I whisper.

"First door to the right." He nods toward the hall. Sebastian resumes the call while watching me as I make my way out of the kitchen.

I give the living room another admiring peep. His place is inviting and warm, in a way that complements him. Reaching my destination, I send my hand to the knob and open the door to an obscure guest toilet. I feel my way over the wall for the switch, flick it on, and turn to face the room. Although the décor is eye-catching with bold ocean colors, minimalist style, and a massive, dark wood framed mirror, one thing gets my attention and dims everything else in my view. There's a message, written in red lipstick, on the lovely mirror. Despite my limited knowledge of the local language, I still manage to simultaneously translate the note.

Tian,
Thanks for last night.
xo,
Lola

I stare at the red letters and shake my head. Idiot. What an idiot. That would be me, of course. What have I gotten myself into? It's one thing having whatever we have going on, it's a completely different story doing it with someone who has a Lola thanking him for last night. The warm, needy feeling I've been nursing – since I stepped into his home, since the first time he touched me tonight – at once turns into an appalling burn right at the center of my belly. Truth be told, it might also be reaching toward my heart. I shut the light and open the door. I remain silent for a beat, listening to the sound of his voice, making sure he's still on the phone and tiptoe my way back. Only it's back toward the front door. I gently close the door behind me, making sure my escape is as stealth as possible. *Fucking liar*, "*are you involved with anyone, infidelity is a hard limit for me.*" *Men!*

I hail the first taxi that passes by and urge him to step on it. I look out the window, fuming. What a jerk. I couldn't be more pissed, at him and at myself. What did I really expect from a guy I slept with before knowing his name? That he'd be completely honest and genteel? Well, the blame is all mine. God, I can't believe I slept with someone else's man ... several times. I feel sick to my stomach.

I pay the taxi driver and hurry inside my house. I lock the door and lean on it. Wound up with agitation, I take a deep breath and kick off my shoes. I close my eyes and the realization sinks in.

I left him.

Woe betide me, am I ready to let go of all that's largesse? (And "largesse," it is. I kid you not, I'm a walking, glowing ad of just how large-sse it is . . .) I'm telling you, it's not curiosity that killed the cat, it must've been pure greed that killed the glutton pussy. Couldn't resist yet another bowl of all that's sizzling, delectable, and oh-so-orgasmic. Well, I'm not a spineless feline. I'm a mature, sensible woman. I can resist a delicious treat – no matter how addicting it is, no matter how it makes my body scream for more, and no matter how it makes me feel about myself.

And anyhow, it's high time I got back to using this thing inside my head that's there for the purpose of reasoning and reflection. Forgive me, brain, for I have sinned; it's been days since I've used you. Good Lord, I've became a needy airhead. And it's all courtesy of one Sebastian Noé Balle.

Chapter 12
"Warning Sign"
Travis

A flash of adrenaline enfolds me as soon as I hear a motorcycle hum coming from outside my door. Less than twenty minutes after I got home and steamed down, to a degree, persistent knocking colors the quiet space of my place. I slowly walk toward the invading hard pounds, contemplating on how to thank him for being a dishonest ass and send said ass to Lola's hands.

I open the door and meet his questioning, muddled stare with a hard one. I don't speak; I just glare at him, my eyes narrowed.

He shakes his head. "Care to explain?" His hands fall to rest on his hips in questioning accusation.

I run my eyes over his handsome, mildly irritated face, memorizing it for lonely nights (in heat) to come, and say, "Well, color me conservative . . . what can I say? I'm not the ultimate STD fan. Neither am I keen of crablouse."

"What the hell are you talking about and what the fuck is craploose?"

"Oh God, you went to college in the States, right?"

"What does it has to do with my education? What the hell, Liv?" His features harden in harmony to the thickening of his accent.

Now, of all times, we have a language barrier issue? How did this turn into me explaining wingless, pubic lovin' insects?

"Those are cooties, fleas people sometimes get in their . . ." I gesture toward where Lipstick Girl Lola could have left some on him. His eyes follow my hand and bounce back to mine.

"You fucking kidding me?" His brows clasp together. "Let me get this straight, I was making you dinner, and you run off because all of a sudden you think my junk's infested?"

"No . . . that's not exactly how I would put it."

"Ah, no? Really? So how exactly is it then?"

"I guess somewhere between making me dinner and promising a long night you failed to mention *you were seeing someone else*." I fold my hands across my chest.

"Say what?"

It's my turn to shake my head and send my eyes to the ceiling. "You were the one who said, and let me quote you here, 'infidelity is a hard limit for me.' So not only is cheating a hard limit for me too, lying is a secondary creed."

"Liv, what . . . the . . . fuck are you talking about?"

"The lovely red note on your mirror." I tip my head sideways, my stare challenging his.

The expression his face wears clearly illustrates his short musing, which gradually morphs into realization. His eyes narrow as they re-meet mine. He takes a step forward and I take one backward. "You mean the message Lola left me?" he asks in a low voice and takes another step toward me. I take the equivalent backward.

"That one," I say in a hard voice. He takes another step, his eyes running from my collarbone, to my lips, to my eyes.

I take another step back. "I think you should leave."

He cocks his head sideways and takes another step. I take another the opposite direction. He takes another slow step, his eyes a mixture of heat and exasperation with a touch of something sinister. "She thanked me for letting her crash at my place last night." Another step. I take another step back and raise my eyebrow. He inches closer. "She's an old friend. I slept on the couch." He licks his lips and mine slightly part. I take another step back and my rear meets the living room sofa, stopping me. Sebastian takes another step my way, reaching deep into my personal space. I trace my stare to his blazing one. "Why did you run off? Why didn't you simply ask what it meant?" His proximity unnerves me and excites me at the same time. He sends his hand to cup my cheek.

"I guess I misjudged the situation." *And acted like an impulsive teen.*

He shakes his head. His hold on my face lightly tightens, he inches closer, his leg moves to part both mine. "I think you were jealous, Liv."

I shake my head; a light warm blanket of thrill covers my alert body.

"I like that."

"Don't flatter yourself. I wasn't. I was disappointed. I thought you were better than that. I thought *I* had better judgment," I say in half a coherent utterance, half on a breath.

"Well, thank you for the vote of confidence." He inches

closer. "How can you do it?"

"What?"

"Do everything sexy."

I blink. He is good.

"You pissed me off, and I find you even more irresistible," he says and brings his mouth to hover next to mine. "You don't run away again." He gently bites my lower lip. "You have something to say, say it." His mouth is so close, his other hand crawls to my breast, and I let out a choked breath as his fingers find my hard nipple. I nod; nothing to argue with here, he's right. "I'm still pissed, Liv." His hand leaves my breast and trails down to cradle my rear. "There are consequences."

"Consequences?" I whisper, and the implication of the simple word couldn't turn me on more.

"Si," he pushes me by my rear against him, *to feel him.* "Consequences." Both his hands move to grab me by my hips and tug me to straddle him. The fabric of my skirt ends crumpled in a heap, exposing my thighs wrapped around his waist. I hone my lips in on his neck and taste his skin as he walks us toward my bedroom.

As soon as we enter the room, Sebastian takes one step and drops me to the bed. I lightly bounce at the contact with the mattress. He crosses his arms over his chest and gazes at me with eyes that insinuate pure sin. He scrapes his teeth over his bottom lip. "Take your clothes off . . . slowly." He remains standing firmly, watching me. The room is dimly lit by early evening soft light, still bright enough for me to take in all his rough beauty, yet dark enough to set that special ambiance, a perfect one for what's about to happen between us.

"Undress, Liv." Mirroring his intent gaze, I slowly start to unbutton my blouse. "Leave it open like that," Sebastian orders, and I leave my blouse dropped to my sides, framing my purple, black laced bra. I thread my thumbs into my skirt, slightly raise my pelvis up, and push the skirt down my thighs. Sebastian finally makes a move, falling to his knees at the edge of the bed. He seizes my skirt and helps pull it off me. He leans in closer and in a gentle, painstaking caress trails his flat tongue over the delicate fabric of my thong. I whimper and he grabs my thighs and spreads them wider for him. A low groan leaves his mouth as he nuzzles me.

I close my eyes and drop my head to the mattress as his tongue slowly moves down and traces up my inner thigh. He reaches the hem of my panties, leaving warm breaths and light kisses on my skin in his wake. As the flutter of his mouth fades, I sense his fingers traveling toward my panties and moving them sideways. I moan to the sensation of his thumb subtly hovering between my folds. Gentle, arousing, teasing touch. He leisurely strokes my heat to the sounds of my heavy breathing, his light sporadic groans, and the sound of waves coming from outside my window. I let out another choked moan as his tongue takes the place of his thumb.

I rise to lean on my elbows and watch him utterly engaged in pleasuring me. It's the sexiest vision I've ever seen. A halo of raw desire emits from him, from his hooded eyes and intense features, to the light shine on his mocha skin. He is still fully clothed, a snagged gray tee hugging his toned chest, straining around his arms that hold my thighs parted. With his mouth still on me, his eyes trail up to meet mine. His stare burns into me, and so does his tongue on my sensitized middle. I whimper and a breathy, "God," leaves my lips when his tongue sinks into me. Sebastian's eyes don't leave mine, nor am I capable of breaking their spell as he slowly brings me to the edge. Lapping, caressing, kissing, suckling me to lose myself in him. I'm shaking, on the verge of falling over the edge. Uttering incoherent pleasure sounds, I close my eyes, unable to contain everything that's happening to my body. And just when I'm about to shudder, he stops. My eyes rip open, darting his way. He shakes his head.

"Wha?" I barely manage to express my immense frustration.

"Consequences, Liv." And his thumb moves to lightly press on my throbbing clit.

"Sebastian."

"Ever heard of edging?" I shake my head, beyond hot and bothered and about to beg.

"Let me enlighten you . . ." he says and dips his mouth toward my middle. His finger sinks into me, and I drop my head back. His tongue joins; his rhythm slower now. He tilts back and blows over my overly sensitive skin and I arch my back, yearning for him to release me from this torturous sweet pain. He inches closer and resumes his divine torment. And I build up, faster than before, harder than before. It's becoming unbearable. I let out rapid pants, every inch inside of me clenched, ready for him to release it.

And he stops.

"No," I cry. And his lips are back on me.

By the fourth time he brings me to an almost breaking point and unceremoniously halts, I start begging.

"Sebastian, stop torturing me. I can't take it anymore."

In place of an answer, he props his arms on either side of my legs and pushes himself up to stand. Silently, staring at me, he shoves his hand into his front pocket and produces a condom. He quickly discards his clothes. I drink him in as he covers himself, aching for him to touch me again. His hand fists his significant, strained shaft, and the other rolls the condom down. His abs slightly twitch at the action and I gape at him fascinated, dazed by his exquisiteness and by my urgent need for him. He settles between my parted legs and guides himself above me, teasing me. I'm literally shaking, holding my breath, waiting. I rise my pelvis to encourage him.

And he sinks into me.

But stays halfway out.

"Sebastian," I almost scream, at the verge of losing my sanity.

"No running again. Next time you talk to me."

I nod. I'd agree to anything that he says at this very moment, as long as he gives me what I want.

And he does.

Oh, my God.

Oh. My. God.

He moves in me. Heavenly. In precise, perfect motions that hit deep and wonderful. His mouth meets mine in a wild game of domination. He picks up the pace of thrusts, artfully playing on each of my aroused nerve endings.

And I come for him so hard, the world around me blackens. His name strings out of my lips in a chant. The orgasm comes in waves, spiraling from the center of my body to every part of me. The high is so strong I'm not even with him as he continues to thrust in me, rapidly and forcefully. I'm too caught up in the sensation enfolding me. I never in my life have felt it as resilient, as mind and body shattering. It's too much and it's beyond perfect.

Some long moments after, or hours for all I know, Sebastian finally stiffens and then groans my name before falling on me.

He tips his head back from my neck and lightly presses a kiss to my mouth before rolling to my side. We both lie in silence, bringing our heart rates and breaths to steady.

"Wow. That was . . ." I whisper.

"Pleased with the service?" His voice husky, lined with amusement.

"It was beyond any expectations."

We both lightly chuckle, spent and blissfully exhausted.

"Edging?" I ask now that I've gathered my wits about me.

"Uh-huh. It's when you bring yourself or your partner to the edge, stop just before the release, and repeat it several times. Eventually, the orgasm is more intense." His lips impishly crook. "And my mom always says, 'hay más felicidad en dar que en recibir.'"

I translate his words in my head and end up mirroring his grin. *There is greater joy in giving than in receiving.* Smart woman, his mother. Did an impressive job raising and educating such a giving son.

"Oh." Oh, wow.

"Oh?" He turns his head to look at me.

"Oh, I like it. Very much." His lips tug higher at the edge.

"Duly noted."

. . .

"So, I have this business event next weekend," Sebastian says as he passes me a glass of wine. We are having a light dinner on the porch after we've finally left the bedroom to refuel. I lean my back onto the fluffy crocheted pillow resting on the arm of my swing. My feet rest on Sebastian's lap as he lightly rocks us with a gentle motion of his legs.

"What business event?" I ask and take a bite of my pan con tomate. Divine.

"Wine tasting. I'd like you to join me."

I send him a glance over the rim of my glass.

"It's over the weekend. I have a couple of seminars to give and a bit of mingling to do, but I'll be free in the evenings. It's in Masquefa." His eyes search mine. "What do you say?"

I quickly evaluate the implications. "It's your family's business that you're running, right?"

He affirms with a nod. Sebastian sets his wine glass onto a small mosaic end table by the swing.

"Will they also be there?"

"Yeah."

"I guess I'll pass this time." I don't miss the flit twitch of his lips at my reply.

"Why?"

"As I've mentioned before, I think I'd rather have our 'agreement' kept as it is."

"What agreement?" He takes a deep breath through his nose. "Listen, I'm not into arguing again, just think about it. I really want you there with me. It's a beautiful place, good food, good wine. We'll have a great time."

I've already made up my mind. I'm not going. But I leave it

to rest at this point. I, too, have zero inclination to argue, again.

"I'll think about it," I murmur.

He nods, gazing ahead at the night as it colors the sky and the sea in a blanket of velvety black. Slowly, Sebastian cranes his neck to look my way. With our eyes firmly secured, he slowly inclines my way. I follow his lead and lean closer till our breaths mix. We kiss with the softest of touches. The light night breeze flutters across my skin as Sebastian's lips brush mine again, warm and supple.

"Let's take it inside," I murmur to his lips.

. . .

It should be long past midnight when we finally disengage from devouring each other, once more. I'm tired, spent, and utterly sated. My head rests on Sebastian's bare chest, his arm around my shoulder. Sebastian talks and I listen, eagerly indulging in his voice and his accent.

"It's a grape originating in Jerez, here in Spain, which we recently brought to our smaller sixty-acre vineyard. In that one, which is my favorite, we focus on making balanced, ripe wines that reflect the soils and climate's typicity. In order to get the signature characteristics of the grape from which it was produced, you need to start picking grapes at their ideal ripeness and then preserve that character through the actual winemaking process. I'm quite pleased with the results so far." He turns to plant a light kiss on my shoulder. "Okay, enough about my work. I want to hear more about you."

"What would you like to know?"

"Tell me about your family," he says in a soft voice, his finger drawing small circles on skin.

"Honestly, there's not much to tell. I'm an only child. My mom was a stay at home mom who took the role of a perfect housewife once I left home. My dad is the epitome of a hardworking, kind man."

"Remind me, what's 'epitome'?" Sebastian stops me. His English is nearly fluent; I tend to forget that it's not his mother tongue.

"It's the essence, ultimate type."

He nods.

"Anyhow, he retired last year after working forever for the IRS, and I guess now he's working on trying to survive full doses of my mom on a daily basis." We both chuckle. Only mine has nothing to do with humor. "What about your family? Do you have any siblings?" I ask, deliberately redirecting the attention back to him.

"Two older sisters, Bianca and Amaia. They sort of spoiled me rotten growing up. Although they gave me plenty of shit, especially when we got older, and I was very much into their friends."

"I see, so older ladies is your thing."

He lightly chuckles.

"I'd never admit to that. Anyhow, it's not important. What's important is that my current *thing* is you." It's my turn to smile and for the warmness in my stomach to expand. "Bianca lives with her boyfriend in Madrid. She's a primary school teacher. And Amaia is studying to become a vet abroad in the UK. I adore them both. We are pretty tight. They'll like you."

I disregard the last comment albeit it powders warmness in

my belly. "That's nice. And your parents?"

"Well, my mom is the *epitome* of a Spanish lady. She's beautiful, elegant, smart, and has my father by the balls." He snorts a chuckle and I grin at the dark ceiling. "And her kids are always her first priority. My father is a good man, a little rough around the edges. But his family always comes first. He worked me to the bones before he let me step foot into the office that was always waiting for me. He didn't show me the ropes; he'd hit me with them so I'd know nothing was guaranteed. He made sure I knew I had to prove myself first."

He speaks passionately about his work and I listen, wrapped up in the moment. In the intimacy. The mystic dimness, the pulse of his voice inside of me, the gentle caress of his fingers on my skin, the subtle trace of his warm, masculine scent. It's dark and it's intimate and our quiet little whispers draw us closer . . . against any of my sensible wills.

"Hey," he whispers after a long while in which we lie in pleasant silence, his fingers lightly brushing my hair while I'm snuggled on his chest.

"Hmmm . . ."

"Aren't you going to kick me out?"

I smile to his skin. "Later," I mumble, feigning a sleepy voice.

I can sense him smile as he tucks me closer under his arm.

Early dawn light is just starting to drip through the curtains, but I couldn't be more awake. Every part of me is awake, especially my overloaded mind. Overloaded with everything Sebastian and this night.

The thrill of visiting his place.

Him making me dinner.

The stub of pain, the sting of jealousy, seeing that note.

Him "edging" me.

His beauty, his charm, his warmness.

Him.

Us.

This warm, fuzzy feeling that enfolds me and won't leave.

How serene I feel in his arms.

And mostly, how I don't want to, and shouldn't feel this way.

I've let this evening take a turn I'm not ready to repeat.

Chapter 13
"Infidelity"
Skunk Anansie

I leave my hand on the door, slowly soaring down from the impact of the Sebastian effect. The beam illuminating my face won't leave even when I turn on my heels, heading to start my day. I eventually pushed Sebastian out the door as I promised him, only this time it was after he spent the night. He woke up with a start, hurriedly fishing his clothes from the flotsam and jetsam of our evening together. After downing a double espresso and giving me a kiss that still feels hot on my lips, he left. I take another step toward the bedroom and stop at once when my eyes hone in on the facing down photo.

Somewhat astonished, I lift Kai's and my photo to stand upright. I shake my head. He's done it again. Somewhere between kissing me silly and leaving my place, Sebastian turned the framed picture on its face. I let out a short giggle at the absurdity of the notion. As I take another step, I'm stopped again, this time by knocks on my door. The smile returns to my lips at the thought that it might be Sebastian.

My face scrunches in puzzlement as I open the door. The last person I'd ever expect to show up at my doorstep stands before me, puffing smoke in a whistle-like huff from the side of her mouth, and says, "Bonjour, so it was Sebastian that just left, oui?"

My mouth opens to speak, but words fail me with the many concerns marching through my mind. Beginning with what on Earth is the French bitch doing at my doorstep? To how bad is it that she, of all people, knows Sebastian just left my place? And mainly, what the hell is the French bitch doing at my doorstep!

"You can relax, chéri," she mutters. "I have greater things on my mind," she adds and proceeds to invade my home, making me sidestep as she lets herself in.

I gaze at her back and then at the door and shut it closed.

"Um, coffee?"

"Scotch."

My eyebrows lift up.

"I don't have any strong stuff around here; the strongest might be red wine."

"That'll do."

Okay . . .

I fix myself another cup of coffee and a glass of wine for my surprise guest who's sitting on the sofa, staring out the window.

I hand Dominique her drink and take a seat in my generously sized, gray upholstered recliner, studying her cautiously.

"So," I start, wanting to get some hint of the nature of this unusual visit. My lips clamp at once as I watch Dominique down the glass in one long, not her usual elegant grace, series of swallows. My stare widens when she wipes her mouth with the back of her hand.

She sets the glass back down and says to the table where her eyes are directed, "I didn't want any empty consolations. I wanted to talk about it. I wanted to bitch it out as you Americans say."

I nod, still, to be frank, mildly staggered.

"I just found out dzat my beloved husband has been screwing his apprentice for God knows how long." She shakes her head. "Dzey are in love," she adds with utter scorn. I cringe with empathy. "Je suis un tel cliché." She sighs. "I'm such a cliché. I gave up my dream for a man who gave up on me a long time ago, only I wasn't willing to see it."

"You are not a cliché, things like this unfortunately happen. People grow apart, people change."

"Change enough to fuck a twenty somedzing under my nose?" She sends me a bitter smile and turns to pour herself another serving of wine. "But you know what; the fault is not his alone. I decided to live in a different city. I put the distance between us. A long distance relationship is a long distance disaster waiting to happen. People grow apart; closeness, physical connection, intimacy helps concur obstacles. It's not the cure, but it sure helps the lifeline pulse. He wouldn't have been looking had he had it all . . . you don't go looking when there's nothing missing."

"Dominique, I don't think you did anything wrong. After being together for so long, you don't hurt your partner this way. You can talk, say how you feel, instead of choosing the easiest way, sans confrontation."

"Allez savoir pourquoi, I'm not sure where dzis is coming from, but I want to do somedzing stupid. I'm so mad. I want to hurt him. I want to step out of my poise and do somedzing vindictive and juvenile, like burn his clothes or physically injure him."

"Oh, there's a reason and a mighty good one. He betrayed your trust; he cheated on you, for heaven's sake. I'm pretty sure I wouldn't stop at burning things, I might go full-on Lorena Bobbitt."

"Lorena Bobbitt?"

"Um, she's famous for chopping her husband's penis off for being unfaithful."

"Très joli! A genius." She takes another sip of her wine and levels her eyes with mine. "I like you, Liv."

"Well, I think I've just became fond of you, too." I send her a genuine smile.

"So friend, would you help me pull off an embarrassedly juvenile stunt and never again speak of it?"

"My friend, I'd be honored to."

. . .

"Dominique, I can't let you do this, don't! It's unholy to burn Dior. We'll go to hell." She twists her mouth and tosses the sacred garment into a burning pile. I cringe, cross myself, and send a silent prayer of forgiveness to the gods of haute couture. Dominique lets out an amused snort.

We both place our legs crossed by our ankles on the railing of Dominique's elegant beach house balcony. We stare ahead at the waves; the fire burning couture inside a metal barrel between us sends streams of gentle heat our way while dancing in joy.

"What's next for you?" I ask and Dominique shrugs.

It takes her a few good moments to finally say, "I like it here,

I'm not sure I'm ready to go back to France."

"I like it here, too. More than I thought I would," I murmur.

"I came here because of him, dzanks to him, and I dzink I'll stay here *for me*." Her lips coil in a painful smile. "Emotions are a funny thing. It amazes me how much resentment you can suddenly hold for someone who you've loved and admired for the greater part of your life."

I nod. Her words reverberate inside of me, and even though she is talking about her husband, the vision of my mother appears before my eyes.

"Alors, now dzat dze burning part has been successfully accomplished, tell me about Sebastian."

A reflexive smile hones in on my lips at the way Dominique pronounces Sebastian's name, in a nasal French twang. Say-bas-tyawn.

I make sure to keep my stare fixated ahead while saying, "Not much to tell."

She snorts in response, prompting me to look her way, "Having Sebastian leave your house in the morning cannot be a 'not much to tell' answer."

"We are seeing each other, I guess. Casually."

Her trimmed eyebrow rises, encouraging me to go on.

"Dominique, it is what it is, and whatever it is, I'd like to keep it under wraps. It's nothing that will last too long, so no need to make an issue out of it." The sting I feel saying the latter part of my sentence surprises me.

"Why?"

"What do you mean by 'why'?'"

"Why would it have to end soon?"

"He is young, younger than me, that is. We're both not looking for anything beyond having a good time with each other. And I'm planning to go back eventually, so yeah."

She shrugs. "I wouldn't go and declare anything and just flow widz it. Why do you have to already set a pending termination date?"

So I won't get hurt . . .

I smile at the notion of the tight embrace Dominique and I depart with.

"I like this warmer version of you," I tease her as I step down the first stair of her balcony.

"Don't get used to it," she admonishes. "I have a reputation to keep."

Chapter 14
"All You Never Say"
Birdy

"Happy anniversary," Sebastian announces, leaving me staggered both by his kiss and, to a greater extent, by said declaration.

"Come again?"

"I will, soon." He grins at me. My lips pull up at the playful sin he transmits.

"Anniversary?"

"Four months since we've . . ." his smile gets wicked, "gotten to *know each other*."

"Oh, no, we don't do that."

"Right, excuse me, my bad," he says, his smile dims some by a touch of annoyance. "Happy fuckversary."

Although I'm sure it was meant to be humorous, something about his last words and my sudden uncertainty of our, whatever we are, makes me frown.

"How do you even know how long it's been since . . ." I shake my momentary funk off.

"It was the night before I left for Madrid for an important meeting. To which I showed up a total mess, tired and with you all over my mind. A night to remember."

"A night to remember," I repeat under my breath. Our stares meet, and Sebastian opens his mouth to speak, but a gentle cough coming from the waiter standing by our table makes him keep silent. Sebastian's lips shut, but his stare remains on me for another lengthy beat before he turns to the server.

"A bottle of Cordornìu Cava," Sebastian says. "The lady will take care of the food part."

I reward him with a soft smile before dictating a long list of small dishes to the patient waiter.

"Sure you got it all?" Sebastian teases.

"What can I say; I just love the food here." I close the menu and set it on the table. "This place has been a long orgasmic culinary joyride for me." My eyes run greedily over Sebastian in a suit. "Um, this place is a long orgasmic joyride. Period," I add, earning a small side smile by my dinner partner. Small, albeit embedded with such great promise.

"I thank you on the behalf of myself and my people. Our great nation is both humbled and honored to have made your experience orgasmic thus far, and we look forward to continuing your pleasure and satisfaction for the rest of your stay."

"Sebastian, are you sure we are there? You ready to commit to doing that for so many more months? It's a serious commitment, not to be easily promised."

"I do." His smile progressively fades. "Actually, it would be great if you'd drop your going home deadline."

I gape at him.

"Think about it, Liv. It isn't set in stone, it can be modified."

My heart hastens its pace.

"So, I'm not wearing any underwear," I blurt, dangling a sexy promise before him, knowing full well that this bait will surely steer us away from the previous topic.

"Then, what do you call these?"

"Hmm . . . I thought it would sound sexy, like in all those trashy romance novels."

His lips coil in mild ridicule.

"I never thought you'd have your fingers up my alleged nakedness, before I had the chance to finish the sentence."

"Do you even know me?" he asks through a chuckle. "A chastity belt wouldn't keep me away from inside of you."

I join in his playfulness, loving the sound of his words on so many horny levels that I can't even begin to count.

"You see what I mean, that is actually something you would never do. You're too uptight."

"Oh, come on. I can't believe we're back to that," I huff. "After everything we've done." He cocks an eyebrow. "Seriously, I can't believe you still say that."

"Prove me wrong then."

I fold my arms over my chest and tip my chin. "What do you have in mind?"

His eyes slowly move from me toward the restaurant's window. A devilish grin settles on his lips.

I crane my neck to follow his stare. I frown at the few shops before us and turn back to him in query.

He gestures to the direction of a specific store. "We're going to visit that one after we're done with dinner."

I narrow my eyes and a soft, "Oh," leaves my lips at the tacky sign, blinking "Sex Shop" in neon pink letters. "And we're going to get one another the most bizarre thing they have and try it . . . for dessert."

A toy from a sex shop for dessert. Touché, Sebastian.

"Like I haven't done that before."

Sebastian tilts his head to the side and studies me with crinkled eyes. "No, you haven't." The cocky jerk is right, of course. Too bad the wine we're having is good; otherwise, I'd probably splash it over his irritating, teasing smile.

We refuse the waiter's offer for individual plates and ask him to leave the many small dishes between us. Sebastian brings a fork of grilled and lightly peppered squid to my mouth as he tells me about an interview he had today with a local radio station about his family's winery and his life in general.

"They asked me if I could name an event that shaped me as a teen." He takes a taste of his half-empty glass of red.

"What was your answer to that?"

"When my father had a heart attack."

My eyes shoot to his above the rim of my glass.

"He gave me *the speech* while lying in his hospital bed. The 'you'll need to take my place and take care of the business and our family if something happens to me' one."

"That's a heavy duty speech. How old were you?"

"Seventeen. It was some kind of an omen not to fuck up. I've always known I'd be involved in the family business, but it was the first time he actually told me what he expected of me. What was yours?" Sebastian catches me off guard.

A few monumental events of my youngish life pass through my mind before I say, "It's not an event, it's actually a few that together formed *the effect*."

Sebastian runs his cloth napkin over his lips and drops it back to his thigh, his stare coaxing me to go on.

"Ever since I can remember, every year my parents made me switch schools. It was more my mom's idea, but my father never confronts her, so there was essentially nothing to stop the crazy."

"Did you guys move a lot?"

"Funny, but not at all," I say flatly. "We lived in the same house since the day I was born. The thing is that when it came to me, nothing was good enough for my parents. I mean my mother." I sigh. "Even though my grades were always nearly perfect, my mom was never content with any of the educational institutions I went to. So, basically I started a new school every year."

"That's crazy."

"Yeah, you're right, there's no other way to describe it. No matter how much I tried to fight it, she wouldn't hear any of it, and this madness went on till the day I graduated."

"That must have left quite a mark on you."

"Oh, it did. By the third year, I had mastered not getting too attached to anyone, and what I like to call a 'sayonara sans emotions' mechanism. I don't do good-byes, or I do, but don't really care. It's my gift." I don't even bother to conceal the bitter bite of my words, nor do I elaborate about the not getting too attached to anyone part, either. "I can be your friend for so long, and in a blink of an eye, let you go, no emotions, none whatsoever."

"Won't happen with me," Sebastian says. "You won't be able to let me go." For a moment, we stare into each other's eyes, and something passed between us, wordlessly.

I break the tense moment. "Believe me, you're no exception."

"You sure know how to make a man feel special."

"Like *you* need any more strokes to your ego."

His response is a twitch of his lips.

Thankfully, the rest of our meal flows with a lighter ambiance, less disturbing topics, and some utterly delicious food.

"Ready to get some toys?" Sebastian asks, leaving a couple of notes on the table.

I return with a cheeky, bring it on smile.

. . .

The young, stylish guy at the register with a creepy smile gives us both a knowing wink as soon as we enter the debauchery parlor. Having penises in all shapes, colors, and sizes present themselves to me from every corner makes me want to hold my head up and blow this scene (pun intended). I'm definitely out of my element here – the mother of all understatements.

"Remember, the most bizarre thing," Sebastian whispers next to my ear, giving my waist a soft squeeze.

"Shouldn't be a problem, everything around here is uniquely unusual," I murmur, and he snorts a chuckle.

Something about this situation sends sparks of excitement through me. Sebastian, whose eyes burn to mine above the aisles, is looking for something to pleasure me. I counter his stare with one no less heated. As his attention drops to something behind the packed shelves separating us, I squint my gaze, dying to get a glimpse of what it is. With Sebastian's attention elsewhere, I turn to examine the abundance of lascivious gewgaw before me.

I shriek when large hands grab my shoulders from either side. "Does it excite you?" Sebastian asks, his lips next to my ear and his chest pressed against my back. His hands slowly trail down my arms.

"I don't need any accessories to get excited when it comes to you. I get turned on just looking at your wrist."

"Good to know."

I nod.

"So, I'm ready to go whenever you are." His hand moves to my waist and traces up to caress the side of my breast.

"You got me something?" I say.

"Yeah." His lips flutter under my ear. "I'll wait for you outside."

"You're leaving me alone in here?" I ask in blunt dismay.

Sebastian chuckles and kisses the top of my head. "You'll survive. After all, it's nothing you haven't done before, right?" And he leaves, a smirk decorating his lips.

Oh God, what am I doing here? Pig tail anal plug, really? What on God's green Earth is a Clone-a-Willy? Oh, not . . . it's not . . . my cheeks catch fire as I read the illuminating label. "Make an exact vibrating clone of any penis." Not that Sebastian's equipment is not clone worthy. On the complete contrary, it is very much worth replication, but still, no way in hell. Just when I'm about to grab the lovely G.I.L.F, aka the Inflatable Granny that comes with a set of false teeth . . . for the full experience, of course, I find the grail of the weirdest holy.

I snatch the item that in my book is by far the most bizarre pleasuring toy and in utter discomfort walk toward the clerk. I swallow hard and, yes, want to die, as I hand it to the cashier. I look everywhere, ensuring I don't meet his eyes even by accident.

"So let the record show that I, Liv Bliss, stood the test. And so help me God, if I ever hear the combination of the words *up* and *tight* ever again," I tell Sebastian as soon as I meet him in front of the smut establishment.

Sebastian grins at me. "You would what?"

I bite on my smile. "Never again. You hear me?"

. . .

Sebastian lies on his side on my bed, his head supported by his hand as he gazes at me with a hint of amusement. I kick my heels off and tuck my legs sideways under me.

"You go first," he says, drinking me in.

I hand him the black bag in my hands.

He shakes his head and his lips tip up. "Show me."

Thrill laced edginess enfolds me as I set the bag between us and sink my hand inside. I expect Sebastian's stare to follow my action, but it stays fixated on my face. I finally get the item out and put it on the bed between us. Sebastian's eyes study me for an additional beat before they slowly descend. His eyebrows shoot up as he takes in the box standing between us.

A low chuckle rolls off his lips when he snatches the box and examines it closely. His stare arrows at me, to the box, and back at me again. His expression morphs to mild surprise with a hint of mirth. He turns to me with an air I'm not able to decode.

"Do you really want to watch me fuck a can?"

Of all of my most embarrassing moments, this one skyrockets to first place. Leaving me telling Kai I'd definitely do his dad, with the father person himself standing behind me, in the dust. "You got me a Pussy in a Can, Liv? I guess it's true what they say, it's always the reserved ones who are the kinkiest." Sebastian bursts into guttural, free laughter.

I hide my face in my hands and can't stop my own laughter. I couldn't be more embarrassed, but still, the situation is beyond absurdly amusing, not to mention Sebastian's contagious chuckles.

Our laughter mixes when warm hands peel mine from my face. Sebastian's dancing eyes trace mine. He holds both of my hands in one of his and with the other brings the box forward for display. He makes a whole production of studying the item again.

"Okay, read me the instructions," he says, and our amused cackles take a higher note. "Seriously," he adds through a chuckle. "I'm not accustomed to fucking cans. I think I need guidance."

"God, can you just stop, I can't breathe," I say, having a hard time breathing, my insides burning from the uncontrollable laughs. He shakes his head with the broadest grin and tosses the disturbing can aside. I dry my eyes and still chuckle when I ask, "So, what did you get me?"

He presses a soft kiss to my lips and sends his hand to his pocket. I watch him curiously as he produces a small bag and hands it to me. I slide my hand inside the plastic bag and scrunch my eyebrows, feeling the lacy fabric. With two fingers, I fish out a delicate, lacy thong. I give the panties a short perplexed peek and turn to Sebastian.

"That's the wackiest thing you were able to find for me?"

He shrugs and his hand caresses the skin of my throat, moving slowly to curl around my shoulder, pulling me closer for his mouth to hover over mine.

"Thought you'd look great in them."

"Um, isn't this kind of missing the point of finding the weirdest, err, sex thingy?" I say to his mouth.

He takes a taste of mine, slowly kissing me. He eases back to look at me, our mixed breaths noticeably heavier. "I never intended to go through with it."

"So, it was all about tutoring me." I gently push his chest.

He bobs his head. "It was fun, though?" He grins at me, and I echo with an amused beam.

"So, no toys then?" I ask, not the least bit disappointed.

Sebastian pushes back to lean on the headboard and extends his hand to help me straddle his thighs. He brushes his fingers through my hair, holding my face next to his. He leans in to swipe a feathery brush on my lips. "I'm not into toys. To be honest, it doesn't do it for me. I'm more into experiencing the body like it's meant to be."

I can't even begin to express how much I like the words coming out of his beautiful mouth, how every part of me finds it enticingly promising.

And how much I love the tour his mouth starts on my skin — my neck, my breasts, my thighs. A tour that ends with us both blissfully exhausted in each other's arms.

I close my eyes and rest my cheek on Sebastian chest, indulging in the pleasant blend of warmth and incredible scent.

"So, am I now forever exonerated from the being windup charge?"

"No."

"Wrong answer, dude."

He huskily chuckles.

"The thing is that I like that part of you. I find it incredibly sexy how one minute, you can be so lustful and sensual and the next, timid and demure. In fact, I like everything about you."

"You're okay, too." I smile to his skin as he slaps my butt. "Good night, Sebastian," I whisper.

"Aren't you gonna kick me out?" he whispers back, wrapping me tighter in his arms.

"On our anniversary? That would be ruthless!"

We both lightly chuckle. I leave an airy kiss on his skin. My lips smooth into a calm stretch thinking how in fact, I more than like everything about him. How content I feel in his embrace. How incredibly right it feels. To an alarming, dismantling degree.

Long moments pass in which we lie in easy silence, tangled in each other, both in our own bubble of thoughts, slowly falling asleep.

Sebastian's low voice breaks the tranquility. "You know what, Liv? Sometimes it's the things you aren't telling me that I like best."

There's a twinge in my heart as I make a decision to keep silent and not tell him just how much I like him, too.

Chapter 15
"Say Something"
Great Big World

Stephy, in a red tee with "Shoe Addict" plastered on the front, paired with cute distressed jeans, sets four cups of heavenly smelling coffee on the table and takes a seat to my right. Dominique peels off her black blazer, adjusts her silk cream blouse onto skinny jeans, and gracefully takes the seat on my left.

"Morning," Vivian says, making her way toward us with generous pieces of Tarta de Santiago on a tray, my recent favorite, an almond, rich in flavors cake. Vivian licks her icing sugar tinted thumb, smooths her maxi tribal dress, and plops onto the last vacant chair.

"Gérard and I are not together anymore," Dominique says dryly and takes a sip of her coffee. I give her hand a squeeze under the table while taking a sip of mine. "Alors, dzere will be none of dzat." She points her finger at our friends who regard her with bemused yet compassionate eyes. "We are not discussing this, and you are not consoling me. I'm done mourning."

We all nod, some more reluctantly. I can see the many questions on Vivian's face and the great job she is making to honor Dominique's request to "zip it."

Stephy forks her cake. "Oh my God, Vivian, this cake is unreal," she gushes. Which immediately leads to Dominique and me forking our own pieces. A unified moaning moment follows our tasting of the baked orgasm.

"You're getting me worked up with the noises you're producing." Vivian grins widely.

Dominique pats her lips with a napkin. "Stephy, tell us one of your dating stories; I need something to lighten my mood."

"I can do that," Stephy answers, polishing the last piece on her plate. "Remember the guy I told you about from the UK office who came for an orientation week?"

"Cute ginger guy?" I lightly chuckle, recalling how Stephy dreamingly said she'd like to lick each one of his freckles, all over his body, if given the chance.

"Same one. Hot freckles, delish accent."

Vivian eyes crinkle along with the shake of her head.

"On the last day of the orientation week, we stayed late, and he offered to buy me a drink. The power of the freckles intensified after the second glass of wine, and eventually, we ended up in my bed."

I snicker and Dominique sends me an amused glance.

"So we are about to get busy, and all of a sudden, he starts asking questions."

"What questions?" Vivian says.

"Oh, a whole lot of questions," Stephy says and starts a hilarious impersonation of a robot. "Can I kiss you? Can I take off your shirt? Can I take off your bra? Can I kiss you here? Can I kiss you there?"

"C'est ridicule," Dominique says.

"Ridiculous, indeed," I confirm.

"It was such a turn-off, so odd. It was like robot sex."

As our hoots subside, I turn to look out the window and my smile immediately dies. The cake in my stomach all at once feels like a brick. In some sort of an unexplainable sadistic penance, I keep watching the couple on the street as they disengage from a lingered tight embrace. The beautiful lady with the tight ivory blouse and knee length, snug pencil skirt smiles wholeheartedly, looking up at the guy. She tilts her head back; her silky dark ponytail jerks with the move and bounces back as she inches up on her killer crimson heels to kiss Sebastian's lips. He grins at her as she cleans lipstick off his lips with her thumb. My stomach clenches. They keep smiling amicably at each other while exchanging some more words before Sebastian's hand hones in on her lower back and they turn the other way. I watch them absorbedly till they disappear in an alley that leads to the main square at the old city center.

My insides feel queasy when I rerun the scene I've just witnessed before my eyes. The reasonable part of my mind objects to conjuring an incriminating scenario, while the emotional one counters with red lips kissing Sebastian, the fond smiles, Sebastian's hand low on her back, and sadly so, how good and . . . happy they looked together. Reason argues against irrationality and says they're just platonic friends or business acquaintances. Not jumping to conclusions, injured emotions dispute in bitter disdain with: he was in his running clothes, and almost shouts, "she cleaned lipstick off his freaking lips." That pretty woman just cleaned the lips that told me they liked everything about me a few nights ago, the same lips that kissed me softly and deeply before they left me last night.

"Liv? *Liv?*" someone says. I'm not even sure which of the ladies looking inquiringly at me has asked the question.

"Uh . . ."

"You seem, très troubled," Dominique determines.

"Sorry, I was just, um . . . never mind. What's up?" My friends trade flit glances between them before turning back to me.

"Should we buy you a ticket to the show on Friday?" Stephy asks.

"What show?"

"Oh, for heaven's sake, did you listen to anything we said?" Vivian eyes me, mildly exasperated. The look on my face calls for them to repeat the exchanging glances part again.

"Liv, dze flamenco show. On Friday?" Dominique comes to the rescue.

"Right, sure, why not. Of course."

. . .

No matter what I do, I can't seem to make the images flashing before my eyes go away. Her thumb brushing his lips, their intimate smiles, his hand on her back.

"That's about it, so what do you think?" Saul's voice over the phone snaps me out of my niggling reverie. I turn to watch the endless blue water and push my toe against the wooden floor to keep the rhythmic swinging.

"Sounds interesting."

"Right, huh? Interesting enough for you to actually take a look at the numbers and maybe draw up an offer?"

"Yeah. Hold up, what?"

Saul lightly laughs. "Would you like to have a look at the numbers and . . ."

I cut him off mid-sentence. "That part I got. If I were to agree, what does it really mean? I'm not coming back you know, at least not in the next few months." Saying I'm not the least bit interested in Saul's offer would be a gigantic lie. I'd be more than thrilled to help him with the offer to the client I essentially brought in. It was my baby; this new software company we've been working with forever to persuade to take us on. It was my baby just before I handed him to Saul, the assigned adoptive mother, just before leaving for Spain.

"Do it from there."

"Do I have a deadline? As tempting as it may sound, I'm not too keen on working like crazy again."

"How about a month?"

I furrow my brows. For whatever reason, Saul is giving me way too much time to get this work done. We both know that if I take my time doing it, I can have it done and polished in less than two weeks. I can't help but wonder what the catch is.

"I can do that."

"Great. When you're done, and if you're interested, I just heard that we got shortlisted on the Buchman and Fearnley RFP."

A tingly buzz covers my skin. "You're kidding me? Wow, that's just . . ."

"Yeah, it is."

I can just imagine the smile spreading on his face.

"What are you trying to pull off by dangling B&F before me?

Are you trying to get me back?"

He chuckles in response. "Always. I'll send you the files later this evening."

I gaze at the phone in my hand with an excited smile. The thought of working again couldn't have been better timing. To be completely honest, these past few months have felt a bit mind numbing. I've been feeling this prickly restless itch to do something more substantial, like actually using my brain for something other than easy conversations, beautiful views, and everything Spanish lover. A little bit of sinking into analysis and numbers would be perfect.

The roar of a motorcycle makes my heart slightly rattle in my chest. Excitement laced with a pinch of disquiet washes over me as I watch Sebastian kick down the stand with his heavy boot clad foot. He takes off his helmet and my heart does yet another little jiggle. He climbs down the sturdy vehicle, helmet tucked under his arm while he runs his fingers through his hair with the other. As he lifts his eyes, after unzipping his black leather jacket, they immediately find mine. A side smile nestles on his lips as he pauses to admire me. I smooth down the fabric of my cotton, white dress till my fingers reach the crochet hem ending mid-thigh.

Sebastian takes the stairs, keeping his eyes on me. With one final step, he halts before me. He bends at his waist and sends his hand to the side of my face, leans forward, and brushes his lips on mine. He says, "Hola," and leans back in for another kiss. I stiffen and pull back from his kiss when the thought of him with that woman earlier today invades my mind, again.

"I'm getting a drink, get you something?" I straighten to stand, no longer sure how to act around him. He follows me inside, leaving the helmet on the dining table. "How was your day?" I ask and inwardly beg for him to tell me about his earlier encounter. If it were just an innocent happenstance, he'll surely tell me about it, no?

"Nothing much, went for a run, worked from home, and packed for tomorrow."

I wait, willing him to go on. Sebastian moves toward the fridge.

"That's it?"

He cranes his neck to look at me over his shoulder, holding the fridge's door. "Yeah." His answer makes me take a step back and hug myself. "Beer?" he asks. I shake my head.

"I saw you earlier today." I tensely wait for his reaction.

Sebastian twists off the beer's cap and turns to fully face me, leaning his hip on the counter. "Why didn't you come to say hi then?" He takes a swig.

"You seemed busy."

"Busy doing what?" He eyes me.

So here's where I have two options, the classy one – tell him that I saw him with a pretty lady – or go with the next thing that comes out of my mouth and I regret about half a second later. "Having someone clean your lips after she had soiled them." Go rational, sophisticated behavior.

Sebastian's face scrunches as he ponders my words. He cocks his head, gazing at me. "After she had soiled them?"

Hearing him repeat my sentence out loud has me squint my eyes toward the floor; maybe there's a loose tile I could crawl under. I shrug, not sure how I could possibly rectify my approach of the soiling topic now. Adding assault to injury, his eyes crinkle at the sides and his lips curve up from behind the bottle's neck.

Sebastian crosses his legs at the ankles. Amusement dominates his eyes when he scratches his bristled cheek and looks at me from under his lashes. "It might be a language barrier here, but I'm not sure I understand what you mean by someone soiling my lips."

I grimace while sidestepping him on my way to the fridge and murmur, "Having fun?"

Sebastian's firm arm circles my waist, flinging me back against his chest, and pulls me backward. "It's more than fun; I love every second of it."

"Glad for you."

His bristled cheek grazes below my ear as he nuzzles my skin. "I'm glad to hear you are bothered by someone kissing me. It means you care."

I'm about to reply with a sharp comeback and stop short when the words "someone kissing me" pummels at my stomach. I try to wiggle out of his hold while muttering his name in a low warning tone.

His hold on me tightens. "It was this old friend of mine I told you about. Lola. We met on the street after my run, and I walked her to her meeting on my way home."

Sebastian gently turns me to face him. His arms wrap around my waist and he tilts his head just enough to align our stares. I trail my eyes over his handsome face – his high, hard cheekbones, long lashes, and creamy brown eyes. He dips his chin lower as I rise to stand on the heels of my feet. We lean in an inch closer, our stares heating up. An inch closer and in a shaky intake the blend of his scent and breath reaches all the way inside of me. An inch closer and our lips meet in a feathery touch.

"I don't want to be kissed by anyone else," he whispers.

With my next kiss, I show him that I feel the same way. My hands reach his chest. His trace my back. He tips his head sideways, deepening our kiss. I dictate our pace next, skimming his tongue, seeking more. I bite his lower lip and slide my tongue right back with an urgent pant. His firm body against mine, his hands touching, caressing, grazing over my neck, collarbone, chest, cheeks, everything about him, everything about our intimacy sets fire to lick up from my thighs to ignite the rest of my body.

"So, are you coming tomorrow?" he asks out of the blue while lightly sucking on the heated skin below my ear.

"Where?" I breathe.

He presses a swift, chaste kiss on my lips and rests his forehead on mine. He takes a deep breath and to my utter reluctance, leans back, leveling our stares.

"To that wine event I told about."

Oh, that.

I bury my hand under his white tee, slightly grazing his warm skin. "I don't think so."

"I really want you to come with me." The graveness in his voice makes me carefully choose my next words.

"Maybe some other time. I have this thing my former boss asked me to look at and I might go to a show with the girls."

"Okay and the real reason?" The impatience in his voice tells me that we're probably not about to continue the blessed, blessed activity we were so engaged in less than an irritating question ago.

I add a dash of sweetness to the smile I work to put on my face. "We've been through this before. I don't think it would be . . . the right place for me. For us to be together."

"Can you hear just how little sense you're making?" He inches backward and crosses his hands over his chest, clearly signaling for me to back off. My hands drop from under his shirt.

"Whatever we have between us is not that kind of . . ." I wave my hand, trying to find the right word to name our *thing*. "Relationship."

He shakes his head. There's a vein noticeably pulsating in his neck. Dangerously ticking. "Increible." He shakes his head again. "And here I thought we were past this casual phase. Liv, we've been seeing each other for months. Months."

I gaze at him, somewhat shaken while having the mother of all internal battles. It feels like it's one of those moments in which you've frozen in place, knowing full well you're watching an advancing train wreck, one that will leave *you* wrecked.

"Why are you blowing this out of proportions?" I say in a dainty voice.

"Am I?" His eyes burn into me. "Because, as I see it, I'm trying to give this a chance to actually grow into something meaningful while you keep going one step forward and ten back."

"Sebastian."

"You know, Liv, I wouldn't be pushing this if I had the slightest feeling that there is indeed something paramount behind your reason not to join me, but I know, just as you do, that it's only because, for some reason that's beyond me, you are afraid to give us a chance." He takes a step forward and frames my face with his hands. "Can you please stop this . . . how is it called? Pretension."

"Pretense," I say.

"This pretense of yours. We both know that what we have is much more than what you pretend it not to be. Joder! Liv, you were jealous just a few hours ago because a friend kissed me. I don't get you." To my silence he says, "Okay, you know what? Go ahead, name my wrongs, have at me. Maybe finally I'll fucking understand why you keep pushing me away."

"There's nothing wrong with you." *There's something wrong with me because I'm afraid to let you in.*

"You are doing a great job of making me believe the very opposite," he drawls.

I'm not even sure what it is that makes me stubbornly keep my walls up, what is it that I'm so scared will happen if I let him in.

"So?"

I slowly shake my head.

"I see." He drops his head and heaves loudly. He lifts his eyes into mine and my breath hitches at the anger laced disappointment staring back at me. "I guess that's it then," he says with a shrug and starts toward the door. My eyes grow wide and my lips slightly part as I watch him walk past me. I turn to follow him with my gaze and call for him as his hand reaches for the doorknob.

"Don't leave. Not like that." My heart is pounding wildly in my chest.

He turns back to look at me and I fidget by the fury wafting from him.

"Oh, I'm so sorry. My bad. I forgot to fuck you, right? After all, this is what it's all about, eh, Liv? I almost forgot the rules you set," he retorts while retracing his steps till he is towering over me, ire radiating from his rigid demeanor. He darts his arm to my waist and pulls me against him, leaving tenderness aside. "So, how do you want it this time?" His mouth is aggressively on mine. His other hand, not less rough, grips my thigh, wrapping it around his pelvis. "Bend you over the sofa, go down on you on the floor?" His lips on mine are hard, demanding, and intrusive.

I squirm out of his firm hold and press my hands to his chest. "Stop it. No, Sebastian." He draws back immediately. We both catch our breath, our eyes collide with so much heat and muddle that it feels like we're trading flames rather than stares.

"No?" he questions with unconcealed contempt.

I hug myself, trying to ease my trembling.

"So tell me, what is it that you want from me? Because whatever I'm offering seems to not be good enough."

I open my mouth to say something, make it better, stop this senselessness, but words fail me. "Say something, Liv," he says with softened lining.

I try to control the lump forming in my throat. "Maybe we should talk about it when you're back, when we both had some time to think. When you . . . when we're less testy." My voice traitorously shakes.

He sighs in blatant frustration. "No. If you're not coming, then I'm done." He waits for a tense moment. To my silence, his lips flatten and he starts for the door. I follow him with my eyes. With each step that he takes toward the door, the spring in my stomach tightens.

Sebastian shoves his hand into his front pocket and produces a small card. He leaves it on the dining table, takes his helmet, and continues to the door. I hold my breath as I watch him leave. I flinch at the thud of the door as it slams behind him. Still hugging myself, I listen as he brings the bike to life, and I remain frozen as I listen to the roaring sound of the vehicle as it winds away.

As silence enfolds the house, the tears I've held back become impossible to restrain.

Chapter 16
"A Mistake"
Fiona Apple

Even after a night's sleep, if tossing and turning could be constituted as sleeping, my emotions and thoughts are still all over the place. Pored over and unknotted. I'm confused, upset, gloomy, and angry. The anger part though, is mostly, if not completely, with myself. I've royally screwed Sebastian and my "thing" with my bare hands, or silent mouth, or ridiculous bipolar behavior, or all of the above.

I push the half-empty cup of coffee away and slide my open notebook closer below me. I lightly touch my lips with the pads of my fingers and close my eyes. Puffing out a heavy exhale, I reach for the card Sebastian left on the table right before he left yesterday. It's silver, textured with black wording. A business card of the resort where the event is being held, or as I like to call it, my Last Chance card. By leaving this card, Sebastian has wordlessly told me that I could still make things right. Stop my pretense, as he said. I try not to ponder the implications of me not showing up. His words haunted me all through the night. "If you're not coming, I'm done." I rest the card next to the notebook and reach for the pen nestled in the gutter. I take another deep breath and start writing.

All answers are correct but choose one for the full mark. The correct answer that best elucidates my resentment for not giving in last night and having this unyielding guard when it comes to Sebastian is glaringly simple. I'm a coward. I'm scared.

I'm scared because he wasn't a part of my grand plan.

I'm scared because I lose control when I'm with him.

I'm scared of how my feelings for him solidify each time we're together.

I'm scared because we couldn't be more different.

I'm scared because I'm so afraid to let him in and then let him go.

I'm afraid because our togetherness has an expiration date.

And mostly, I'm afraid I'll never again feel the way I feel when I'm with him.

Am I ready to let him go without even giving us a real try?

Am I ready to let him go?

I write down the answer, the one I had all along but was too hesitant to embrace, and retrace it a couple of times till it screams back at me in bold, black enlightenment.

NO.

I push back the chair and head straight to my bedroom. I'm not even sure what I'm shoving into the open suitcase. There are a couple of dresses, a few pairs of heels, and an assortment of lingerie from all the varieties of the sultry to subtle spectrum. Adrenaline is rushing through me, building until I don't even know what I am throwing in the bag anymore.

. . .

As I stand before the friendly receptionist, the wind is slightly taken out of my sails. Okay, I'm here. Now, what? I don't have a room, and I'm not sure if I should get one. I'm not even sure where the event is being held, or how Sebastian will react when he sees me here. And what if I waited too long and he's already given up on me? Showing up, under those circumstances, would be a huge mistake.

"Bienvenida a Can Bonastre Wine Resort, Señorita," the friendly receptionist greets me, pulling me out of my concern bubble. "En qué puedo ayudale?"

"I'm here for the event?" I offer, tentatively.

"Of course, Miss. Would you like to check in first?" He smiles, nodding at my luggage.

"Can I have it stored for the time being?"

"Sure, Miss."

"Could you please direct me to the event?"

"Here is the agenda. The current session *News and Innovations, Textures and Tastes*, started about twenty minutes ago, but you can still get in."

It doesn't take me long to find the conference hall. Slowly, I pull back the round handle and try, as quietly as possible, to open the bronze door. I hold my breath as the heavy door slides back in a loud, lingered squeak. I inwardly curse when the same sound repeats when I try to close it gently behind me.

Disregarding the few heads turned my way, I make a quick peek of the approximately hundred guests, searching for a vacant chair. I spot one a couple of rows closer to the stage and quickly, yet stealthily, make my way toward my target. I smile apologetically at the couple sitting next to the vacant seat, nodding at the empty space. I wiggle through the small space between the lanky gentleman and the back of the seat of the next row. Another cautious step and I almost make it safely to my seat. *Almost*. The awkward, embarrassingly loud way I land onto the chair is more akin to a collision with the inanimate furniture. My pointy toe boot somehow manages to get stuck behind the leg of the chair of the lady I've tried to gracefully pass, and I end up diving onto my seat with an involuntary yelp and way too much ruckus.

At this point, *all* heads turn my way. Heat covers my skin as I offer a timid, apologetic look at whoever is in my direct view. My next remorseful gaze directs to the stage, to the person holding the mic whose attention I've apparently also managed to steal.

He brings the mic held still in his hand near his mouth and resumes his lecture, albeit his full attention remains on me. A clan of butterflies *on LSD* start dancing in my stomach to the fusion of our stares. My lips curve into a relieving, earnest smile when I notice the little pull of his lips, partly hidden behind the microphone. When he finally turns his attention back to his attentive audience, I get the full spectacular that is Sebastian on stage.

He moves in easy grace, the timbre of his masculine voice coated by his blood-simmering accent doing things to my imagination that I shouldn't entertain in a room full of people. Thirstily, I drink the sight of him. His handsome face, closely shaven and naturally tanned. His crew cut styled up in a semi-tamed fashion. His impeccable body clad in a snug black tee that's stylishly paired with a charcoal two-piece suit, perfectly accentuating his fit build. His fluid monologue colors the room till with a side smile and a wealth of charisma, he thanks the audience and announces a fifteen-minute break before the next presenter.

My nerves, just like the parting audience, scatter around in disorder as I wait for Sebastian, who's closing the distance between us. We hold eye contact even when he excuses himself from people who pause him for a handshake or a short chat. The longer it takes him to reach me, the more agitated I grow.

A small step away, he leans toward me, close enough for his lips to soar next to my ear. "You are here."

"I am."

He inches up, eyes me for a beat, giving me enough time to stew, to contemplate whether I made the right decision coming here. The pull of his lips at the side liberates me from these doubts. His dimple makes an appearance before he leans in toward me once more, only this time it's for his lips to touch mine with a chaste kiss. One that bathes me in tender warmness and his heady scent.

Sebastian takes my hand, suggesting I should follow. And follow I do. *As if there's anything else I'd rather do . . .*

"What are we doing here?" I ask Sebastian once we enter a small room packed with wine crates and clattered marketing collateral.

"I need to get some more samples," he says while setting a few red wine bottles onto a high table. "And taste you."

A soft smile adorns my lips when he turns my way. We study each other for a silent pause, a slow journey from each other's eyes to mouths and back. He takes another step to close the space between us. "Not necessarily in that order," he murmurs, his lips honing in on the pulsing vein on my neck. "Your smell . . ." He nuzzles my lightly heated skin.

Gradually the mass of his body covers mine, and we start a slow-motion dance of exploring each other. Sebastian leans me backward against the wall, and I gladly surrender, letting him lead. My hand travels to the back of his neck while the other cradles his firm rear. His fingers caress my collarbone, curling around my shoulder, pulling me deeper into our kiss. Roaming slowly over my curves, his other hand palms my ass. I slightly incline my mouth to better absorb his tender, yet determined tasting of me. Sebastian's thigh moves slightly to part my legs. The silence of the room soon fills with heavy breaths and occasional sounds of pure need as our desire to devour each other intensifies.

"Oh, God, you taste . . ." My words come out on a breath, right into the heat of Sebastian's intoxicating mouth.

"Sebastian? *Ay*, lo siento . . ."

My eyes rip open and cautiously trail toward the voice. Sebastian huffs and inches back. My already heated skin's temperature feels on fire. My partner in crime, utterly collected, turns to the gracefully matured, handsome version of himself.

"Papá." He shifts to fully face his dad. "This is Liv."

"Oh, *the* Liv? Great pleasure to meet you, I'm Miquel." Sebastian's dad, clad in a three-piece navy pinstripe suit takes a few steps to reach me. Before I'm able to respond, try to decode "*the* Liv" comment, or attempt to subtly make amends with what I'm sure is my disheveled state, his hands rest on either of my shoulders and he leans in to kiss both my cheeks.

"Likewise." Words scrape out of my mouth. I clear my throat and his eyes morph a shade wickeder.

The same tone is sent his son's way via a long side-glance. "I came for some extra samples, but I see you beat me to it." He gestures to the bottles Sebastian left aside before we began our "getting reacquainted" session. "Bueno, I'll see you both later." He winks at me and leaves.

Patting my hands over my outfit, I smooth the unfussy ensemble, ankle-cropped boyfriend style jeans and olive-green fit blazer which I've amped up with a stylish leopard scarf. "Nothing's better than a good first impression, uh?" I murmur.

Sebastian regards me with a mirthful sidelong peep. "Don't sweat it. I'm pretty sure he'd high five me if he didn't think it would make you even more uncomfortable." Sebastian smirks and I shake my head, however with a dainty arch of my lips. He extends his hand to me. "Let's get back. You can either stick around for the next session or go to the room. Thought you might want to rest."

"I could use a little nap," I say, indulging in the feel of his palm against mine.

"We'll probably wrap up in a couple of hours, and I'll come up then. Oh, and dinner is at eight. I'll have to be at the bar about half past seven though, for mingling." The last part is uttered with an accompanying eye roll.

I assist Sebastian by carrying a bunch of brochures as we make our way back to the foyer where guests are scattered in little groups, chatting and tasting wine till the next lecture begins. Sebastian leaves the wine crate with one of the servers, briefly instructing him where and how the samples should be placed.

Same goes for the marketing material.

Having a sense of being watched, my stare is pulled toward the opposite side of the ample space to where an elegant woman donning a mauve suit and a silky, dark bun nods at Sebastian with a heartfelt smile. Her attention is drawn my way with the slide of Sebastian's hand to my waist. Her expression hardens, deepening in scrutinized interest. I return her stare with no less curiosity. When Sebastian's father reaches her side and enfolds *her* narrow waist, I put two and two together. The mother.

Sebastian drops a light kiss on my temple and squeezes my waist. "Let's go say hello to my mom."

I have an urge to argue, but in the same breath, I decide to remain silent. If I am here, I may as well just go with it. By joining him this weekend, I've nonverbally agreed to more. The cards of our "rules," the ones I've religiously kept thus far, have been shuffled.

"Nice seeing you again," Sebastian's dad nods at us politely, a hint of a knowing glee decorating his features.

"Oh, you've already met Sebastian's, eh . . . friend?" Sebastian's mother's neatly made-up face turns to her husband with overt keenness.

A side smile adorns Sebastian's dad's smoothly shaven face. "I had the pleasure of running into the lovely Miss Liv while she was tasting one of our special vintages."

Sebastian raises an eyebrow, rewarding his father with a mischievous grin. Warm heat washes over my cheeks. A flush that deepens when Sebastian's mom asks me, "And how did you like it?"

"Very much. I've never tasted anything like it," I say, willing my convicting rosiness to evaporate. Both men's eyes light up in cheeky elation. I bite my lip to keep it from widely stretching.

"I'm glad to hear that. I hope you'll have the chance to try more of our wine this weekend."

"I'll make sure of that," Sebastian says, and his old man gifts me with a wink.

"So you're staying for the entire event, then, Livia?"

"It's Liv, Mom," Sebastian corrects his mother.

"Um, I guess I am." I chance a glance at Sebastian.

"I hope our son got you one of the suites in the south wing. They have the best view of the resort."

I send Sebastian another glance, not sure how I should respond to that.

"I did. *Liv* is staying with me," Sebastian answers in an idle tone, nodding at a gentleman who raises a full glass his way.

His mother's demeanor seems to muddle for a flit beat. When she recomposes, she darts a look, which I can't gauge, toward her husband and son in tandem. Alas, it's her expression when she pivots my way that leaves *me* less than composed. "Oh," she says, her eyes narrowing at me, but her question is directed at her son. "I thought Lola was sharing your room. Is this a last moment change?"

A few things happen in succession after the last of her words drop between the four of us. A blow that pummels at my stomach. Me trying to subtly wiggle out of Sebastian's hold. Sebastian's arm securing firmer around me, keeping me next to him. Miquel ducking to whisper something to his wife while giving me a genuinely rueful glance.

"Lola was never supposed to share my room." Sebastian's low

voice holds more than the irritation he radiates; there's a warning carried somewhere along his tone.

"What was I never supposed to do?" The woman in subject appears out of thin air. With her shine, almond eyes, and blood-red lips, she adds the last necessary detail to make me feel like I'm exactly where I don't belong. I'm not sure what to make of the caution embedded gentle headshake the man holding me tight to his side sends his friend Lola.

Both women trade a short glance before turning in unison my way. The entire situation makes me second-guess the decision I took to join the event in the first place.

"Lola, have you had the chance to meet Tian's new friend?" Sebastian's mom asks Lola with a blatant "can you believe this?" look. Or maybe it just appears that way to me. Whatever it is, there's clear displeasure echoing from her small gesture.

"You must be Liv!"

I can't hold any resentment toward Lola with the kind smiles she peppers my way.

"I'm Lola." She hugs me and plants two airy kisses on either of my cheeks. Truth be told, at this point, I'd be more than happy for the joyful gathering to end and for the welcoming committee to break up.

"Nice to meet you." It takes great effort for me to sound as amicable as I do.

"So, I guess we'll see you guys later at dinner," Lola continues with a cheery voice. She threads her arm through the crook of the older lady's and says, "We should go, Celeste, we'll miss our spa treatment." That last tidbit wraps up the stingfest my stomach has been hosting for the last few minutes perfectly. Just when I finally decide to give a chance to Sebastian and me, I find out that his mom could probably live without the idea of her son seeing me, and that she's more than fond of his fine-looking friend. Same friend that not only looks more radiant up close, but also kisses him on the lips and leaves him "thank you for last night" notes. With goddamn red lipstick on his mirror.

I can't help the stare I have trained on the ladies, following them as they disappear through a narrow corridor, joined by their semi-embrace. Miquel leaves us next.

Sebastian's arm on my shoulder pulls me closer to him. "Hey," he says in a voice that makes me believe he knows that the little gathering made me uncomfortable. As much as I try to play it cool, I can't wipe the unease that has just been infused to every part of me. Sebastian stoops, his eyes searching mine. He slants closer to plant a soft kiss on my lips. "Don't take my mom too seriously."

I nod, daze fogging my thoughts. "I guess I'll go to the room now."

"I wish I could join you, but I need to attend the next session. I'm already running a bit late." Sebastian produces a keycard from his pocket. "I'll be there as soon as I can." He is about to head back to where people are swarming back into the conference hall and takes half a step back. He cups my cheeks and startles me next when he kisses me as though there's no one around us – tongue, intensity, and heat.

"I'm glad you came." He dips his chin for another kiss, a light one, and leaves, too.

Chapter 17
"I'll Drink to That"
Outasight

Trolley in tow, I leave reception to find our room, almost missing, for the second time, the beauty of the resort. Pushing away malignant thoughts that threaten to ruin this weekend for me, I stop to take in the view. The view I missed when I rushed in this morning, equally anxious and hesitant.

Lying at the foot of the spectacular Sierra de Montserrat Mountains, the resort has the perfect hideaway setting. The main building, our haven for the weekend, is an eighteenth century country house surrounded by acres of vineyards. It is heaven on Earth, and it is ours. And I'll be damned if I let anything, or anyone, ruin that for me. Not an overprotective mother, an attractive friend, or even a damned force majeure will hold me back from enjoying our time together to the fullest. With a grin plastered on my lips and a determined "fuck that" in my heart, I enter our room. The smile on my face might have just reached its full elasticity.

I take a short tour of the room, admiring the contemporary, cozy style that transcends all aspects of the space. Mahogany wood elements that bring warmth and beauty to the minimalist design. Though there is so much to take in – the details of the room, the glass enclosed shower dominating the space, and the marvelous view from the small, charming balcony – I choose to focus on the deserted black tee loosely draped on the headboard of the wide bed. Bringing the shirt to my nose, I take a lungful, closing my eyes. Sebastian's scent of warm chocolate and earthy seeps in, stirring my insides in the best of ways. In record time, I strip off my clothes and shrug the shirt on. Wrapping myself in the cuddly comfort only a well-worn shirt can induce, the smell of the man I wish was wrapped around me right now bathes me. Snuggled under the plump down comforter, it doesn't take me long to drift into deep, serene sleep.

I flutter my eyes open into a dimly lit room. I'm alone; the balcony door is open, bringing in a gentle evening breeze. I jump at the sudden escalating mechanical bell jangling that rudely disturbs my mellow wakening. It takes a few additional monotonous chimes more till I realize it's the alarm clock on my phone that's screaming at me to rise and shine. I send my hand for the exasperating device on the nightstand and hurry to turn it off. I can't help the giggle rolling off my lips when I notice the little note left for me next to the phone.

Get your perfecto ass out of bed and come join me for dinner.

A quick shower, thorough application of honeysuckle and spices scented lotion, and dramatic evening make-up, then I slip on a semi-sheer black silk maxi dress. I turn to examine my back via the standing mirror and beam at the way the low-cut, strappy back detail showcases my milky skin. The dress might be a tad daring given the blurry line between where the arc of my lower back ends and the curve of rear begins. Nevertheless, or in spite of, I leave it on, knowing full well how my dinner companion will appreciate the effort.

. . .

Patrons in small groups engaged in conversations around tall tables dot the misty bar. Seeing no familiar faces, and no Sebastian in sight, I decide to wait at the bar till dinner. I'm about to ask for one of the fruity cocktails on the menu when my eyes fall on the row of wine bottles on display on the wooden surface. Noticing the labels exhibiting Sebastian's family winery, I ask the graying bartender with the crisp apron for the Riesling.

A gentleman next to me tips his head in greeting. Eyeing me, he lets the bartender know he'll be taking care of my bill. I thank him and he asks for my name.

"Jario." He introduces himself, taking a taste of his dark drink. He tells me that he is from Madrid, and that he came to the event to choose new wines for his restaurant that specializes in traditional paella dishes. His smile grows when I share with him my great love for the Spanish cuisine.

"So, how about you reserve time for me for an evening walk after dinner?" he asks next, moving his hand to rest next to mine.

A light brush of warm fingers tickles my exposed back; my skin rises to the delicate flutter and to the presence of the man who's now leaving a soft kiss on my shoulder. I thank Jario for the drink, and kindly refuse the offer for the walk, explaining that my evening belongs to Sebastian.

"I hope that much more than just your evening belongs to me." Sebastian twirls me to face him.

"Depends what you're offering." I smile into my wine glass.

Sebastian shakes his head with a faint smile of his own and holds his heart as if I just shot him right through.

"Have I told you how beautiful you look tonight?"

"No, and you should rectify it immediately."

Sebastian's dimple makes an appearance.

"You look stunning. Join me for dinner?" He offers me his hand. I take it and follow him with a butterfly, or two, dancing around in my belly.

After a short introduction to our dinner companions, a couple of wine aficionados, and a cork manufacturer from Portugal and his wife, Sebastian pulls my chair back and waits till I take my seat.

He bows to leave a kiss on my cheek and whispers next to my ear, "You look so delicious, I wish I could skip this damn dinner and eat you."

I try to conceal the lick of desire now burning within me with the simple act of placing the dinner napkin on my thighs.

Savoring the entrées, an assortment of lightly grilled seafood seasoned with a hint of salt, I admire Sebastian who's attentive and patient to the wine enthusiasts that bombard him with questions about new lines, vintages, and whatnot concerning his business. He'd changed into a dark fitted suit paired with a white button-down, top buttons undone. His hair is tamed in a slick back style, his hard jaw and strong cheeks neatly shaven, his eyes twinkling with that special glee they take on when he talks about his passion. I find it hard to unglue my stare from him when the guy to my right engages me in a conversation. We don't interact much with each other throughout the evening; nevertheless, the loaded connection between us is ever-present. With "accidental" brushes, the constant buzz looping between us, covert smiles, the intent chance glances while conversing with others.

A delicious main course and dessert later, I let Sebastian do his thing and head to the balcony with a cup of Cortado. I'm in need of a breather after having just enough of everything wine, too much dinner party hum, and frequent, unpleasant glances from a certain Mrs. Balle, aka the mother of my lover. Bracing my elbows on the wrought iron railings, I enjoy the lovely night enhanced by the moonlight's soft halo and sporadic twinkling dots. The heavy patter of footsteps coming from behind prompts me to resurface from my private moment and turn back to Miquel, who's approaching me in a tailored navy suit.

"Good evening," he says and sends his hand to the cigar nestled in his ivory pocket square.

"Good evening to you, too." I turn to face him fully, taking a sip of my coffee.

"How are you enjoying the event so far?" He tilts his head toward a butane lighter, cigar wedged between his lips. I watch him as he inhales in short puffs till the end turns an evenly illuminated cherry-red.

"Leisurely." A thin smile raises my lips.

"Sebastian asked me to step in tomorrow so he could spend more time with you," he says, positioning himself next to me, leaning his back on the railing.

With a warm cloud in my stomach, I grin into the night.

"Doesn't happen too often," he adds.

I study his face lightened by the supple moon glimmer. Getting an image of how Sebastian might look in his sixties. Same strong jaw, beautiful dark eyes, creases and silver, full hair that enhance the gracefully aging appearance. A very promising foretell.

"It's been a while since he got seriously involved with someone." He exhales a long cloud of white smoke. "After what happened with Lola and all. But I'm sure you already knew about that."

A feeling that weighs heavily on my stomach prevents me from telling him that I actually don't already know anything about what happened with Lola and his son, and that only the sound of it makes my mood drastically deflate.

"Sebastian says you're into financial consulting. Are you practicing that here as well?"

Talk about a change of subject. Still reeling from his last statement, I mumble a short, "Um, no. I'm here to purely enjoy your beautiful country."

"I see. If you change your mind, we could always use another set of eyes on this business opportunity we're currently examining."

"Oh, even though I'm not officially on duty, I'd be more than glad to assist, if I can."

"Whatever he is offering, say no." Sebastian's voice reaches us from across the balcony. We both regard him with a friendly grin.

"Oh, sorry sir, no can do. What he is offering is far too

tempting to refuse." I wink at Miquel who seems pleased with me poking at his son.

"And once again, they end up falling for you, Papá." Sebastian enfolds his arm around my waist, drawing me closer to him. "I'm here to save you," he says in a feigned whisper. He releases his hold on me next, only to shrug off his jacket and wrap it around my shoulders.

His father gives my swooned expression a peep and says, "Enjoy your night," before leaving us to ourselves.

Sebastian embraces me, his arms surrounding me by my waist. His eyes tell me how happy he is to see me just before his lips do the same. "Let's go enjoy our night," he says, breaking our kiss.

. . .

By the time I take the jacket and heels off, Sebastian has already changed to black training pants. I inwardly high five myself at the sight of him sauntering into the living space with nothing but those sporty pants that hang low on his hips, exposing delicious, tanned, taut skin, ornamented by a no less enticing dark trail.

Still in my dress, with Miquel's earlier comment still hounding my mood every now and then with perturbing little jabs, I tuck my legs below me, nestling on the sitting area's plush rug, leaning my back to the beige loveseat. I follow Sebastian with my stare as he crouches next to the minibar, absorbedly studying the rich content.

"Hola, Don Julio," he beams at the bronze liquid's surf in the clear bottle. "So glad this day is over," he comments as he settles on the rug by my side. He sets the bottle on the table and reaches for my legs, helping them over his bent ones. He leans closer for his lips to cover mine for a long taste. Easing back, he turns to uncork the bottle of tequila. "I've arranged it so that we'll be able to spend most of tomorrow together."

"You didn't have to do that for me. You're here for work, after all."

"Didn't have to . . ." He presses a light kiss on my bare shoulder, bottle still in hand. "Wanted to."

I snatch the bottle from him, and in a much un-ladylike manner, I take a generous swig that ends with my insides literally catching fire. "I'll drink to that," I croak via the body-wide shock my poor intestines go through, recuperating from this toxin disguised as booze. "Can't wait to spend the day with you," I say, looking at him from under my lashes, not sure if the heatwave tinting my skin is a product of my admission or the lethal alcohol.

He reclaims possession of the bottle and brings it to his lips. "I'll drink to that." He cringes, swallowing. He strokes my legs ever so slowly, thigh to knee. "I think my dad has a crush on you," he beams and turns my way, radiating his soft expression to me.

I smile to the bottle's mouth as I bring it toward my lips. "I'll drink to that." This time, wisely enough, I make it a wee sip. "Your mom doesn't seem like my greatest fan, though."

He shakes his head. "I need a drink for that." We both grin. "I'm glad you came. I didn't want to have to give up on you."

His words pull at my heart. "I'll drink to that," I whisper and take another light sip. "I'm here, for *everything* being here represents."

"I'll drink to that." This time his voice is the one saturated with gentleness. Throwing back another drink, he dips and coaxes my mouth to join the taste. I tilt my head and flutter my eyes closed, dissolving into the feel of our tongues dancing slowly through the burning liquid.

As we slowly pull back, the space around me sways a little. I'm not sure if it's the effect of the alcohol that I've been consuming without a care, or the intimacy we are sharing that makes me say, "I want to visit Barcelona with you." Out of the "what the hell" blue. "And Paris. Wow, Paris and you . . . You and me in Paris . . ."

"Sure, drinking to that." He grins. "I want to have you on our yacht in Barcelona and in Paris." The sinister grin doubles.

My face must be some spectacle, a blazing, joyful one. "Shut your face, you own a yacht?" I blink, and he casually nods. A little smirk pops on his lips, undoubtedly a product of my graceful articulation. "I'll drink to that." I take another drink that feels like it might just kill me. The room becomes a blurry blend of soft lights and solid dark objects, which I think might be the furniture, or rocks, or dancing trees. With zero control over my thoughts or mouth, I blurt, "I kissed a girl in college."

Sebastian's wicked chuckle trickles through me just before he murmurs, "most deserved shot ever. I'll drink to that." And another mouthful is consumed. "I like this buzzed side of you. I want to hear about the full experience, in detail, when you're actually in control of what is coming out of your mouth."

"*I like you.*" I giggle. "Like, I like you. Like a whole lot of crazily like you!" I giggle again, patting his cheek twice.

Watching me heatedly, he swallows another taste.

Next my mouth is swallowed. And my neck. And my

collarbone. And in record time, I find myself sprawled with my back to the carpet and with Sebastian between my parted legs. His hands and mouth are all over me. I close my eyes, indulging in his heated, eager attack. The indulging part, though, lasts for exactly two and a half seconds. Everything around me spins, everything inside me turns and everything the person on top of me is doing should stop right now.

"Sebastian, I'm going to be sick," I manage a feeble whisper to Sebastian's mouth. What happens next? I have no clue because I pass out *cold*.

Chapter 18
"Feel This"
Bethany Joy Lenz

I try to straighten my stiff back, but it hurts.

I try to swallow over my dry mouth, but it hurts.

I try to force my eyes open, but it hurts so damn much.

An involuntary groan scrapes from my mouth as I finally manage to carefully flicker one eye open. It takes a sluggish moment for my surroundings to register. I'm in the bathroom, "gracefully" slouched somewhere near the toilet. Feels like my bones have left my body. My eyes drop to run over myself and check for overall damage. Somehow, I'm in a fresh pair of panties and a large tee that ends in a pile of fabric around my hips. Around me, supporting me on either side are masculine legs, and my pillow, as it seems, is a warm body. I shift my head slowly, very slowly because it hurts like a son of a bitch trying to look at Sebastian. To my own shifting, his body behind me starts stretching in lazy motions.

"How do you feel?" he rasps.

"I want to die," I whisper. His chest lightly shakes in harmony to a soft animated snort. My lips make an attempt at settling into a semblance of a smile. What a task.

Behind me, Sebastian inches some. "Hold on, let me get up," he says in a low voice and my thudding head and I couldn't be more grateful for the low decibel. Sebastian towers above me, studying me in assessment. With a ghost of a smile, he bends to hook one arm under my knees and the other under my arm and effortlessly lifts me up. He carries my lethargic body à la romance movie style toward the living area. The only difference is, in romance movies usually the hero doesn't look like he could use a good night's sleep and a shave and the heroine is not a total mess.

Carefully, Sebastian sets me onto the sofa, arranging a couple of pillows behind my back. He leaves an airy kiss on my forehead and turns toward the minibar.

I gape at him with utter puzzlement as he tears open a bag of gummy worms and piles a few in the palm of his hand, which in my current state, looks like a psychedelic pile of Jello. With his other, he flings open a small can of soda. Sebastian scoots close to me on the sofa and brings the colorful contents in his hand to my mouth. With a gentle arch of his lips and a motion of his eyebrow, he gestures for me to open my mouth to the mound of sugar.

"What's that?"

"Hangover remedy."

To my frown, his dimple appears.

"I don't think so. I'll throw up."

Amused expression intact, his eyes caress my disheveled appearance. "I wouldn't worry about that. I don't think there's anything left in you."

I got to give it to him, at least he has the decency to try and subordinate his smirk by biting on it.

I bury my face in my hands, a motion that calls for a new wave of thudding to strike at my temples. Hands still covering my cheeks, my eyes trail up to Sebastian's as I ask, "How bad was it, err, last night?"

"Let's just say, I've never had anyone barf on me after I've kissed her. It was, ah . . . unique." He lightly chuckles.

"God, now I really want to die."

Another soft chuckle.

"I should pack now," I murmur. "Our thing will forever be haunted by my barfing – God, this is so embarrassing. You'll never want to attempt to kiss me again, let alone... I killed our thing." I stop, shaking my head at what a mess I made of the evening.

"You haven't killed anything. Anyway, our thing covers so much more than just sex."

The severity of his statement and the way it comes out takes me aback a little. "Now, open up," he orders. I open my mouth to about half a dozen gummy worms. "Don't chew them yet." And he brings the small Coke can next to my mouth. "Take a generous sip and just let it soak for a while."

We share a prolonged gaze, him with a need for a shave that just adds an extra roughness to everything that's already handsomely rough. And me, I must look just lovely. I can't even imagine the disaster on my face given the make-up I haven't removed from last night and well, the shenanigans that followed.

In an attempt to make some sort of amends with my appearance, I bring my hand to my hair. In a reflexive, innate motion, I run my palm over the side of my face to brush my hair back and stop short. I lightly pat my head next in several places and my brows furrow. In one hard gulp, I swallow the sickeningly sweet contents of my mouth and my eyes fly to Sebastian. To my confounded stare, he cocks his head. It takes me another whole beat to intellectualize my findings.

"You braided my hair?" I whisper in a voice that brims with emotion.

"Yeah." It's his turn to appear perplexed. "After I washed you and helped you into fresh clothes. I didn't want it to get dirty again . . . you know, get it out of the line of fire." He ends his explanation with the sweetest of boyish smiles and a dimple. The hangover has nothing on the effect our short exchange has on me. I tilt forward; cradling his prickled cheeks in my hands and bring my lips to his. It's a chaste kiss. A chaste kiss full of something new, something that has his name all over it. Overtaken by the iron grip on my heart, needing to make sense of it, I excuse myself to freshen up.

"Hey, do you mind being in a room that's less illuminated and has a bed?" I ask, returning from a get a grip and a quick face and mouth wash break.

Sebastian beams at me. "The magic potion didn't help?"

"Oddly enough, it did tone it down a little, but I guess a horizontal position and dimness will help even more."

We lie facing each other on the bed, our cheeks resting on our palms over a pillow. I made sure the curtains and the door are shielding us from the outside world, leaving the bedroom dimly illuminated.

"You mentioned my mom again yesterday, a few times, actually.

Don't worry about her, okay?" he says, his eyes owning mine.

I sigh. "Well, I guess I'm just not a mom person. Even mine doesn't think I'm all that."

Irritation seeps into the stare he has trained on me. "Why would you say something like this?"

My lips curve in disdain. I leave my pillow and shift to rest my head on Sebastian's abs, fixating my stare at the ceiling. "I mean, my relationship with my mom has always been, um, complicated." I halt for a moment. His fingers comb through my hair, caressing in light strokes. Something about him, something about how he makes me feel lifts a dam I've managed to keep securely locked for a very long time. "*So complicated*. I've always been empathetic toward her; she's my mom, after all. But, I never could diminish the distance I felt toward her. It's hard given she's always unsatisfied with everything I do. I feel like the greatest failure of her life, and it's not the easiest cross to bear. Frankly, it's the hardest subject of *my* life. I guess some of the distance I needed from home was essentially from her."

Sebastian's other hand moves to rest in the hollow between my collarbone and throat. Our deep intimacy and his ever-present nonverbal support make it easy to talk to him, and I go on. "Funny, I've always believed a mother's first and foremost role is to make her child feel special, no matter what. I guess mine was absent from that crucial lesson." In a way, I feel purged after pouring out my heart. The adrenaline fueling within me also makes me . . . gutsy. I turn to lay on my belly, my chin on Sebastian's stomach. His eyes meet mine, and he is about to say something, but I cut him off.

"What's the real story between Lola and you?"

Chapter 19
"Torn"
Natalie Imbruglia

He nods. I couldn't appreciate more the fact that he doesn't try to play it as if he doesn't know what I'm talking about or try to brush it off. In the same breath, I'm not sure I want to know the real story, particularly with his soft expression morphing into edged solemnity.

"We've been friends forever. I guess she's what you'd call my best friend. She's also essentially a family member. Our moms are close friends. They always teased us about how we'd get married when we grew up. Though I always assumed there was much more behind the joking.

"We were inseparable. Lola even followed me to study abroad. For the sake of our friendship, we used to have 'the talk' every now and then, about how we felt toward each other and how it would ruin our friendship if these feelings were other than platonic. I never had any feelings for her, in that sense. I always thought she looked good, but I never found her attractive. She's always been like a third sister to me. She used to insist she felt the same way about me." His eyes drift from mine to the ceiling.

"That was until one of our friends from college died in an accident. It was hard. We were pretty close to him."

"I'm sorry," I say in a small voice. Sebastian nods to the ceiling. I kiss his bare stomach, and he resumes.

"Lola was devastated. She dated him a couple of times. It didn't work out, but they remained friends. When we heard the news, an immediate memorial gathering took place in one of the rooms in our dorms. Lola didn't want to go; she felt it was too painful and wanted to just be with me. We ended up in my room, passing a bottle of cheap scotch between us in silence. When she asked me to hold her, I did. It was the most natural thing in the world."

And as the plot thickens, the less I want to hear. The tighter my stomach twists.

"Then she kissed me and asked me not to stop." He sighs, his tongue moves to stroke his front teeth. "We were sad, we were shocked and shattered, and we slept together." His eyes search mine. "I've never regretted anything more in my life."

I nod.

"The morning after, when she told me that she had feelings for me, I told her I didn't feel the same way. She swore it wouldn't change anything between us, and that she didn't want to lose me as a friend." Sebastian's jaw tenses. "Lola found out she was pregnant a couple of months later. For her, coming from a Catholic family, keeping the baby was the only option."

My stomach clutches. I keep quiet, watching him attentively.

"When a child and the closest person to you are involved, you choose them over yourself. I told Lola I'd marry her and that we'd raise the child together."

Many questions run through my mind. All of them leave an acidic taste in my mouth.

"I felt like I was giving up my life at the age of twenty-one."

I tense, waiting for the rest of his story.

"When we came back home for Christmas break and told our families, Lola was already three months along. Our mothers couldn't contain their joy, regardless of our young age or the fact that I was torn." His voice dims. "I was about to give up my life . . ." Another dejected sigh leaves his mouth. "There were complications and she lost the baby two weeks later."

"Sebastian," his name is a whisper on my lips. I lace my fingers through his in empathy.

"It tore me apart. I was broken. I felt like somehow it was an unspoken wish of mine fulfilling itself. I hated myself for the longest time for the simple relief I felt."

"Sebastian, you were trapped in something you didn't want, and yet you stepped in and was about to give up your own future and happiness just to make sure others were taken care of. That's such an incredibly selfless thing to do. It's not your fault that the pregnancy ended that way."

"I'd never let myself get into such a commitment again unless I'm more than a hundred percent positive it's what I want. Hell, I can't even think about going through anything like that again."

I couldn't agree more. Nevertheless, I can't ignore the heavy press his words have on my heart.

"So, that's the story," he concludes. "We are still good friends, friends with substantial baggage," he adds in bitterness. "And I can only assume my mom's attitude toward you comes from the fact that she never really got over the idea that Lola and

I will never get married."

"Wow," I breathe. There's so much to process.

"You feel better?" he asks, catching me by surprise. "The hangover?"

"I think I do," I say, unfocused, pondering what he just laid before me.

"Let's go for a walk. There's something I want to show you."

Chapter 20
"Poison and Wine"
The Civil Wars

I sit at the garden café, having a glass of Cava, waiting for Sebastian, who had to meet his dad for a short recap of the day. I cross my legs under my A-line, floral halter-neck dress, tapping my green slip-on shoes against my heel, while contemplating the way I've opened up to Sebastian about my mom and thinking about a fragment of a conversation I had with Dr. Schmurtaz before I left for Spain. Thoughts that make sense of my recent actions, choices, and mostly, my inner dilemmas. "*You* have to take on the job of changing your patterns *yourself*. An answer from *me* won't get you anywhere, it will just be a waste of your time," the doctor said. His words keep echoing in my head to a point, which makes me question therapy in general.

Perhaps, it is time I started changing my own patterns. Perhaps, instead of finding so many ways to be troubled by what Sebastian shared with me earlier, I should just be glad he shared it with me, opened up to me, and let me in. With the next sip of my bubbly drink, I decide to take a break from therapy once we are back home. Take a break from overthinking, and everything that threatens to overshadow my current bliss.

"Ready?" Sebastian offers me his hand. I gift him with a thin smile, admiring the sight of him in casual attire. Black cargos and a black snug tee. Simple, yet delectable.

"Where are we going?"

"Have you ever been to a wine cellar?" The mischievous expression on his face makes me think he might have asked something much less innocent.

"Not yet."

He brings my hand to his mouth for a gentle kiss. "Let's go."

After a short walk in the gardens, we return to the main house. Sebastian holds the door for me and nods at the lady at reception. He guides us to a wooden door adjacent to the restaurant and then to a flight of stairs that ends in a darkened, cave-like cellar. He sends me an intense look as we walk through a thick brick walled corridor.

We are welcomed by a musty, moldy scent once we enter a vast room with rows and rows of wooden barrels lying against natural stone walls. It's chilly, humid, faintly lit, and majestic. I run my hand over one of the cold surfaces of a barrel, and lift my eyes to the stoney arched ceiling. I take in the dusky place and turn to look at Sebastian.

"It's beautiful, in a perfect murder setting kind of way."

Sebastian's lips tip up to the side. "There's more." Sebastian's low voice echoes in the opulent room. I follow him to a smaller room covered wall to wall with bottles of wine nestled in dark wood racks. The wall of large barrels hides the room; a small cave in the darkened underground cellar.

"Would you like a taste?" he asks.

My eyes trail to Sebastian's. I hold his gaze and glide my tongue over my lower lip. "Yes," I say softly. "Of you."

Sebastian takes a step forward. He brushes my hair back over my shoulder. Slowly, he tilts his face, nearing my collarbone. He flutters his lips over my skin, raising bumps in his wake. Even slower, he leaves a trail of supple kisses up my neck, to my cheek, toward my mouth, while gently guiding me backward with his weight.

My back meets the round belly of a barrel when I send my hand to Sebastian's neck and pull him to me for our mouths to fuse. Sebastian's hands skim over my dress, tracing my curves. One of his hands roams under the hem of my dress, slowly grazing my thigh, reaching higher. His other pulls down the straps of my dress and bra, revealing my lace covered breast. Leaving my mouth, he suckles my skin, kissing my neck, descending in igniting bites lower and lower. He wraps his warm lips over my nipple that hardens under the lacy fabric barely covering it. He sucks hard, biting, sucking again and leisurely laps his tongue to soothe the heated peak. My eyes roll back in my head and a soft moan funnels through my lips. I keep my head tilted back, savoring Sebastian's touch. I bring my hand to his hard chest and stroke his defined ridges toward his belt. I slide my hand under the belt till I reach him. I wrap my hand around the taut, warm skin and watch him halt then drop his forehead to my chest, his eyes closed. His breathing picks up as I gently squeeze him, rubbing my thumb over the head.

"Liv," he growls.

"Yeah." I stroke him in long lingered strokes while pushing my middle against him. Sebastian inclines his head to look at me with a stare that melts my insides. He keeps his eyes locked on mine as his fingers graze over my underwear. With his eyes burning mine, he rips my panties off me, tucking them into his pocket. His hand reaches back to me. His thumb dipping between my pleats, slowly pressing harder as he caresses it in long, slow motions. We hold our stares firm when he pushes a finger into me and I stroke him firmer, reaching the base and cupping him in my hand.

"God . . . Sebastian," I breathe.

"Joder," he groans.

Sebastian sinks another finger in me and my head drops back. "Unbuckle my belt," he commands. In a matter of a few short beats, his pants drop to a pool of fabric at his ankles, and my dress is lifted to my waist. He grabs me by my thighs and lifts me to straddle him. I wrap my legs around him. One of his hands moves to a higher barrel, holding the weight of us both. His other cradles my rear, holding me right in front of him.

"Take me inside you," he rasps.

Holding his gaze, I reach for him and guide him closer. I rub him against my arousal as his stare on me darkens. I position him right where I'm burning for him and when he pushes in, in a fluid thrust, we both freeze at the sensation.

"I want you so much." An irresistible urge coats my words. And he pulls out and pushes in, this time harder, just like I need him to. "Harder," I cry out and he submits. To my rapid breaths and rough tug on his hair, he increases his thrusts to a forceful, intoxicating pace. He pounds harder, repeatedly, in a rhythm that makes me build up faster. The ample room echoes with the sounds of our erratic breaths, pants, curses, the sound of flesh against flesh, and our names on each other's lips. He drives wildly into me, filling me completely, his wide length touching all the right spots. I grip him harder, one hand in his hair, the other around his neck. I dip my mouth to reach his firm shoulder and bite it hard as I absorb his raw, blessed attack. I become slicker and greedier, feeling him grow thicker in me. He slows to steal some hungry kisses from my lips. I squeeze him deeper, tighter, as I climb to the very top through my ecstasy. And as he slams into me with undeniable fire, I let go with his name enlaced through my cry. Not long after, Sebastian chases my climax with his own.

Chapter 21
"Matters of the Heart"
Tracy Chapman

They say each day we die a little more. Physiologically, it obviously couldn't be more true. In a sense, even mentally we do. Life has a tendency to wear us out, even when it's good to us. Even through moments of great happiness and bliss, we still age. However, since the moment I arrived here, since the moment I met the girls, and mostly, since the moment I met Sebastian, I feel like I'm getting a little more alive every day. Though I haven't done anything truly momentous or grandiose, these past months have been the happiest I've been in a long, long while.

"Coffee?" Vivian asks from where she fusses about with a few orders behind the counter. Resurfacing from my philosophical musing, I send her a questioning stare. "Would you like a cup of coffee, Liv?"

I nod, still somewhat pensive, my thoughts pulling me back to earlier this morning. To when Sebastian left my place. To how he kissed my lips, lustful and ardent enough to leave me yearning for more while he's away. Sebastian left this morning for Lisbon for a week. A business trip to further negotiate the new opportunity his father mentioned when we were at the resort, which feels like ages ago now. My lips settle in a calm arch as I think of what's coming next, at the end of the week. This coming Friday, I am to meet Sebastian in Barcelona, where we plan to stay on his family's boat for the weekend. I'm not sure what excites me more about the weekend, Barcelona, which I've wanted to visit since I arrived in Spain, spending time on a boat with Sebastian, or just simply spending the weekend with Sebastian.

"Everything okay?" I ask Vivian, who settles into the seat beside me. She continues to rub her hand on her chest, a hint of pain soaring over her face.

"Si, si. It's just this pain; it comes and goes, started last night. I think I just slept wrong. It's nothing, I'm sure. It'll go away." She puts her ever-present smile back on.

"Are you sure?"

She dismisses my concern with a nod. She eyes me for a lengthened moment, bringing a Carquinyolis toward her mouth. She bites into the Spanish biscotti version, eyeing me curiously, her stare narrowed as though she's trying to read me. I glance backward, checking if any of our friends have arrived yet.

"I'm seeing Sebastian," I say in a low voice, answering some unspoken question. "I spent the weekend with him in Masquefa."

She doesn't say a word, her lips tipping up behind the biscotti she holds next to her mouth.

"I'm going to tell the girls, but I really don't want to make a big deal out of it."

Her eyes joyfully join her smile.

"I thought I'd tell you before, since you know him and all."

She keeps silent, her calm smile unbroken.

"And since it's just a temporary thing, with me leaving in a few months . . ."

She nods with an easier smile. "I'm glad for you." She squeezes my hand and rises to stand. Uncharacteristically, she doesn't add a word and instead heads toward the working area. Her reaction, the enigmatic bright expression she has on makes me think of a gypsy fortune teller who has just found out what your future holds and for some reason is not willing to share the revelation.

I stare at her, confused. "That's it?"

She glances at me over her shoulder. "Yes. I'm glad for you, both." The flat undercurrent of her response and that little secretive glint in her eyes leaves me bothered, even concerned.

Dominique is the first one to join us. She kisses me airily on both cheeks and glides to the seat at the head of the table. "Is everyone coming?"

"Embar has a thing, she said she might drop by later."

Dominique nods. "I see you had a good weekend," she determines after throwing me a brief, yet exhaustive side-glance. I smile at her in response.

Stephy joins us just as Vivian sets an aromatic duet of Manchego cheese fondue and chunks of crusty, crackly bread on the table. When Alma shows up moments later, Vivian adds small dishes of jambon, cubes of apples, marinated mushrooms, and gherkins.

"Dzese will go great wiz a Chenin Blanc," says Dominique, gesturing to the fiesta on the table.

Vivian tells Dominique to check the pantry and I can't help

cringing at her wince when she rubs her chest again. I listen to my friends as they rave about the flamenco show they went to over the weekend, the one I was supposed to join them at. Every now and then I send concerned glances Vivian's way. She is not her usual, vivid self. Something about her is off.

"Hold up, Liv, weren't you supposed to join us?" Alma says, prompting everyone's eyes to focus on me. Uh oh. Okay, I can't keep hiding my relationship with Sebastian. That would be simply ridiculous. However, the last thing I feel like doing right now is plunging into a discussion about my lover, which I'm sure is inevitable. Noticing Dominique's subtle grin, I decide to announce the news Frenchie Bitch style.

"So, I'm going to tell you something and each one of you gets to comment on it in three words and then we drop the subject. Okay?"

Alma and Stephy's brows furrow on cue and Dominique's smile expands. Vivian just sends me a soft glance. I down the rest of my wine.

"I'm sort of, um, I'm in a relationship with Sebastian Balle."

Stephy's mouth drops and Alma's smile is so wide I fear it might split her face right in the middle.

"You lucky bitch." Dominique winks at me and takes a drink of her tall glass.

"Wow, good for you. Both of you, I mean." Alma's grin doesn't lessen.

"That was nine words, but I'll let it slip," I counter with a smile of my own.

Stephy's baffled expression gradually fades. "You and Sebastian?"

I nod.

"What, like, he's your boyfriend?"

I nod once more.

"Awesome!"

I let out a light giggle. When I turn to Vivian, all I get is that glee in her eyes, the one she had when I told her about Sebastian in the first place. I make a mental note to talk to her alone later and find out the root cause for her strange behavior.

By dessert, the fizz over my news progressively subsides and our usual conversation turns full gear. Stephy pops a raspberry into her mouth; an ornament of the delicious Crema Catalana, Vivian's signature dessert. She chews on it in a pensive air.

"I had one of those mid-shower eureka moments earlier today." With such a preface, we all turn her way. "I came to the conclusion that women are such hypocrites."

"Excusez-moi?" Dominique's nosy tenor question verbalizes what I believe is our combined thoughts.

"Okay, let me ask you something before I tell you all about my revelation," Stephy says. I shrug and turn to crack the burned sugar crust of my creamy dessert. "Appearance wise, what attracts you most to a man?"

"Easy, height," Alma says, bringing a spoon to her mouth, which ends with a tiny moan.

"I agree, height. Love the feeling of having someone wrap me in his arms completely," Stephy adds.

"Eyes," Vivian says.

"Height," Dominique contributes to the discussion.

"For me," I linger on the thought. "I think the strength they exude."

"Doesn't count, it should be an actual physical feature," Stephy chides.

"So I guess, me too, height."

"Uh!" Stephy says with vigor. "Would any of you disqualify someone just because he was short?" She pauses, letting us process her question. Not waiting for our replies, Stephy goes on. "I was on a date with this nice guy yesterday, Enrique. I thought we sort of hit it off. And just before we were about to say good night, where I thought he might kiss me, he thanked me instead and told me he probably wouldn't call me."

Everyone's brows crease in stereo.

"He said that though he thought I was sweet, he couldn't date me because he dated only skinny women. Ladies, let me tell you. I was flabbergasted."

"Asshole," Alma grunts.

"No, he wasn't," Stephy corrects in a knowing voice. "At first, I thought he was. I was actually so riled up before going to sleep, I was about to boycott the entire male species. But after a long night's sleep, *the* eureka moment came. He was just being honest." She shrugs. "And I realized just how much of a hypocrite most of us are. If a guy says something like that we scream sexism and are ready to take to the streets carrying signs and pitchforks. However, it's more than okay for us to only date tall guys, right?" Seeing there aren't any counter arguments coming from our side, Stephy just smiles at us, really saying "you see, I'm right."

Dominique and I stay after everyone leaves, including the last patrons, to help Vivian close up. Swiping a cloth over the last table, I turn to Vivian, who labors on reassembling the clean parts of the coffee machine. "Are you feeling well, Vivian?"

Dominique braces her elbows to the counter and eyes us both.

"I'm just a bit tired and stressed. The café is doing great, and I shouldn't complain, but it is a lot of hassle running it."

"Can we help somehow?" Dominique asks, beating me to it.

"Thank you, queridas, but it's just a phase. Nothing to worry about, it'll pass. Don't you worry about me."

We continue with the last tasks to close for the night when Vivian breaks the comfortable silence. "Liv, have you thought about what's next?"

"What do you mean?" I ask as both Dominique and I turn her way.

"I know you still have a few months till the year is over but have you thought what you'll do next? Will you extend your stay? Are you planning to go back? Now that you have something, excuse me, someone else, to consider."

Her questions catch me off guard. My friends gaze at me in silence, waiting.

"I have no idea," floats out of my lips on a breath, a product of a momentary haze. An answer that carries along a multitude of questions I've tried not to entertain lately because I'm afraid of where the answers may lead me. Places I'm not sure I'm ready to go.

Chapter 22
"Sin Miedo a Nada"
Alex Ubago and Amaia Montero

"You have such beautiful eyes," says the man sitting on the bar stool next to me, twirling the dark drink in his sturdy tumbler in circular motions. The guy is in a full-on flirtatious mode, pulling all possible shticks men believe will get a woman to go home with them. I have to give it to him for trying, though, he definitely falls into the category of a charmer, and what's more, he is far from being an unpleasant sight to feast your eyes upon. Although, even with said merits under his belt, he has nothing on the man I'm actually waiting for.

Sebastian and I had planned to meet in this charming tapas bar. A little gem hidden in one of the side alleys in the Gothic Quarter of Barcelona. I check my watch and my heart semi-teeters; Sebastian's flight should have landed almost over an hour ago, which means he should be here any minute.

"How long are you in town for?" asks my courter, inching closer.

"For the weekend." Nonchalantly, I take a taste of my light Sangria.

"I'd love to show you around." To which follows a suggestive grin.

"Perdón Miss, is this seat taken?" A voice that evokes all kinds of whirls in my belly asks. We both regard the orator, me and the guy next to me. In an attire composed of dark jeans, a blue gingham shirt, and a camel blazer, casual-style personified, Sebastian raises an eyebrow.

"Um, no. Please, go ahead." I send him a coquettish beam.

He leans his hip onto the high chair, gazing at me. "Una caña, por favor," Sebastian orders from the bartender, eyes never leaving mine. I return his stare with a hint of a smile, waiting to see where he is going with his "strangers" play. He reaches for my hand and takes it in his. From the corner of my eye, I notice the clasp of my suitor's brows.

"Nice to meet you, my name is Sebastian Noé Balle," he says and brings my hand to his mouth, lingering the press of his lips on my skin till the guy next to me coughs in evident disapproval. "What's your name?" He looks up at me from under his lashes.

"Is that even your real name or did you just make it up?" I say with a cheeky air, pulling my hand back.

Sebastian tilts his head back with a chuckle. "No, beautiful, I'm sorry to disappoint you, but it's the name my parents gave me."

"Well, if this is your *real name*," I enunciate *real name*. "Then my name would be Miss Lust."

Sebastian's smile tips higher.

"Do you mind? We're in the middle of something here," the guy next to me says with an annoyed bite.

Sebastian's eyes bore into mine. "Why don't we let *Miss Lust* decide who she'd like to talk to?"

I raise an eyebrow and fold my arms over my chest.

"I bet if you see what I have in my pants, then you'd want to have your drink with me," Sebastian adds.

The guy to my left clenches his jaw, eyeing Sebastian with utter hostility.

"Is that so?" I cock an eyebrow, biting on my smile.

"Yeah, and I'm sure you'd want it in your mouth." Sebastian's tongue grazes his front teeth.

"Miss, would you like me to have him thrown out of here?" the gentleman at my side growls.

"No, thank you." I lift my hand, in an *it's okay* gesture. "I think I can handle this one by myself," I say, not tearing my stare from Sebastian's, loving the little mischievous grin he has playing on his lips. "I'd want it in my mouth, you say?" I slowly lick my lips.

"Yeah." Sebastian's hand moves to rest on my thigh as he leans in closer as though he is about to tell me a secret. "And once you have it, you'll be begging for more."

Overtly, I drop my eyes to Sebastian's crotch. "Um, will it fit in my mouth?"

"You'll have to open wide for me."

The guy at my side downs his drink and asks for another, watching our little play in sheer astonishment.

"So, can you close your eyes now and open wide for me? As wide as you can."

I lean forward, prop my arms on Sebastian's knees for support, close my eyes, tip my head back, and open my mouth. After a beat in which I sense Sebastian reach inside his pocket, I hear a soft crackling of a wrapper and soon after a sweet square is placed on my waiting tongue. I suck on the sweet goodness with exaggerated pleasure noises and slowly open my eyes to Sebastian, who greets me with a wink.

"So? Will you be joining me on my boat?"

"I'd join you anywhere you ask as long as there's more chocolate," I say and wrap my arms around his neck.

Sebastian tips his head to the side, looking at the guy next to me. "Never underestimate the power of chocolate, hombre."

"I missed you." He plants a kiss on my smile next and our unhappy spectator grunts with a headshake.

. . .

"So, what's the plan for the rest of the day, not that I'd mind staying here just like this for the rest of the weekend." I flutter my lips over Sebastian's bare chest, where my head is resting as we both indulge in the after bliss of our lovemaking. A long session that started at the boat's threshold then moved on to the small dining table, continued in the shower, and ended on the bedroom's queen size bed.

"Do you know La Orja De Van Gogh?" he asks.

"Of course. Love them. They are my favorite Spanish band."

"I got us tickets for their concert tonight."

"Are you serious? How? Aren't they usually sold out within the first week?"

"Let's just say I know a guy who knows a guy." A naughty smile twists his lips.

I snicker, putting on a whole show of rolling my eyes.

"What's that supposed to mean?"

I find myself with my hands pinned above my head under

Sebastian.

"What?" I ask through a giggle. "You're so lame. *I know a guy.*" I imitate his voice.

"Lame, eh?" His thigh spreads my legs apart. My giggles gradually dissolve into his mouth.

. . .

"You're so beautiful," Sebastian says, the tender undertone in his eyes backing his words.

"Stop doing that," I tease.

"Doing what?" He takes a step toward me, where we meet on the deck, ready to go to the concert. Well rested and changed into casual jeans, we stand facing each other.

"Stop putting me on a pedestal. For the life of me, I'm not sure why you think I belong there. I'm afraid it's so high up that I'll eventually fall down flat on my medium-size ass."

His eyes lit in subtle danger. "I can't believe you sometimes. It's not a pedestal, Liv, it's exactly how I see you. Smart, and beautiful, and funny, and incredibly sexy. Maybe it's time you paid a visit to a mirror and took a careful look; see all the things I see, the ones you seem to be missing."

And that's the first time he makes my heart severely twinge tonight. I doubt I would survive a second one; the feeling is so intense.

Thoughts entwining with thoughts make me freeze in my spot as we are about to enter the concert hall. I'm pushed, almost losing my balance, by people streaming in on either side of us, jostling their way in. Fragments from when Sebastian told me about Lola and him, snippets of the way he looks at me, Vivian's questions the other night, and my impending return home all mesh in my head at once. Sebastian, who's a step ahead, turns to search for me.

"Liv?" He hurries my way.

For an expanse of two beats, I just look at him, and all of a sudden, it dawns on me. I've developed such strong feelings for him. The revelation leaves me startled, maybe even frightened.

Abruptly, another group passing us to get in flings me forward to crash on his chest. Sebastian catches me, pulling me closer against him.

"Are you okay?" He tilts his head back to look at me.

I nod.

"Don't worry." He smiles. "It's just a concert, nothing too special. You won't fall in love with me tonight. I won't let you." His smile turns sinful. "I promise."

I know it's his way of trying to lighten my mood, but I can't help but allow his words to seep in with a resilient effect. I inwardly shake off my muddle.

"You promise?" I return his smile.

"Promise," he says and kisses my forehead.

The tunes beat all the way inside of me. It's a magnificent duet of the band singing together with more than a thousand people as their choir. Multicolor clusters of light spot the crowd and return to the band. Sebastian's arms hold my waist and slide to hug me as I lean my back against his chest. We move to the rhythm amid people singing and dancing to the music. The lead singer tilts her mic toward the crowd and a chorus of voices fills the enormous concert hall. Songs soften into one another, coloring the hall in easier tones. Sebastian moves his hand under my shirt, stroking my belly, making my features mellow into contentment. I lift his free hand and bring it to my lips, pressing light, supple kisses on his skin. He dips his face to kiss the base of my neck. I close my eyes, resting the back of my head on his chest, indulging in the feel of him wrapping me in his arms, and the music playing in the background.

I open my eyes when the music winds down and the lead singer thanks everyone for being here this evening. "We have a surprise for you," she announces.

The mass of people roar and she sends an airy kiss our way. "We have a special guest with us tonight," she says and a new wave of cheers and whistles erupts. Next, the heavy lights weaken into a subtle halo on the stage and easy tunes funnel the dimmed space. When a guy carrying a silver mic makes his way from the back to the center of the stage, the crowd goes wild. The new addition to the group kisses the lead singer on the cheek and nods at the rest of the band.

He turns to the audience. "Buenas noches, Barcelona!"

Roars, claps, and whistles come as a response. He smiles at the blond singer, takes her hand in his, and with his other brings the mic to his mouth. He sways for a few more piano tunes and starts.

I crane my neck to look up at Sebastian over my shoulder. He dips his head for my mouth to reach his ear. "I love this song," I say.

He nods, his eyes beaming at me.

His hand on my stomach moves to my waist, and he turns me to face him. I wrap my arms around *his* waist and smile at him. His liquid brown eyes blaze at me as he brings his hands to hold my face. Shielding my sight to see just him, he leans in, his lips close to mine, our faces framed by his large hands, and he softly presses a kiss to my lips.

"I'm dying to hear you say the things that you never say," he translates the song for me. The lyrics trickle down to the very depth of me. Another soft kiss covers my lips, and he continues. "How long are we going to wait?" Our next kiss is longer; our lips wrap around each other and retrieve for a softer touch. "I'm dying to know you, to know what's on your mind." The weight of the words, the timbre of his voice together with the tender air in his eyes makes my chest squeeze tight, in sweet aching. I slide my hands under his shirt, caressing the warm skin of his back with the tips of my fingers and inch on the heels of my feet to reach his lips once more. The whirlwind of emotions playing inside of me is guiding my tongue as I taste him. We ease off, staring into each other's eyes.

You know that moment, that tiny moment that when it happens, it becomes so clear? The moment your heart expands to an impossible size and embraces the person in front of you to its very core. Wraps him in so tight it hurts. My heart just did that.

"I'm dying to explain to you what goes on in my mind." Sebastian continues to translate the song for me. The tune wrapping us escalates gradually, intensifying the heat of the music. Both singers on stage reach the chorus in magnificent harmony, stretching their voices to a larger-than-life climax. And we find ourselves lost in our own bubble, embracing each other closer, our mouths uniting into a heated fusion.

In his embrace, in a cloud of his scent, with the taste of his lips, everything around us drowns. I sense nothing but him. And it's powerful, and it's taking over every part of me. I'm dissolving into him and he into me.

Songs begin and end, the show around us carries on while we are in our own world of two. We don't let go of each other till the second encore winds down and the last keys are played.

My chest feels heavier. It feels like my heart is lodging in my throat when I look into Sebastian's eyes as we make our way out to the night. Something has changed, something that causes mayhem inside of me. Inwardly, I whisper, "Liar, you promised I wouldn't fall for you tonight . . ."

. . .

The next day, Sebastian plays the part of a tour guide to a T. However, over coffee and fruits on the sunbathed deck, he tells me there won't be any banal touristic monuments included in our tour. "Except for a few of Gaudi's more known works, which are a must, as they make the Barcelonian landscape what it is. Besides that, you'll see the city and its real beauty as we, the locals, do."

And he holds on to his promise and so much more. Making this day one of the best days I've ever had. Sebastian takes us to unique, hidden places that just make me fall deeper for the city . . . and him. A small tapas bar with delicious food that caters to less than ten people and even then is not very spacious, yet feels homey. A couple of Gaudi's hidden treasures located on random streets. A tiny café with the best churros I've tasted thus far (sorry, Vivian). And we end the day with the spectacular – Magic Fountain of Montjuïc, a beautiful display of color, light, motion, music, and water acrobatics. Only we don't admire it with the crowds assembled at its feet. I get to watch its magnificence enveloped in Sebastian's embrace as we lie on a wooly blanket in one of the close by play gardens.

Chapter 23
"You Could Be Happy"
Snow Patrol

"I feel different," I told Dr. Schmurtaz. "And it's not about how he makes me feel; it's about how *I* finally let *myself* feel."

Our weekend in Barcelona together not only deepened the connection between Sebastian and me, it solidified it. It also made me make the needed switch in my head from spending time with him to actually *being* with him. The doctor listened to me when I explained that once we returned, I realized how content I was. And not just because of Sebastian, but because of how I've been enjoying my journey. I felt connected to my new home now, to the new friends I made. How for a while now I haven't had to second-guess choices I've made. I even got to catch a glimpse of a smile in the doctor's eyes when I told him how dedicatedly I've been writing in my journal. And what surprised me the most, was how easily he agreed with my decision to take a break from therapy for the time being.

"Any last words before you let this cuckoo bird spread her wings?" I asked.

"Firstly, I'd say don't refer to yourself as cuckoo, not even jokingly. Liv, I think you're heading in the right direction. Don't let setbacks threaten you, it happens to all of us. And you need to remember that we are, in fact, our toughest critiques. And most importantly, stop overthinking everything."

And on that educational note, he concluded a few years of therapy. Okay, not exactly. His last words weren't as memorable, they were simply, "I'll send the bill over right away."

"Bueno, querida. Here, I'm done. I'm all ears," says Vivian, yanking me out of my little brooding break as she joins me where I wait for her, having a coffee at one of the outside tables. I made sure to arrive before the rest of our friends so we could finally have a private conversation.

I study her face, glad to come up with the conclusion that she looks like her usual vibrant self again. She stares right back at me; her curvaceous body hugged by a simple black cotton dress, her thick dark curls a wild halo around her face, a perfect pair with the darkest red decorating her plump lips.

"Well, I wanted to make sure you felt better. You've been sort of tuned out lately. Is the pain gone?"

She regards me with a genteel air in her eyes. "I'm fine, I'm fine."

"You look great, love the lipstick." Her smile stretches. "And I wanted to talk to you about your reaction . . . when I told you about Sebastian and me. I guess I didn't expect that reaction from you, of all people. You didn't say much . . ." I linger on the last word, searching for her expression.

That twinkle in her eyes from when I told her about Sebastian makes an encore. "My reaction expressed exactly how I felt about it. I was, and still am, glad for you. I've known Sebastian since he was a little, mischievous boy."

I wince and sigh, "Oh, God."

"What's with the *oh God*?"

"When you speak of him that way, of him being a child. That you knew him back then, just makes me think of our age gap. It's not something that makes me feel too good about the situation."

"That's nonsense," she admonishes with a wave of a hand. "Liv, I am much older than you; it's not a surprise that I've known him since he was a little child. The gap between the two of you, eh, I wouldn't even give it a second thought." She drops her palm in dismissal. "I was genuinely glad for the both of you. When he first asked about you, I thought, perfecto. They'd be great together."

I can't help the plunge my lips take.

"So, si, my reaction was exactly what I thought. I was happy. Period."

"You're quite the romantic, uh? I never thought of you this way." I send her a cheeky grin.

Her smile lights up her face, pushing her beauty mark higher. "Are you kidding? I'm as romantic as they come. I'm a product of the eighties' ballads. Romance runs in my blood. I have dreamy stars embedded in my irises. These songs were chemically manufactured in a lab after experiments had concluded they could leave a human heart melted and swooned."

We laugh it off and greet our friends next as they start to arrive.

"It's official; you're my favorite person on the planet," I tell Vivian after tasting each and every dish she'd concocted for us tonight. Vivian smiles in utter joy, nodding.

"Seriously, you've outdone yourself this time," Stephy confirms. "Ladies." She turns to us. "Whatever you've been told about sweets not being healthy, it's a big, fat lie. A propaganda. Nothing makes me feel happier than sweets. And what's healthier than happy?"

We all eye the wealth of goods spread before us with an agreeing nod. Vivian went all out with tonight's menu, a dinner composed of nothing but mouthwatering desserts. Chocolate praline bites, crumbly walnut and rum cookies, Crema Catalana, homemade pistachio ice cream, salty caramel fudge squares, pears in liquor and brown sugar, and so many more little perfections of delight.

"Speaking of deceptions, what's the greatest lie you've been told that eventually turned out to be a brutal misconception?" Alma asks, then adds, "Mine was that you're safe from catching STDs if you only sleep with your partner." She snickers in contempt. "Sorry, there are actually two misconceptions there; the second is that if he truly loves you he won't cheat on you."

"Ouch." Stephy cringes.

Dominique twists her mouth in annoyed disgust. Perhaps empathy.

"You know what the hugest misconception of them all is though?" asks Stephy. "I'll tell ya." She narrows her stare at us. "Sex goes on *all night*."

The next words literally fly out of my mouth filter-free as I dig a spoon into the chocolate mousse. "Oh, I beg to differ."

Vivian and Dominique practically burst out in laughter. Alma giggles and Stephy eyes me with big round blue eyes. With the spoon still held between my teeth, I send them a gigantic, sassy grin and shrug.

. . .

"Don't you have people coming over to watch a game?" I ask when Sebastian attempts to free me from my cute top.

"Hold on, this is not just a *game*." Solemnness composes his features. "It's *El Clásico*."

My brows almost meet when I regard him, clueless as to what the *El Clásico* might be. Sounds like an old western to me. The Good, the Bad and the Ugly, part II: El Clásico.

"It's a match between Barcelona and Real Madrid. And it's almost the most important game of the year. Only five games left to play in La Liga, and Real have a four-point lead, meaning this game will probably decide who will win the league title this season. And just to make it clear, we are cheering for Barça."

He might as well have spoken in Mandarin with a northern dialect for all I know, as I didn't understand a word. But I did enjoy watching his lips move.

"Oh, Barça. Aren't they the team with the hottest guys in the soccer world?"

"Not sure about that . . ." An overt eye roll follows the low murmur.

"That Piqué guy."

Sebastian's smile expands as I say the first name and immediately sinks when I mention the second.

"And Casillas."

He drops his head, closes his eyes, and slightly shakes it from side to side. "Casillas plays for *Real*. He's their captain and goalkeeper. Please, whatever you do tonight, *don't* repeat that, okay?"

I grin at him. He gives me a once-over that ends with him pulling me by my hand toward his bedroom, which make my lips stretch wider. A little pre-game match. I'm totally game.

Once we pass the bed and enter the walkthrough closet, my gaze at Sebastian's back becomes a query. In the middle of the confined space, Sebastian sends his hands to the hem of my lace inset black cami and peels it off me. When I'm about to give his dark blue tee the same treatment, he nimbly careens toward the shelves. He pulls out a scarlet and blue stripped shirt and helps me shrug it on.

Just when I'm about to protest the style choice, he says, "Wow, you look so hot in this shirt." And . . . shirt stays on. One of his hands moves to cup my jaw and the other curls around my waist, pulling me slightly toward him for a hungry kiss. I reciprocate with an equally greedy exploration of his mouth. A short game of tongues, taking turns dominating our connection, and hands ravenously running over each other, we find ourselves on the floor with me seated across Sebastian's groin. I almost rip his shirt off and he kisses me as faint groans bubble from deep inside his throat when a loud knock comes from the direction of the living room.

"Mierda," Sebastian growls through gritted teeth and drops his head back to the floor. He takes a deep, bothered breath and looks at me with a boyish glint and the most adorable dimple. "Um, can you get the door? I sort of have to calm the situation down."

I giggle and gift him with another juicy kiss before standing up.

"Not helping," he murmurs, and I send him a flirty smile over my shoulder as I leave for the door.

When Sebastian joins his friends and me in the living room, he sends me a sinful smile that makes me want to call off the damn *El Clásico* and send everyone home so we can continue the game *we started* a few minutes ago.

There aren't any tedious introductions; it's all casual and flowing. "The guys," six of Sebastian's friends, introduce themselves to me, a couple over handshakes, some with the traditional kiss on each cheek gesture, and the last one, Pepe, with a wide grin and eyes zeroed in on the Barça logo proudly decorating my healthy chest. Sebastian slaps Pepe on the back of his head and drags him to help fetch the many six-packs chilling in the fridge.

There's another knock on the door. Seeing that everyone seem too busy doing whatever guys do pre an important game, I open the door. So far it was the guys and me, now the powers have slightly shifted. Now it's the guys, me, and Lola.

Lola wraps me in a hug that seems genuinely warm and turns to give the same treatment to the rest of the gang. I'd be shamelessly lying if I said it didn't bother me when she lingered a tad more when hugging Sebastian. I decide, however, to let it slip for the sake of keeping my good mood intact.

By the time the coffee table piles up with empty beer cans amid snack debris, I've enriched my Spanish expletives by eleventy percent.

"Vamos, Barça, vamos!" Sebastian urges the players on as he leans in to press a soft kiss to the crown of my head, where I'm sitting on the rug, leaning against the sofa between his parted legs. I tilt my head back and smile at him, only to receive another quick kiss, this time on my lips. When I turn back to the game, I catch Lola's eyes on us. Meeting my gaze, she swiftly careens back to the screen.

More than thirty minutes into the game, right after a sharp gasp erupts from one of the guys, a sudden tense silence enfolds the room. I watch everyone curiously as they wait, appearing to hold their breath. Lola buries her face in a pillow. Abruptly, high fives fly above my head and sighs of reliefs fill the room, accompanied by a few juicy curse words.

"The bad guys missed a penalty kick," Sebastian whispers to my ear, mirth lacing his words. I grin and continue watching the game. When there's a close-up of a tackle between Casillas and Piqué, Lola and I exchange an appreciative stare that concludes with thin smiles.

The ceiling almost flies up by the shouts of joy and roars of elation that boom the room when Barça scores next.

"Goallllllllllll," the commentator yells not less than five minutes later, when Barça scores yet again, making us go wild. We all stand up at once; it's a jungle of high fives and hugs in the room.

Till it isn't.

Till Sebastian grabs me for the mother of all kisses. At that exact moment, I decide that soccer is my favorite game.

As we see our guests to the door, after everyone helped with the cleaning, a warm sense of belonging washes over me. Though it was the first time I've met these people, they've treated me as their own, including Lola, despite her sidelong glances at

Sebastian.

"Hey, I'm going for a run, wanna join?" Sebastian asks as I return from freshening up.

"No thanks, I'll pass. I don't do the whole running thing. My preferred sports are breaking food into smaller pieces using my mouth or sex, which sometimes also includes intense mouth activity." I hold the point of my tongue between my teeth flirtatiously.

He grins, a darker flare to his eyes. "I'll be more than delighted to help you with the latter when I'm back. Keep the shirt on."

"Sure, shirt stays on. I'm just going to finish up this proposal I've been working on." I refer to the project Saul sent me a short while ago.

By the time I'm done with the side notes, my summary of the overall project, I stare at the screen of my notebook and wait. I wait for the surge of satisfaction I've always felt when I was done with a project. The sense of fulfillment, the little thrill of doing something I supposedly love, but this time it doesn't seem to arrive. What jumps out at me though is a realization, enlightenment, of just how much I haven't missed it. With the thought of "this is not what I want to do" fogging my mind, or rather clearing it, I head to take a shower. I need a break before working on the very last tweaks.

When the front door opens, I'm back in the living room, my legs tucked under me on the sofa, notebook on my thighs, wearing only the tee I promised to keep on with a tiny matching crimson thong and a towel wrapped around my wet hair. I click send, shooting off my work to Saul, together with a preface suggesting a call. A call in which I'm planning to tell him that I'm not interested in taking on any other projects. I lift my eyes to find Sebastian by the door kicking his running shoes off. Given my position at the opposite side of the living room, he doesn't notice me at first, and I get the chance to drink him in. A light sheen covers his tanned forehead and temples, and a flush enhances his sharp cheekbones. His black tee clings to his ripped torso, darker moist spots coloring the front. He has black training pants on decorated by three long white stripes on each side. He seems to be deep in thought, listening to music on his player in an armband wrapped around his bicep.

When his brown eyes accidently meet mine, I respond with a tender smile. He stills for a beat, his stare on me growing intent. Not breaking our connection, he starts toward me, taking slow steps, seeming somewhat undecided. Something about the way he carries himself as he closes the distance between us, something about the way he looks at me, makes *me* tense. Less than a step away, he drops to his knees in front of me. I cock my head, waiting, not sure for what. By the light tilt of my head, the towel wrapped around my hair is released and drops to the floor. My wet hair falls, scattering around my shoulders and a thick cluster clings to my cheek.

Sebastian brings his hands to his ears and pulls out the earbuds. He moves his hands to my face, proceeding toward my ears. Along the way, he brushes the lock of hair aside and gently helps the earbuds to my ears. He holds my face and I blink at him as the music registers. The softest of smiles curves my lips as I gaze back at him, listening to *the* song from the concert. Sebastian still holds my face, his eyes gazing into mine as the chorus comes. He mouths something to me next. Something that makes my heart expand so wildly that it blocks my throat. My hands slowly move to my ears to pull out the earbuds, wanting to hear what he said.

"Me estoy enamorando de ti," he says, validating what I thought he just said.

An army of butterflies marches in my stomach as I move to reach his lips. Softly, I brush them with mine. Gently, I skim them, sending my tongue to taste him. I close my eyes and there's nothing else on my mind but this moment; the taste and feel of him and the words he just told me. "Me estoy enamorando de ti." His statement keeps twirling in my head. "I'm falling for you."

I leave my place on the sofa and move to sit on top of him on the floor. I reach for the player and unplug the earbuds, letting the music fill the room. I grab Sebastian's face and kiss him with the flood of emotions that he just released in me. I kiss him with the warm feeling that's pressing on my chest. I kiss him with how much I wanted to hear him say that and didn't even know. I kiss him with such ferocity; I don't think I'll ever want to let him go. In easy pace, filled with passion and tenderness, we peel each other's clothes off. With even further gentleness, he sinks into me as I glide over him. We hug tightly as we move against each other in deep, profound motions. Up until our ecstasy reaches us, we never break eye contact. With my face buried in the crook of his neck, we continue to embrace, letting our heartbeats calm down.

Chapter 24
"Protect Me from What I Want"
Placebo

I remain seated by the screen long after I end my video call with Saul. A call in which we discussed my notes and I politely refused, more than once, to take on more projects. A call that ended with me telling him that I've officially made my decision to resign. Contemplating for a few moments more, I decide that I'd better have a glass of wine by my side for the next call I am about to make.

I take another look at the table I've set in the kitchen; a silver tablecloth, white china, and a couple of short trimmed roses in a low, round bowl. I turn to lower the oven's temperature where an aromatic dinner I ordered earlier is warming. I leave the kitchen with a thin smile and a generously filled glass of wine. Taking a deep breath, I take a seat at my desk. "Here goes," I murmur, take a long sip of the wine and press dial on the video chat.

I have an urge to laugh at the absurdity of my immediate relief when my father's face greets me via the screen and not his so-called "better" half. So far, I've managed to stick to phone calls but seeing my dad on the screen fills me with warmth. Sincere affection lines his features as he asks me how I've been; telling me how much he misses me, and mostly how happy he is to hear I'm having a great time. My smile tones down when a French manicured hand curls around his shoulder and my mother's voice comes from the speakers, asking my dad to let her talk to me.

"Hi, Mom," I start with a great attempt at staying mellow.

She sits straight-backed against the chair, observing me. "Hello, darling."

I smile at the screen. "How are you?"

Her lips coil at the edge, almost forming a smile. She sends her hand to her pearl necklace and says, "I see they have good food over there."

And with one single comment, she makes me want to end the call. "They actually do; the best I've ever had." I don't let her lead me in the direction she's clearly aiming toward.

"Mmmhmm." Flat and annoying. "So, what have you been up to since our last call? Are you ready to come back?"

Calling for my patience to stay intact, I take a deep breath and answer. "Traveling. I've been to Barcelona recently. It's so relaxed and beautiful, Mom. You'd love the architecture." I continue telling her about less than meaningful things, making sure to keep whatever is important to me off topic. Making sure she won't be able to ruin it for me somehow from afar. I'm too caught up in trying to force this conversation to stay away from an argument that I miss Sebastian coming in.

I'm a second too late to signal that I'm on a call, a second too late to prevent him from twirling me in my seat and planting a keen kiss on my lips. When he breaks off the kiss and tells me,

"Hola, you," his eyes meet the screen. Or better yet, meet my mom's wide eyes, and none less wide, open mouth.

"Mom," I clear my throat. "This is Sebastian."

Sebastian grins at the monitor. "Nice to meet you, Mrs. Bliss."

"And you are?" My mom's baffled expression doesn't waver.

"Your daughter's boyfriend," Sebastian answers and drops his hands to rest on my shoulders. "I see where Liv gets her stunning beauty from," he says.

I think he just deliberately enhanced his accent. I move my face from the screen and mimic shoving a finger down my throat, making Sebastian smirk. I make a quick assessment of the situation and come to the conclusion, why not, he's a big boy, he can handle her. Anyhow, he should be punished for that last cheesy comment.

"I'm going to check on dinner," I say and quickly disappear toward the kitchen. Sebastian doesn't seem bothered as he takes my place in utter nonchalance, facing the monitor.

I shrug on oven mitts and bend to retrieve the duck dish. As I set the fragrant roast on the kitchen counter, I freeze and my entire face scrunches. *The hell?*

There's a light giggle coming from the living room. The sound is new to me. Wow, is this how my mom sounds giggling? *He made her giggle?*

My mom expresses herself in so many varied and polished ways. She frowns, grimaces, scowls, glares, admonishes, and snaps. Oh and her signature expression, the one she reserves mostly for me, scrutinizes. Giggling is definitely not a part of the Jane Bliss repertoire.

"Oh, Sebastian." And another coy laugh.

I shake my head. He made her "Oh, Sebastian" him? Really? I let the swooning linger for a few moments more before I head to rescue the swooner from the swooneree.

"It was a delight talking to you, Jane."

Yes, he's definitely working extra Spanish drawl to his accent. The player.

"Likewise, Sebastian," my mom almost sings.

"I'll take a quick shower," Sebastian says low and grabs a hunk of my rear, which is not visible to his new fan.

On cue, as soon as Sebastian leaves the room, my mom's face quickly shifts back to her usual displeased expression. She eyes me for an additional moment before conceitedly asking, "I guess he knows you're sitting pretty?"

"Pardon?" I can't even begin to hide my surprise.

"He is twenty-eight, Liv, and such a handsome young man."

"No, you did not just suggest he is with me for my money." My jaw drops, and I'm reeling in ire and bewilderment.

She straightens her poise and scrutinizes me for another stretched, silent moment.

Unbelievable. Even from a thousand miles away, she makes me feel self-conscious and doubt myself. My mom is the master of nonverbal communication. She can make me feel like shit with nothing but a tiny twitch of her lips.

"Liv, honey, what are you doing to yourself?" She lightly shakes her head in clear disappointment and sighs. "Maybe you should just pack your things and return home. If you're having an early mid-life crisis, there are specialists to help with that. You don't need to take a younger man to make you feel beautiful again." I'm too flabbergasted to even comment. "Liv, this young man is the poster guy for lipstick on a collar. What are you doing with him?"

"Mom." I hold my hand up. "You know what? Just stop. I don't want to listen anymore, unless you have something positive to say to me. Thank you, but I'm not interested in your opinions."

She twists her mouth again.

"Darling, this guy will never have a future with you. Stop wasting your time on dreams. Just come back home and stop playing."

"Have a lovely day, Mom, I'm going to have dinner now." I don't wait for her response and press end. I'm so riled up that just the mere thought of food makes my stomach turn. I bury my face in my shaky hands and try to calm down my exasperation, and in the same breath, push away the little doubts she's masterfully seeded in me.

I raise my eyes to the sound of Sebastian's steps, hoping with all my heart that he didn't hear any part of my conversation with mommy dearest. I meet his eyes with my cheeks still held in my palms. He walks my way, toweling his wet hair, wearing faded jeans with the first two buttons undone. "You okay?" he asks, gazing at me.

"How do you feel about marriage?" The moment the words leave my lips, I regret them. I have no business asking him that. What's wrong with me?

"Are you proposing?" he asks with a smirk. When I don't return the humored gesture, his features recompose. "I don't think about it much, to be honest. I don't think it's something I see myself doing in the near future, obviously not after what happened to Lola and me. It's not something I'd jump too quickly into. Not unless I was a hundred percent sure and ready."

I love and hate his answer at the same time. It's sincere, candid, not bullshit coated. I hate it because it, in a way, validates what my mom has just sowed with utter malice.

He takes a step forward and holds my cheek in his palm. I lean into his hand. "Liv?" Low and concerned.

"She has a tendency to mess with my head. You go ahead and eat; I'll take a short walk to clear my mind and then join you."

Sebastian nods, but instead of heading toward the kitchen, he turns to grab a shirt of his left on one of the chairs and shrugs it on. He sends me his hand. "Let's go for a walk together." The fact that he doesn't just run away from my crazy but wants to help me get through it touches me.

We walk by the water in silence; Sebastian's arm embracing my shoulder, and mine tucked in his back pocket. I take a lungful of the evening salty breeze, closing my eyes for a brief moment.

I turn to Sebastian. "Thank you."

He ducks to press a kiss to my temple and we continue our stroll till the only thing I can think of is how I need him to make love to me and make everything go away.

Chapter 25
"Who Says You Can't Go Home"
Bon Jovi

"You make me happy," I tell Sebastian, a little heady from wine and a greater part heady from him.

"I'm glad." He pulls me closer. "I can't wait to make you even happier, smile from within."

We both break into laughter at the cheesy innuendo.

"Now say it again, only add *mi amor* at the end for some extra corniness."

"Are you making fun of me?"

"Well, yeah . . ."

Sebastian swats my rear and twirls me by my hand to collide with his chest. He lifts me some for our mouths to connect. I melt into the kiss, thinking how great the past week has been and how the last thing I want is for him to leave now.

As though reading my mind, Sebastian says, "I wish I didn't have to go now. But I really need to get everything done before the meeting tomorrow."

He walks me home after our night out. I burrow under his arm, pressing my cheek against his shirt, loving the feel of the warmth of his skin through the crisp fabric. Throughout the week, we've been spending every free moment together. Right after I managed to exorcise the last remnants of poison my beloved mother managed to infuse in a short call. Not willing to allow any of it to resurface and mess with my head any longer than it has, I shake my thoughts off.

"You expecting anyone?" Sebastian asks, the hint of edginess in his voice summons my stare to arrow his way and then to the door.

"Oh, my God!" My perplexity softens my voice, weakening it into a meek whisper. Not giving it much thought, I let go of Sebastian's hold and speed right into Kai's arms.

"Well, someone missed me," Kai's familiar husky voice sounds so sweet in present. I inch on my tiptoes and give him a noisy smooch.

"What are you doing here?"

We both turn to Sebastian's heavy steps on the stairs. I beam at him in complete joy. He nods at Kai.

Kai mirrors Sebastian's gesture and says in a clear voice, "You were whining about missing me so I came for a visit." I can't help wincing at the way both men size each other up. I swear their chests inflate a size.

I take a step back to stand next to Sebastian. "Sebastian, this is my Kai." I wince again, this time at the ticking of Sebastian's jaw.

Kai holds his hand out, eyeing Sebastian with an air I'm not sure I'm the biggest fan of. "You must the new *friend*."

"*Boyfriend*," Sebastian reciprocates curtly. From where I'm standing, the gripping and shaking of the hands thing between them looks more like arm-wrestling than an innocent gesture of greeting. They are so absorbed in their stare down that for a whole beat I feel like they've forgotten I even exist.

"Should I get a ruler?" I ask, annoyed and to a degree astounded by the immature absurdity on display.

"You'll need an industrial size in my case," Kai says in his trademark cockiness.

"Then I guess you'll be able to share."

A brief grin touches Sebastian's lips at my retort. Unfortunately, it disappears just as quickly as it came.

I hand Kai my key and say, "Kai, can you give us a moment?"

He sends us a glance, his mouth set in a smirk, and turns to unlock my door.

"Hey." I wrap my arms around Sebastian's waist. Sebastian dips his chin to gaze at me. "So, I'll see you tomorrow?"

The tick of the jaw returns. "You kicking me out?" It's the first time he says these words with zero humor. It's the first time they make me cringe.

"Of course, not." I tip my face back, looking at him in query. "You said you had to go home to finish . . ."

"I'll do that later," he cuts me off before I'm able to finish my sentence and steps inside the house.

Fine, then.

"Scarlet, where should I put my shiz?" Kai asks as soon as we get inside.

"In the bedroom. Want something to drink?"

"Beer," Kai calls as he makes his way toward my bedroom.

"Where is he sleeping?" Sebastian asks briskly, following me to the kitchen.

"On the sofa."

"The hell he is."

An answer that makes me turn his way with a start and a sprinkle of annoyance.

"Please tell me you're kidding."

"Do I look like I'm kidding?"

No, he doesn't look like he is kidding. And it's not amusing me in the least bit. I take a deep breath that does nothing to stop my growing impatience. "Let me get this straight. My best friend traveled halfway across the globe to visit me, and I should ask him to find a place for the night?"

Sebastian's eyes narrow, and I can clearly see the wheels in his brain working. "He can stay here; you'll come sleep at my place."

"Oh, for the love of God. Sebastian, don't you trust me?"

"You, I trust. Him . . ."

"So that should be enough. Though, believe me, Kai is more than trustworthy, especially when it comes to me. He is the big brother I never had."

Sebastian throws his eyes to the ceiling and I need to kill the urge to growl. Finally, after having a drink with us and seeing that Kai is not as bad as he seems, I manage to persuade Sebastian to go home. It's not that I don't want him to get to know Kai better. I actually wouldn't mind having him by my side all the time, but he does have a long night ahead of him.

"Why were you being a jerk?" I ask Kai once Sebastian leaves and we turn to sit on the porch. I'm snuggled under a knitted, wool blanket, my legs on Kai's thighs.

He shrugs. "So you've passed the no-strings-attached phase, uh?"

"Long ago," I say, rather dreamingly. "How long are you

staying?"

"Tomorrow evening."

My calm smile melts.

"I took this job in Madrid, a quickie, so I could visit you. Right after, I'm heading back home. Funny, it's the first time I really miss home."

I gaze at Kai. His features take a serious tone. "I spoke to this friend of mine, the photographer I covered for with the nature gig. His son was born a week ago." Kai drops his elbows to his knees and cocks his head my way. "He sounded so peaceful and content."

I nod.

"He made me think."

"What are you saying?" I say in a soft voice.

"Dunno. It made me think about life in general, nearing forty, my lifestyle."

"I spoke to my parents last week. My mom made me think about that too, in her own special way. She basically asked why I am still wasting my life." Gentle smiles touch our lips, but they are not of the animated variety, but of the scornful realm.

"Liv, I'm willing to give us a try."

My eyes rip open and I study Kai carefully under the dimness of the night.

"I mean, our pact. If there's anyone I'd consider sharing a life with . . . it's you."

I find it hard to bring my lips to close.

"Kai, what are you doing? Why? Why now?"

He pushes a breath out of his lips. "Do you see yourself staying here? There aren't many months left to renew your lease. I guess you have some sort of an idea what's next, no?"

I shake my head. "No, I don't. I love it here, but I don't know."

"What about him?"

"We are together."

"Did he ask you to stay?"

His question is like a blow to my stomach. "Not in a direct way, no. He didn't ask me to stay for him. He told me that I should stay a while ago, but there was no promise along that line."

Kai scoots over closer, and his fingers caress my cheek. "I'm not just saying this, Liv. I'd really like to give us a try. You don't have to answer right away. Just think about it. When you come back home, we could see how things go."

"Wow, Kai," I whisper under my breath.

"Okay, now that I've successfully managed to mess with your head, love of mine, let's go for a walk."

By the time we return from our late-night stroll, it's almost midnight. A couple of hours have passed in which we told each other about the past months we were apart. Miraculously, or not, we managed to brush off the bomb Kai dropped earlier and quickly got back to being us.

I pile up a pillow, blanket, and a towel in my hands and head toward the living room, to make the sofa for Kai. As I round the corridor, I collide with Kai who's on his way to the bathroom. I let out a screeching yelp and lose my balance only for Kai's nimble hands to stabilize me. We stand facing each other, the pile of fabric huddled against my chest and Kai's hands holding my forearms.

"Phew, that was a close one." I grin at him.

Kai's crooked smile sparks at me and immediately fades away. Before I register what's happening, Kai's face slowly nears mine, near enough for his lips to cover my stunned mouth. For the briefest instant, I let myself get caught up in the moment, maybe as a tribute to my younger self who had the hugest crush on him, but the moment my eyes flutter close, all I can see is Sebastian's face.

It feels like a bucket of cold water poured over me once I make sense of what just happened. I push Kai's chest back, the pile in my hands dropping to the floor between us.

"Kai!" My voice is an angry scold. "What are you doing?"

He stares at me, seeming as confused as I am.

"That was such a dick thing to do. I'm in a relationship. Kai, I love him." I wince, utterly dazed by the words that have just left my mouth.

"Wow, I didn't think it was that serious." *Neither did I, Kai.* He leans back against the wall and drops his head back. "I'm sorry, Liv. I don't know what came over me."

I huff and bend down to pick the mess up from the floor. Kai follows my steps as I walk toward the living room. I drop the linen on the sofa and turn to him.

"I'm going to chalk this one up to our list of idiotic mistakes and let it slip for the sake of how important you are to me. I care about you a ton, and nothing will change that, even if you act like an ass."

A smile crawls up his lips. A smile that makes my own lips mimic it.

"This never happened."

"This never happened," he repeats.

"Now," I inch up on my feet and press a quick kiss on his cheek, "I'm going to Sebastian's. I'll be back for breakfast. You can just sleep in my bed. Good night."

"I adore you," he calls after me as I close the door behind me.

. . .

I knock on Sebastian's door again, waiting. A few minute pass till I hear the sound of a lock turning. The door is opened to a groggy Sebastian, who looks at me with one eye slightly winked, squinting due to the light coming from the landing behind me. He observes me, fisting a bed sheet wrapped around his waist.

"I'm not here because you acted like a caveman earlier. I'm here because I want to be here."

Sebastian's arm reaches to curl around my waist and pulls me to him. His mouth crashes to mine and the sheet drops from around his waist. He lifts me by my thighs to straddle him. Wordlessly, he turns us toward the hall and kick shuts the door.

He continues walking us deeper inside the apartment in silence. Charged, lustful silence. Silence that licks fire to spread inside of me. When we get to the bedroom, he kick shuts the door behind and drops us both to the bed. I wrap my legs tighter around his waist, meeting his mouth again.

. . .

I let out a beatific sigh. "Good morning," I murmur to the room with closed eyes and a thin smile. The stretch of my lips grows as he plants another luxurious kiss near my hip.

"Good morning," Sebastian says to my skin, leaving hot kisses as his mouth trails south. I drop my head deeper onto the pillow and my lips part as the tip of his tongue tastes my skin a few inches below my naval. "Sleep well?"

"Mmmhmm. And waking up even better."

"Hola." Sebastian's face appears before me. He is propped above me, his weight held by his flexed arms. I give him a thorough gaze and my smile stretches. His hair falls down to nearly cover his smiling eyes. His dimple almost giving me a heart condition by its irresistible combination of adorable and scorching sexy. "How was your evening with your friend?"

Oh, the evening with my friend. We didn't have a chance to discuss *that* last night, as we were too caught up in devouring each other.

He angles his elbows, lowering his upper body for his mouth to lightly kiss across my collarbone.

"It was good, for the most part." An instant inward debate takes my focus away from Sebastian. An argument of whether to tell him everything about last night or leave the part that he'd probably not embrace so wholeheartedly out. "Kai kissed me." Honesty wins.

Sebastian's lips halt amid a kiss. "Did you kiss him back?" he says to my skin.

Though his mouth is still hovering over my skin, his eyes crawl up to mine.

"Umm . . ."

He drops his head, keeping it down for a beat.

"No. Yes . . . I mean . . ."

Sebastian pushes himself away to drop on his back next to me.

"There's only one answer to that question." His voice is so velvety it sends my skin to prickle; not in the good way, though.

"For the briefest moment."

He covers his face with both his hands.

"Till I realized what I was doing, and that the only person I want to kiss is you." I roll to my side, resting my cheek on the pillow.

He rubs his hands over his face; his next breath is an audible one. He drops his hands to his sides and turns to look at me, his cheek resting on the mattress. For a space of a few beats, only our eyes converse, in hard, tense gazes.

"I made sure he knew how I felt about it. Made sure it cannot happen again. And then I came to you."

He takes a deep breath once more and nods. "Coffee?" he asks, sitting up then straightens to stand.

"I never meant to upset you. I just wanted to make sure we are completely honest with each other. I don't want to hide anything from you."

Sebastian's hard stare melts a degree, and he nods again. "I'm making coffee," he says and leaves the room.

I'm not so sure I like his reaction because it seems like there's much more under the surface. A ticking bomb in the disguise of self-control. Though my chest feels leaden, I'm glad I shared this tidbit with him. At this point in our relationship, I'd hate to hide anything from him, even on the account of upsetting him. I let him cool down for an additional moment and head to join him.

I wrap my arms around his waist and lean my head on his back, breathing him in. "Are we okay?" I press a soft kiss on his skin.

He sends a hand to squeeze mine. "Yeah, we're okay."

I kiss his back again and remain embracing him as he pours our coffee into mugs. Sebastian's phone rings and I let go of him. When he turns to fetch the phone from the counter, I bring one of the steaming coffee cups to my lips. I lean my hip to the counter and take another sip, watching him.

It's Sebastian's mother on the phone. From what I manage to glean from the call, they are discussing the next time he is planning to visit. I take another taste of the coffee, and though I'm trying not to eavesdrop, I still manage to learn that the new subject they are discussing is me.

Sebastian eyes are on me as he answers in curt, short sentences. His expression takes a harder tone when he tells his mom that he'll ask me if I'll be joining him. A few more impatient sentences are exchanged before he says something in Spanish along the line of, "Relax, it's not that serious anyhow, it's not like we're getting married or anything. She doesn't even know if she is going to stay here."

I know I shouldn't let it sting as much. After all, he is calling it as it is, but the way he dismisses our relationship hurts, badly. To me, it sounds like it has been deliberately uttered for me to hear. A special message for me after what I shared with him earlier. The ticking bomb's safety catch has been released. Whatever it is, it's not something I want to keep listening to. I rinse my mug, put it in the dishwasher, and head to the shower, the magic of waking up next Sebastian completed eroded.

Chapter 26
"The Beginning of the End"
Tired Pony

"I'll wait outside, okay?" I tell Kai, leaving him and Vivian to continue their vivid conversation about Kai's travels as he waits for our order.

Taking a seat at one of the outside tables, I check my phone, again. No calls. The way we parted earlier, Sebastian and me, as I left to see Kai and Sebastian left for a meeting in Madrid, keeps playing in my head. We separated with our usual hug and kiss farewell ritual, but the tense undercurrent between us wasn't lost on me. It was a charged moment. A moment that left a heavy weight at the pit of my stomach; one that I can't seem to shake off.

Absorbed in my thoughts, I miss Stephy till she's sitting right next to me, eyeing me below creased brows.

"What's with the serious face?" she asks, her sweet smile making me mirror her.

I dismiss it with a brief headshake. "Nothing. How you doing?"

She twists her lips, moving them from side to side. I smile at her pensive state, and the time it takes her to respond to my simple question. Her blue eyes narrow at me, and she huffs.

"I think I'm going to boycott dating."

My lips twitch. If there were a good distraction from everything depressing, it would be Stephy. "Is that so?"

She huffs again, pulling up the sleeves of her stripped black and red cotton dress. "Well, my last date might have just sealed the deal on a much-needed break from men."

"What happened?"

"I went on a date with someone I met online, and it was going pretty well till he asked me if he could take a few photos of us kissing. He wanted to send them to his ex-girlfriend to make her jealous. Needless to say, the promising evening ended long before dessert." She air quotes promising.

I beam at her. "So, that's it. You're giving up?"

"Yeah, I'm done. My vagina is in remission. No more men," she declares and less than a breath after, her eyes round to an expression that could only be described as puppy eyes. "God, have mercy on my ovaries . . ." The last of her words winds down to an almost whisper.

I follow her gaze and nod to myself. *Oh, that.* I've seen it so many times before, the commonly known "Kai affect."

Stephy remains dreamingly silent as Kai hands me a cup of coffee. His eyes drop to Stephy, who seems to be hypnotized. He brings the camera in his hand forward, "I'm going to take a few shots of the area."

"Sure, I'll wait for you. I need to talk to Vivian."

He turns to Stephy and offers her his hand, "Be my model?"

"Mmmhmm," Stephy's reply sounds more like a breathy shriek. Eyes locked with Kai, and rosy cheeks, she stands up and follows him. I roll my eyes with a grin. Shortest boycott in the history of short boycotts.

"So, Dominique is meeting Gérard and some prominent lawyer as we speak," Vivian says, plopping onto an empty seat.

"Sad . . . to think that so many years of marriage end up in a splitting-the-loot get-together supervised by some expensive stranger in a suit."

Vivian nods in affirmation. "And the supposedly closest person to you, your *life* partner, leaves you to continue the rest of the ride by yourself because he couldn't resist putting his hands on a younger chick."

I gaze at Vivian as she stares ahead at the busy pavement. She seems tired again, maybe even worried.

"Vivian, when was the last time you saw a physician?"

She regards me with a troubled look.

"I'm fine, querida. Really. There's just so much going on. A large catering company has approached me. They'd like to collaborate with me. The more I studied their offer, the more I fell in love with the idea of catering."

"It's a good thing, no?"

"Don't know. As much as I like the idea, I'm not sure I'd like to share my business with a stranger. My café, my business, has always been a family thing. My own thing. I'm not sure I'd like to change that. Perhaps you could be my partner?" she beams at me.

"Me? Have you ever tasted anything I cooked? If there's something I suck at, it's everything preparing food related." She eyes me seriously, and I add, "I screw up omelets!"

"Who said anything about cooking? It's a business. Just like any other business, it needs a financial brain, business strategies, or whatever you people do."

I study her as she grins back at me.

"Viv, I'm leaving in a few short months . . ."

Her grin calms into a thin line, *"Are you? Really?"*

I don't get to answer her question as Kai's return interrupts us. The question remains an unanswered one, both to her and to me.

. . .

When the train's headlights advance toward us, Kai tugs on my hand and pulls me into the warmest hug. We hold each other firmly for some lingered moments. He kisses the crown of my head repeatedly while my hold on him tightens.

"Come back home, Liv. I meant every word I said. Come home to me."

Kai bends to leave a chaste kiss on my lips, squeezes my hand with a supple smile, and walks to the train. I watch him till the train's lights become fading red spots.

A wild whirlwind of thoughts seizes my brain so much that I hardly notice my surroundings as I make my way back home. A whirlwind that has been growing steadily and progressively to the point it's the only thing I can focus on.

It comes in three waves that together form a tsunami that presses hard on my chest and leaves my emotions wrecked. Wave one, courtesy of mommy dearest. The doubt she seeded in me. The big question. Am I really wasting my time? Am I wasting my time here? Am I wasting my time on Sebastian?

Wave two carries with it a more profound reservation, one

that keeps nagging at me: Kai would like to give us a try. Is it something I'd want to try if I decide to go back home? Our pact, marrying my best friend. Isn't that what is commonly known as the most profound foundation for a relationship? The strongest couples that have stood the test of time and life's hurdles are best friends first and lovers second.

And the last ripple that nicely adds to the chaos in my head is Sebastian's phone call with his mom and his comment the other day when I asked him how he felt about marriage. When he *calmed* his mom down by telling her that we aren't that serious, he provoked the complete opposite reaction in me, entirely messing with my head. To be honest, my insistent resentment against the whole marriage idea and children has recently wavered. I think it started to weaken sometime after Sebastian told me about Lola getting pregnant. It made me think. What would I have done? A thought that grew to what would I have done if it happened to Sebastian and me. And to be honest, I liked the sound of it. I liked the idea, more than I could even admit to myself at the time. It's not that I'm secretly wishing for him to propose, but yes, that is something I'd be more than glad to say yes to, somewhere in the future. To have a future with him.

I caught myself dissolving into Sebastian's eyes when he made love to me last night, and there was so much more there, so much more than other times. It wasn't about the dark color of his irises or the tender expression in them; it was the actual moment. It was as if I could see a multitude of unborn moments of the two of us together. As though I saw everything I'd like my future to be. I guess at that exact moment, it dawned on me that Sebastian is *it* for me. I understand now why what he told his mother and the determination he uttered it with hurt so much.

I stop cold, passing the post office, and take a few steps back. I worry my lip staring at the yellow and black sign above the door as an idea starts to take shape in my mind. Quickly, I head inside, and buy four large cardboard boxes and double the amount of smaller ones.

Perhaps if I actually start packing, do my thing, put things in order, the answer will come. The answer to what's next for me?

Chapter 27
"Sometimes Love Just Ain't Enough"
Charice

As I organize books and random knickknacks in neatly piled sets while kneeling on the tan living room rug, the haze in my head gradually clears. On the other hand, my heart slowly begins to wilt. Securing tape over a closed box, I take a deep breath and lean my back against the sofa. I think about how when I packed my apartment before leaving for Spain, it felt like I was packing for an exciting adventure, it felt like I was leaving my past for something better. Now, when I sit amid brown boxes in my half-packed living room, it feels like I'm making arrangements I am not full-heartedly ready to make. It feels like this time I am leaving parts of my heart behind. It feels like I'm going to be leaving *me* behind.

I rise up to stand and caress the wall with the tips of my fingers, walking toward the kitchen. I pour myself a glass of cold water and take a sip, glancing out the window. I like everything about this place, and I know for sure that I don't want to leave. I don't want to leave this home, my friends, and mostly, the man I love. But just as these feelings of belonging cushion my heart, the thoughts of what kind of a life I could have here overshadow the momentary bliss. The sound of a lock turning freezes my contemplation. I set the glass on the counter and turn on my heel. I take a step into the living room just as Sebastian closes the door behind him. His eyes meet mine, and a smile forms on his lips.

Everything in my head evaporates solely by the way he looks at me. I return his smile and take a step toward him.

"You are back." I beam his way.

"I cut my trip short," he says, looking utterly panty-dropping hot in a fine, dark suit and a mischievous grin. "Couldn't stay away."

As I'm finally near and am about to wrap my arms around him, Sebastian's head slightly jerks back in surprise. His features harden when his eyes land on the boxes scattered in disarray on the floor. With joint brows and eyes glued to the brown cardboard boxes, he takes a few slow steps forward. He stops above the last box I worked on and dips his chin to look inside. Ironically so, it's a box of books with the picture of Kai and me feigning a kiss right on the top.

Sebastian jaw flexes and he slowly cranes his neck to look my way. "What's all this?"

The rhythm of my heart quickens while I arrange the words in my head. "Um . . . I just, um. I thought that if I . . ."

"You're packing? You're going back?" Sebastian silences my stutter with his loaded question.

"No. I mean, I started to pack to help make things clearer."

Sebastian's hard gaze doesn't leave mine as he takes a seat on the sofa, his leg inches from the box he just stared at.

I lean my back against the wall and hug myself, holding his gaze with mine. "What is it that you want?"

He cocks his head, eyes burning into mine.

"With me. What is it that you see happening between us?" I ask dreading his answer. Dreading my own response to the same question. Dreading my next breath.

He pushes his finger through the knot of his tie, slowly tilting it from side to side. He drops his elbows to his thighs, threads his fingers together, and slowly cranes his neck to look up at me. His eyes are weary, lined with livid flare.

"Be the man you come home to every night. But, I don't really get it. Why does it even matter? Seems like you made up your mind, made the decision for the both of us . . . you're leaving. So why, Liv, why do you ask?"

I observe his handsome face and fight the ring of pain that squeezes my heart so tightly. A clog expands in my throat as I start to realize where we're heading.

"Make me stay," I say in a weak voice, inwardly begging him to ask me to stay, show me how much I mean to him. That he'd never let me go. Sort my dilemma for me.

Sebastian shakes his head. "I won't. I can't do it to you or to me."

"Yes, you can."

He shakes his head again, and to the simple motion my heart both faints and withers.

I bring my fingers to touch my slightly quivering lips as I say, "You don't see a real future for us?" The next words that leave my mouth are a murmur. "My mom was right . . ."

He rubs his hand over his mouth and chin. "Don't take my

words out of context, Liv. I never said that." Sebastian's voice hardens, matching his rigid features.

Ask me to stay, I silently beg. "But you won't ask me to stay."

He shakes his head once more, causing the tears I'm holding back with all my might to sting at the corner of my eyes.

He takes a long breath and drops his head. When he lifts it back to look at me, his eyes are a shade darker, a shade gloomier. "You can't stay here for me. You should stay for *you*, Liv. You should be wherever you're the happiest. I don't want to be the one who decides for you. If you end up staying here because of me, the first argument we'll have, the first time you miss home, will be the beginning of our end. And I'd rather let *you* be happy than force you to make *me* happy."

The pain starts in my stomach and slowly crawls up and up. When it gets near my heart, it becomes almost impossible to bear.

"I am not going to pretend you're not breaking my heart," I say in a shattered voice and a single tear manages to escape my eye.

His eyes soften, but the dejected tone in them stays. "I am not going to pretend you're not breaking mine," his voice rasps out raw with vulnerability, layered with despair, just like mine.

I watch him as he rises to stand. I watch him as he gives the boxes at his feet another gaze that ends with a wince. I watch him in silence as he closes the distance between us. A step away, his eyes skim over me, and I hold my breath. He leans in to leave a gentle kiss on my forehead and envelops me in his arms. I liquefy into his embrace, burying my face in his chest, taking in his Sebastian scent and indulge in the warmth he induces in me.

Fearing it's the last time I'll feel this secure, this loved.

For some long minutes, we hug each other tight as though holding on to each other for some stolen moments and not letting the impending final good-bye separate us.

"I love you, Liv," Sebastian whispers, and his lips find mine.

Although my heart that's in my throat makes it hard for me to breathe, I drown in his kiss. Closing my eyes over warm tears, I kiss him back with everything I have.

We finally ease back after long beats of desperate kisses. Final kisses, kisses of our end. Our eyes are locked in unbearable despair when Sebastian tells me, once more, that he loves me.

"I love you, too," I whisper while his fingers slowly unthread from mine. I follow him with my stare as he walks to the door. And when it closes behind him, I melt to the floor amid the boxes that hold my unwanted future, the tears coming freely.

Chapter 28
"Doesn't Mean Good-bye"
Jon McLaughlin

There's an incessant ache at the pit of my leaden heart that I've been nursing since our "breakup." Be it as it may, I'm not certain "breakup" would be the best terminology for our last encounter. For we've never really ceased to be a whole. He'll forever remain a part of me. As he walked out my door, I buried him in my heart. I knew that any other option would be a deceitful one, to myself. I knew back then, just as I know, full well, right now, that I'm not capable of making myself forget him, nor am I willing to. Even though not many days have passed since I last saw him and told him that I loved him, and let him go. Though not many days have passed since we wordlessly agreed to part ways, my thoughts of him, of how I feel, won't wane. Feelings that make me think of the Welsh word "hiraeth." A word my beloved late grandma used to express her longings and memories of her homeland. It has no exact cognate in the English language, the closest meaning would be "homesickness," but it's so much more. It's wistfulness, yearning, a bond for a home you can't return to, or one that never really existed. It may be about a ferocious longing and connection to a place, but the allegory to how I feel about Sebastian couldn't be more fitting. Bond and ferocious longing, ones that consume you.

The irony is not lost on me no matter how hard it is to gulp down. The one person I thought would help me make the right decision, maybe make the decision for me, the decision I've subconsciously wanted to make, was the one who actually pushed me to realize I've been living in some sort of a rose-tinted fantasy. The person who made me wrap up in the feeling is the same one who shook me well enough to land flat into cold reality. Cold enough to make me realize that there is no such thing as real-life fairy tales. When it comes down to pragmatism, Prince Charming doesn't swipe you away to a happily ever after, he tells you – *you* should find one on your own.

Yes, the verdict has been rendered. Thanks to my own Prince Charming, I'm returning home, early. Great as it was, it seems like my journey has come to an end. If I extend this escapade any longer, I'm not sure my heart will be resilient enough to resist cracking and maybe even shattering, to never be repaired again.

I'm not the kind of person who, though she can, will live a life of pure leisure. I'm a doer. And it's time I got back to the real world, back to doing. Get a job, do the grown-up thing once again after this long, perfect break. I haven't found out what it is that I want to do yet, but I'm sure that the probability of ultimately finding it is not where I am right now.

I jot down a short to-do list right after changing my flight back home to a week from today. The thing that eats at me the most, besides the impending departure, is delivering the news to my friends. Telling the girls that I've decided to go back home.

Saying good-bye is not something I know how to do, or cope with. Especially given the pang in my heart, this new feeling for me each time I think about it. But I have to, and the sooner, the better. Just like I should tell my parents I'm coming back. Just like I should let Kai know.

Kai.

With the thought of my return, the thought of his proposal arises. My answer to his offer is clear to me, clearer than anything. *No.* At least, not right now. I can't think of, or want, anyone else if I can't have Sebastian. Not even Kai.

Before drowning deeper in my deep contemplation pool, I text the girls, asking if they are up for a spontaneous get-together. I'd be lying if I said I was glad at the immediate consent coming from all of them. My reaction is more in the vein of a sudden dread, particularly with the farewell I'm about to bid.

. . .

"Oh, this little break is a blessing. I really needed a break. Thanks, Liv," Alma says, rubbing the nape of her neck while stretching it from side to side. "I swear, the closer we get to the wedding the more setbacks seem to be popping up out of nowhere. It's as if the entire universe has conspired to wear me down before the big day."

"Dzey stopped producing dze nail polish shade you've always dreamed of for your big day?"

The rest of the ladies snort animatedly, but I don't. I don't have it in me. I'm too strung up to appreciate Dominique's snarks.

"You bet your sweet little hiney the shopping tour we have

planned for next week will be pure-freaking-joy," Embar assures Alma and dives her mouth to close around the thick straw in her iced-coffee.

Alma sends Embar a smile and Vivian regards them both with a little motion of her chin. "Barcelona?"

It amazes me how only hearing the name of the city is a blow to my stomach. I close my eyes for the shortest beat and Sebastian's face burns before my eyelids – the way he looked at me, close and so intimate, during the concert.

Alma shakes her head. "Madrid. Shoes and bridesmaid's dresses."

They continue discussing everything wedding preparations, including the fact that Vivian will be orchestrating the food part. Her baptism of fire for her solo catering venture. Dominique, amid frequent concerned glances my way, can't refrain from engaging Alma in a little saucy banter about her army of bridesmaids, which consists of Embar, aka the BFF, Stephy, and Alma's six sisters. I fight to stay afloat and focused, alas, little by little, I dive into the sea of disquiet that is my mind.

"Liv?" Vivian's voice finally manages to penetrate my introspection.

I lift my head to meet five pair of troubled eyes boring into me. I take a breath that doesn't manage to reach all the way through and divulge on an exhale. "I'm leaving in a week."

"Leaving?" Stephy asks and sends a glance to the rest of our friends.

"Going back home."

"For a visit?"

I shake my head and the oxygen in my lungs becomes even

more diluted. "I'm going back." I swear Dominique's eyes have just glazed over, a notion that brings my own eyes to moisten.

"No," Stephy says, sounding a tad like a petulant child. But it's sweet and touching, and presses hard on my chest.

A choir of voices comes my way in varied sets of questions.

"Anyhow, I have just a couple of months left, and I thought I might start hunting for a job earlier. You know, get started on putting my real life back together."

Vivian and Dominique exchange loaded glances and turn to look my way in unconcealed bewilderment.

"What about Sebastian?" Stephy says, her expression manifesting the gloominess that has descended on the room.

Dominique narrows her eyes at me, and Vivian raises an eyebrow, both waiting. My instinct is to brush it off with a silly "what about him?" reply, but I owe them more than this. They are my friends. My close friends. Some closer, some less, nonetheless, I love them all.

"We broke up, I think."

"You think?" Alma regards me with a creased forehead.

And another solicitous glance is traded between Vivian and Dominique.

"You can say we came to a mutual understanding that there isn't really a future for us given we live on two different continents."

"Who says you ought to go back?" Dominique challenges me with a look that's equal measure pissed and sad.

"I came here for an extended vacation, for a good time, but it's time I got back. I never intended to stay forever." A flint, bitter smile accompanies the last part.

"He didn't ask you to stay?" Though her voice is almost a whisper, I still hear it clear and sharp, and painful. So does the rest of the group. We all pivot Vivian's way.

"No, he did not. But even if he would have, it wouldn't change anything, I guess. Come on, what would I possibly do here long term? There's just so much strolling on the beach and having good food one can allow oneself without turning into a spoiled bum."

"You could be doing anything you'd be doing there, here," Vivian counters.

"Only you'd be much happier," Dominique completes Vivian's words.

"I can't believe you won't be in my wedding," Alma says. Her words carry no spite, they are more of a blue recognition, symbolically so, echoing the expression on each of our faces. Right after her declaration, Alma rises to stand and walks over to me. She wraps her arms around me and I almost choke on the swell in my throat. The embrace becomes tighter when Stephy joins, and Embar. And I can barely hold my tears in check when Vivian and Dominique join them. It's unclear to me how long we stand like this, holding each other in our circle of firm bond, but it's enough to tell just how much they all mean to me, and I to them.

Chapter 29
"Every Teardrop is a Waterfall"
Coldplay

"Scarlet, seriously, only if you're hundred and two percent sure. *Are you?*" Kai's soothing voice asks me over the phone.

"Well, I've been stewing over this to no end, believe me. And what can I say, when it comes down to weighing my possibilities, even though I had the best of times here, if I take language, job opportunities, family, and basically everything real life into consideration, I just know that the sensible thing to do is come back home. It started off as a dream and apparently so ends as such." A dream I had. A dream I lived. A dream that will soon become my most cherished memory.

The sound of a long puff comes from his side, followed by a raspy, "It's your mom I hear talking through your voice."

"No, Kai. It's simply logic." My retort is contempt crusted. *He* should know better than to compare me to her.

"Look, whatever you decide to do, I'm with you. Of course, I want you to come back, but mostly, I want you to do whatever is best for you."

"I adore you, Kai." For some moments, after ending the call,

I soak in the small comfort of having Kai to hold on to when I get back home. For I know, in any aspect of it, my return won't be an easy feat. To be putting it mildly.

Just when I wish for time to still, it slips through my fingers like grains of sand. The clock is ticking, and with every tick, my departure is nearing. But it's time. Time to let a dream stay where a dream belongs – a fantasy in the woods of my mind. I have lived my own private dream, and it is time for me to move on.

I slide the phone onto the kitchen counter and resume labeling the last of the packed boxes with color-coded stickers, making sure the list in my hand correlates to the number on each box. I have a sudden urge to talk to a certain diamond pattern, mustard sweater, hair slicked to the side, head healer. On second thought, that might just add to my agitation.

The song in the background is literally slicing through my belly with each word. But I keep on listening because somehow it expresses with its beautiful lyrics the thoughts swimming in my head, the thoughts of Sebastian. A song about letting go of someone you love.

Pressing a red sticker on another box, a motorcycle's hum coming from outside my door stills me.

Can't be.

I try to shrug it off with the simple excuse that there are more than a few bike owners in Serenidad and that it doesn't necessarily have to be the one haunting my every waking moment. I can feel my heartbeat below my ear drumming when the sound grows louder. When it thins down right by my porch, my pulse becomes palpable and frantic. I hug myself, waiting.

Anxious and wistful. In tandem to a knock on my door, my phone chimes, breaking my edgy anticipation. I peer over at the screen and press end on Dominique. *She* can wait, *my heart* cannot.

My lungs detain my breath as I make my way toward the door. A determined knock later, I finally reach it. For a stretched moment, our eyes converse in loaded silence. The singer in the background is crooning in a velvety voice, "Just 'cause I told you that it was over that doesn't mean I don't need you by my side," in perfect harmony to our soulful eye-lock. As though articulating what my eyes are telling the man in front of me. The man with the white button-down and dark jeans. The man with the solemn expression.

The space between his brows puckers as Sebastian's eyes trail over me and creases some more as he seems to be choosing his words. I clasp my hands together, too tense, not sure what to do next. Though I try very hard to avoid the bubble of hope making its way up inside of me, I still can't help but wish with all my heart that he is here to ask me not to leave. And I know full well that I would, without a second thought, do as he asks. If he only asked.

"Liv," he says my name, and it's enough to make me miss a beat.

"Yes." A soft whisper. I get distracted by the motion of his hand and follow it closely with my gaze as it reaches mine and squeezes it gently. With my gaze still rested on our joint hands, I fail to hear the first time he tells me something about a hospital. Entirely focused on the moment, inwardly wishing to hear him say something completely different, it takes me some extra seconds to fully comprehend what he just told me.

"She's in the ER; they mentioned something about her heart. A heart attack. I thought . . ." He inhales. "I thought you'd better hear it from me."

"Vivian had a heart attack?" My eyes rip open and my free hand jolts to cover my mouth.

Sebastian nods. "Come, I'll take you there."

I'm static; swimming in wild waters of confusion till Sebastian secures my hand tighter in his and gestures for me to follow. Before turning to the door, his stare falls on the packed boxes lined on the floor and I can't help cringing at the brief somberness that's obscuring his features. My attention trains on Sebastian's back as I follow him to the bike, and all I can do, besides worry about my friend, is think *he is not here for me.*

On the way to the hospital, I let myself cling to the comfort and rightness of being wrapped around Sebastian's strong, wide frame, his scent, and the warmth he induces in me and on me. Nothing feels more right than having him this close.

. . .

"I tried to ca —" The rest of Dominique's sentence is kept held back when she notices Sebastian by my side. "Sebastian." She nods at him. "I'll wait dzere." She gestures to a row of teal-blue plastic chairs that have undoubtedly seen better days.

"I got to get back to work." Sebastian commences our second and probably last good-bye.

"Thank you," I say through a blocked throat.

He nods, and his eyes flutter closed in affirmation. "When do you leave?"

"In three days."

He sends his hand to the hollow below my chin. His thumb slowly traces my jaw while his eyes skim my own. He takes a breath that to my ears sounds rueful, and leans forward to leave a supple kiss on my lips. "Take care."

I reach for his hand that still holds my face and bring his palm to my lips. I press my lips onto his skin, breathing him in. *God, this hurts so much.* He inches closer and envelops me with his free hand. He leans his chin on the crown of my head and dips to kiss the same spot. I feel his body easing away from me and I want to argue, plead for him not to let me go.

"Good-bye, Liv." Another soft kiss and he leaves me for the very last time.

It's a blur, how much time has passed before Vivian is finally transferred to the CCU, and we are allowed to see her. We've been sitting in the waiting room, waiting in silence. In nail-biting silence, for what feels like a lifetime.

A unified sigh of relief leaves our mouths to the sight of a paler version of our vibrant friend, recumbent on a high bed. The relief factor is due to the faint smile she beams at us, weak and colorless, but nonetheless, still a smile. We stand next to Vivian's bed and rain unrelenting phrases of wellbeing and scolding of welfare at her. Vivian, wearing a calm and patient grin, waits for us to let it all out.

"I'm fine. We caught it in time. It was a minor thing. No one will be reading my will anytime soon."

I shake my head, and Dominique throws her eyes to the white ceiling.

"Now, can you please take a seat?"

I do as told.

"Both of you." Vivian pins Dominique with a look.

"Pfff…" It's the sound of Dominique succumbing. I'm not able to lessen the smile forming on my lips. I think it's the first time I've ever seen Dominique actually acquiesce so easily, or at all, for that matter.

"You need to take it easy," I say with genuine concern.

Vivian's exhale carries frustration. "It came at the worst time. There is so much going on; I can't allow myself to take it easy."

"Oh, you can." Dominique's nosy lilt laces her words. "And you will. I'll make sure you do." To be honest, was I in Vivian's shoes, I'd think twice before replying with anything that wouldn't appease our Frenchie. She is wearing her "do not mess with me" expression. She means business. "Vivian, I'm here for you. I gave it some thought, and I'd like to invest in your business, be your partner if you'll have me."

My chest both swells and pinches at once. I'm touched by Dominique's offer, glad for them both; glad because Dominique has found something she'd like to give a chance, glad at the light in Vivian's eyes that tells how much she likes the idea. The pinch, however, is because I won't be able to support Vivian, support them both. I won't be here.

"I'd love that. There's so much to do though, decisions to be made." My friends eye me for a stilled beat, one from the bed, and the other from the chair parallel to mine. I wince in return. As the laden stare down comes to an end, Vivian resumes with a monologue about what's in store, catering services, and an opportunity to open a branch of Café con Aroma in Barcelona. When Vivian's stream of words becomes excited and she attempts to sit up straight, both Dominique and I jump to our feet, gesturing for her to take it easy.

"Wow, you really thought it all through, uh? But I think that you should try and rest now." I smile at Vivian.

"You should. I'll come by tomorrow and we can put together an action plan. I can start dzings rolling while you get better."

I've never felt as grateful to Dominique as I do now. In succession, we squeeze Vivian's hand and promise to visit the next day.

"Nothing is set in stone, you know. You can still change your mind. No one will think any less of you. On the contrary," Vivian tells me with a faint but sincere smile. Her words keep hovering in my head long after we leave the hospital.

"I need a drink, somedzing good, somedzing French," Dominique says, burying her face in her hands and exhaling. I let out a deflated sigh and nod. Me too, I definitely need a drink, and maybe some Dominique time won't hurt, either.

Three hours, profound conversation, and a couple of Bordeaux later, I lock the door behind me and turn to lean with my back against the cool wood. I kick my sandals off and slide to the floor. I can't make myself walk further inside the house that appears so estranged with its bare walls. I bring my legs to my chest and hug them, resting my chin on my knees. My eyes roam over the room, at this place I've called home for almost a year, at the stacked high boxes manifesting an end of an era, a palpable token of the decision I've made which no matter how hard I try, I can't stop second-guessing. Vivian's last comment before we left the hospital and the long conversation I had with Dominique that came right after irrepressibly dominate my thoughts. A sudden sense of realization sinks to the depths of my recognition. Causing for a surge of exhilaration to simmer inside of me, one that's identical to an equally burning one that emerged shy of ten months ago when Kai told me he'd be leaving for an indefinite amount of time.

Chapter 30
"Home Sweet Home"
Motley Crew

"Who would have thought, eh?" Vivian asks to no one in particular, her eyes zeroed in on some indistinct point ahead.

"Who would have thought?" I echo her through a pensive murmur.

A sluggish moment passes in which each one of us ponders the "moment" before we grant each other an animated glance. We are leaning forward, our elbows braced on the counter, over a display of delicious cakes, the three of us, Vivian, Dominique, and I, gazing at the busy café.

"Who would have thought I'd own a business in Spain." The tip of my lips jumps up as a sense of satisfaction washes over me.

"Who would have thought it would be in the food sector." Vivian chuckles and winks at me.

"Who would have thought one of your business partners would be a French bitch," Dominique deadpans and slowly turns our way, her expression a blend of wickedness and humor. We counter her with elated snickers.

"Okay, shall we start getting ready for lunch?" Vivian asks, making us break off our little joint meditative pause. I head over to the back kitchen to make sure all the lunch orders are packed and ready. Dominique takes over the register, and Vivian does what she does best. Besides cooking ridiculously delish food, schmoozing the customers till they pledge allegiance to both her and *our* café.

Before officially signing the papers, when we'd put our heads together and argued passionately, in an amicable nature of course, about how our partnership would actually work, we came to the unanimous agreement that my part would mostly be behind the scenes and my friends would be the ones who essentially ran the business logistics. In further details, Vivian governs the Serenidad café and the catering, which has been slowly and nicely thriving. Dominique tyrannically overlooks the renovation process of the branch in Barcelona while co-piloting Vivian in the Serenidad café. In the meantime, since both Dominique and I are still reasonably concerned with Vivian's wellbeing, although she had a fairly smooth and rapid recovery, we still try to help as much as we can, or more accurately, as much as she allows us to. Together, Dominique and I work to reduce the stress factor, which leads to our nearly constant presence at the café.

It's been more than three weeks since Vivian was released from the hospital. Three weeks since I decided to abort the going back home mission. Three weeks in which I've been dealing with everything legal concerning registering our new partnership, starting my residency permit process, extending my lease for two more years with an option to buy it later on, and embracing the wonderful feeling of fulfillment, of being whole. Though, truthfully, there is a missing part to ultimately make my wholeness actually complete. Not a single day goes by that I don't think about Sebastian, the key to making my wholeness complete.

It took me a while to fully understand how right he was when he told me that I should stay in Serenidad for me, not anyone else. Staying for him, because of him, would have meant, in a way, that I was surrendering my life to him, when what I really needed was to take control of my life. Now that I've come to the realization of just how fulfilled and happy I am, now that I have found my own way, I agree with his reasoning. However, there's this tiny niggling thought that refuses to leave. The well-hidden wish that he would have fought for me, for us. It's still a persistent cinder weakly burning in the romance struck district of my brain. As hard as I try to extinguish said ember, the damn thing won't go away. I reason it with the whole princesses and ever after fantasies I've nourished throughout my childhood, my naïveté years. What can I say, revoltingly misogynistic as it may sound, after all, my Barbies never ended up running a stellar career while maintaining a monogamous relationship with their battery-operated significant other. They were always the happiest knowing that their well-deserved ever-after was at hand's reach when Ken's perfect Chiclets smile sparkled at them, saying: "Hey babe, I've got your back. Your forever after is on me."

The thought of seeing Sebastian excites me, but in equal measure scares me. Just as time has a tendency to soothe a broken heart, it also has the power to harden one. The more time that passes since I last saw him, the greater my longings grow, but I'm not sure if it's the same case with him, if *his* heart hasn't hardened when it comes to me. The nagging thought, which most of the time I manage to keep at bay, does emerge from time to time, reminding me that thus far he hasn't attempted to contact me. Making me believe he's let me go.

Honoring my so-called "post-breakup" healing process, my friends tried to not interfere, nor mention either Sebastian or the breakup. They kept it up fairly well, besides one little slip-up on Vivian's part when she mentioned Sebastian has been away in Barcelona for a couple of weeks. Which I didn't hold against her because she is, after all, Vivian, and the fact that she held up quiet to that point shouldn't be easily overlooked.

I pack Styrofoam boxes in brown paper bags and add the relevant bill to each bag, getting them ready for takeout pick-ups. I arrange them chronologically on the long table according to the time they were ordered, because OCD-esque as it might be, this is what I do, I put things in order. Troublesome but yet too deeply entrenched.

The cracking sound of the three stairs leading to the back kitchen makes me spin in my place. Following comes Vivian's voice calling for me from the café, but the rest of her words, besides my name, are swallowed by the loud swishing sound of my blood in my ears.

I'm not certain what I find more challenging, properly breathing or keeping my revving heart safe inside my chest. The sudden anxiety that takes over me forcefully intensifies by the reaction to the person now facing me from across the room.

When he lifts his eyes and they land on me, his face flinches back in a confused, staggered jerk. I can't really blame him for his reaction, seeing that in his reality I'm somewhere on the East coast picking up on my life right where I left off before I met him. An eon of silence passes before either of us speaks. Sebastian takes a step forward and pauses. I take a generous inhale that does nothing to placate my inward storm. I stand solid, gazing at him as he returns my stare, standing before me in a pinstriped gray suit, charcoal button-down, and a startled expression on his handsome face.

"You are here." His voice sounds so baffled, it makes it hard for me to determine whether it was a question or an observation.

"I am." I'm not fully positive my words ever reached him as softly as I uttered them. "Yes, I'm here," I repeat, having a déjà vu of when we met at the wine event when I got my second chance with him.

Sebastian's head slightly cocks while the wrinkles on his forehead deepen.

"Um, I've decided to stay, after all. For me . . ." I try to keep my voice coherent, which is not the easiest task, what with everything inside me going wild. "Umm, and give living here a chance."

I can hear his next breath from where I'm standing while the space of a kitchen and a wealth of miscommunication separate us physically and emotionally.

"Are you free for lunch?" Me.

"Let's have dinner tonight." Him.

Our sentences clash, leaving a clutter of words hanging between us. Sebastian slowly walks over, stopping two short steps before me.

"I'm sorry. I already have plans for lunch. I had plans for

dinner too, but apparently they've just been cancelled."

"Oh." I can't help the ring tightening around my chest, caused by the notion of the dinner plans he had. Though he just said they've been cancelled, the thought he might have had a date tonight is too painful to entertain.

"I was supposed to have dinner on a plane . . . on my way to Boston."

Boston? As in my hometown, Boston?

"For business?" I ask, the pace of my heart doubling by the mere implication of his alleged trip having any connection to me.

"For my girlfriend."

I don't think that I've ever had Sebastian's eyes as intently on mine. Their weight is almost tangible.

"You have a girlfriend in Boston?" I bite my lip, both to trap a smile and hold my eyes from glossing over. *You didn't give up on me, after all.* The emotions currently spreading in me are about to overflow.

"I guess I don't. Apparently, she decides to stay where *I live* and chooses not to share it with me." *Ouch.*

I shake my head. "It wasn't like that, Sebastian."

"Oh, it wasn't?" He heaves a frustrated exhale. "I can't do this right now; I have people waiting for me at the office."

I nod, though the last thing I want is for him to walk out of here right now with our conversation left unfinished, my reason unexplained, and probably pestering the man I love, and more than possibly the man I've just royally pissed off. The next exchange between us is too formal, too logistics-esque, too cold. He asks for his takeout, and I hand it over to him.

"Pick you up around seven?" His effort to keep collected

doesn't escape me.

"Yes." I nod, tacking my hands into my pockets, the only way I can hold myself from running after him, hugging him, and burying my face in the broad gap between his shoulder blades.

A clop of heavy steps, a quick dour glance over a shoulder, and I'm left alone in a kitchen saturated with the aroma of cooked food and a multitude of unnerving questions. I don't even get to process the moment or even take an amending breath before Dominique and Vivian's heads pop up in the room.

"Et alors, no sex on dze counter?"

I roll my eyes exaggeratedly and add a small twist of a mouth for good measure. "No sex on the counter, more like a cease-fire with a promise for formal talks between the conflicting parties later on tonight."

"No one is having sex on the counter, any of the counters, ever." Vivian points her finger at us. "We have a precious sanitary license we should *all* endeavor to keep."

Our lips lift up concurrently.

"Ahem, about that . . . There was one time, Sebastian and I . . ."

"Tsk, tsk, tsk," Dominique shakes her head amusedly.

"I absolve you from your sins, my child. Never to happen again!" Vivian twists her lips in a feigned scowl. "Now, what have we missed?"

"Let's see. You missed the part where he told me he was supposed to fly out to Boston tonight, to see me."

Dominique nods with a small smile, and Vivian's face takes that same calm and warm expression she wears each time anyone mentions my relationship with Sebastian.

"Right after, he got upset about me being here for over three weeks without letting him know I decided to stay."

"Querida, what can I say, can you really blame him?" Vivian asks, leaving me in a greater anxiety about meeting Sebastian tonight, one that ripens as the hours progress toward the dinner.

. . .

I'm jittery like a smitten teenager before a date with the boy she's been pining after forever. The guy whose varsity jacket she is dying to wear. The guy she's prepared to pledge eternity to. And just like any other yearned for date, I've dolled up. As in, I have *dolled up!* I smooth my red wrap dress that does to my hourglass figure things any good spandex could only strive for. And yes, the thought of how easy it can be taken off had crossed my mind when choosing my attire, more than once. One little tug at the waist tie and tada! Ready to be served.

The outcome is nothing but classy and subtle though, but boy, the care, trouble, and thought I've given to every inch of my appearance. Suffice it to say, there isn't a single hair out of place on my entire plucked, waxed, scrubbed, and lotioned physique. Though my appearance couldn't be more put together, it feels like my mind is at its most frantic moment to date.

The familiar hum of Sebastian's bike elevates my disquiet to new levels of edginess. I'm stunned by my own reaction, frozen in my place, not sure if I should wait or go to the door. *Okay, this needs to stop, right about now.* I order myself to administrate my crazy and head toward the door.

Body language says so much and Sebastian's is definitely telling me that he is making an effort to keep some distance between us, even before he refuses my offer to come in. Even the traditional two kisses on the cheeks taste controlled.

"Shall we?" he asks, holding his hand out.

Hard as it is to cover my nervous state, I still manage to. "Sure, where to?" I close the door behind me and join him, his hand secured on the small of my back.

His eyes trace over me, hooded and profound. "You look beautiful."

My reaction unsettles me; maybe it's his strange, detached behavior, or my own agitation, but my eyes cast down and the apples of my cheeks warm up.

"We have a table at La Villa."

I can't help wincing at his place of choice for our dinner. It's one of the oldest boutique hotels in Serenidad, and as romantic as it may ring, it's actually at the furthest point on the romantic spectrum possible. It's the place you'd take a client to, not someone you were about to fly over three thousand miles to see.

The loaded post long-separation-vibe looping between us is thankfully forced to take a pause during the ride. Here on the bike where only touch counts, I let myself relax. Where the breeze of the wind wafts through the uplifted visor, and the ever warm and soothing descending Serenidad sun caressing with its warmth. Where I can hug Sebastian as tight as I want. Where no intense stares, no tension taking part. Where we're physically connected. The one thing that had always worked best for us from the moment we first touched, our pull toward each other.

My edginess returns when the ruins of an old fortress, that's part of a national historic site and also a great part of the beautiful scenery of the hotel we're about to dine in, appears in our view.

We're a traffic light away from crossing the mark where countryside backdrop takes over the urban scenery. As seconds drag for the light to change, I feel Sebastian's body tense under my embrace. I flinch as his flat hand smacks the handle with a vengeance. As though he might have just lost an internal argument or won one. Whichever it is, it prompts him to take a sharp U-turn back into the city. I can't even try to communicate with him, to ask where we're heading, as the crazed velocity with which he now maneuvers the vehicle forces me to cling tighter to him. I wedge one hand between Sebastian's back and my front to close the visor and bury my face between his shoulder blades. I ponder what's gotten into him, what made his driving turn combative. I trail my hand to rest over his heart, finding it fiercely pounding. When I dare to lift my eyes from their hiding place, my own heartbeat mimics his as the sight of his apartment building is revealed before me. Sebastian kicks down the stand and hurries to mount off the bike. Wordlessly, he helps me hop off, and then without a word, he takes my hand and guides us forward, both helmets in his other hand. Silently, yet hurriedly, we climb up one flight of stairs. I let out a choked yelp, almost tripping with Sebastian literally dragging me after him.

Wordlessly, he closes the door behind us, discards the helmets, setting them on the oak storage unit in the entrance. Still silent, he takes two more steps inside the dim hallway, my hand in his. Surprising me, he turns back with a start, takes a step toward me, grabs my face, and kisses me like he's been starving for my taste. Once the shock of the past ten minutes evaporates, I reciprocate with no less need. My hands skim over his arms, the pulsating vein in his wide neck, till they reach up to thread through his hair. I tug on it, tilting my face to better absorb his fervent attack. Weak whimpers spill from my throat into our engaged mouths. A full-on moan leaves my lips when Sebastian pins me to the wall behind us, his pelvis firm on mine, his hands all over my body as if they can't decide what to touch first. Thighs, waists, ribs, breasts, collarbone, cheek, neck.

"I should have never let you go," his lips, warm and full, say to a spot below my jaw.

I let out a sigh of surrender. It's the sound of my heated body's admission of defeat to my brain. I press my flat hand to Sebastian's chest, working to calm my frantic breath.

"God, you make my heart beat so wildly."

"That's the way it should always feel." He takes my hand, the one held against his chest, and brings it to his lips.

"We really need to talk." My words still breathy.

"Talk." And his lips are back on my neck. "I can't stop touching you."

"Sebastian," I say but don't do much to stop his renewed touch. "Sebastian . . ."

I'm not sure how exactly, but I next find myself straddling his thighs while he is seated on the floor, his back against the wall. His hands curl around my ribs as his thumbs lightly graze the sides of my breasts.

"You were right not to make me stay," I say, our eyes intently connected under the gentle evening glimmer coming from inside the apartment.

One of his hands trails down my belly and lower till it slides under my dress, making its way up to my panties. His fingers playing over the satin fabric.

"Dios, I missed everything about you," Sebastian says as his fingers crawl under the fabric to caress over my heated skin. We don't need further words between us to understand just how much our bodies beg to connect. I lift myself to allow him enough space to free himself from his jeans, and let him push my panties sideways, then he helps me glide over him. We hold our breaths as I slide down, taking him in as far as I can. I hold still for a beat, letting the liberating sensation of our connection reach every spot inside of me. A unified moan leaves our mouths as I slowly lift myself and even slower slide around him. We blink our eyes open into each other. His hand moves to tug the tie on my waist open while I work my fingers to unbutton his shirt.

"You're too amazing to let go so easily. I was beating myself up for letting you go," he says in a husky voice, peeling my dress off my shoulders, slowly rocking inside of me.

We keep moving gently against each other. I link my fingers with his and he brings our joined hands to rest on his thudding chest, where we are truly connected. He lifts his pelvis, pushing deeper into me, making my eyes roll back in my head.

I re-meet his stare. "I wanted you to ask me to stay so much." I lift my thighs, hovering above him. "But I'm glad you didn't. You were right. I needed to find where I wanted to be and what I wanted to do first." I glide back to him, we gust out a joint, full of desire breath.

"What were you planning to do?" I ask. Knowing full well he understands my question. What was his plan for when he got to Boston?

Sebastian's fingers untangle from mine and move to my waist.

He holds me firmly, helping me better sway on top of him. "Throw you over my shoulder and bring you back." He sends me a boyish grin. His knees buckle next as he thrusts harder. I moan throatily, slightly jerking up. My head drops back as I let the heated ache tidal from my spasm induced core to the rest of me.

"And . . . ?" I ask with my head still tipped back, eyes shut in pleasure.

"I don't know, ask you to come back and maybe work for us." His hands help me better elevate and sink back around his throbbing erection.

I twist my mouth in half a smile that says, "not the greatest idea." When our stares meet again, we're both smiling.

"Desperate times call for desperate measures," he says.

Our grins grow.

"I had to take the time to figure out what I had to do, and where I wanted to do it. I'm sorry I didn't tell you I was here. I was meaning to do that."

His lips find my nipple and suck hard on it. I whimper as he tells my harden skin, "I understand, and I'm glad for you that you found what you wanted."

"Oh, I found it."

He moves to my other nipple. I close my eyes and increase my pace, riding him even more keenly. The dim hall fills with loud moans of our drunken, sensual pleasure. He tilts his head up, leaning in to find my lips. His mouth starts with feathery touches and hastily turns fervent. Gradually, his plunges hasten, matching my pace with sharper, forceful thrusts. We ease back and level our stares.

"I love you." My heart is about to burst with just how much I do.

"I love you." His lips crash into mine, our tongues taking on the trance rhythm our bodies had taken. My release finds me at the edge of oblivion; it's so strong it leaves me shivering from ecstasy in Sebastian's tight embrace.

Chapter 31
"Take Me to Church"
Hozier

4.5 months later

The first tunes of the sentimental "Wedding March" make me slow my hurried steps. I lift my eyes and am taken aback, for the first time tonight noticing the beauty and grandiosity of the old church. Though I've been here many times before, in each of my visits to Barcelona, especially recently during the rehearsals, it feels like I'm seeing it for the first time. Maybe it's the gothic white candles dotting every available surface that sets a majestic ambiance, maybe it's the evening sky echoing through the stained glass windows, or the ornate facades and intricate leaded glass. Maybe it's the priest in a black clergy robe and white vestment waiting at the end of the aisle by the altar, maybe it's the guests sitting in their dressy ensembles, or maybe it's simply the actual occasion. Among the many guests, I look for a set of dark eyes that seem to be looking for me. When Sebastian smiles my way, looking dreamingly handsome in a tux, my eyes become watery. Our locked stare feels more like a physical connection.

I bite on my cheek and hold my eyes open, looking upward, willing the moisture to dry. I can't have mascara dripping over my cheeks, not now. I take a generous breath and beam at the twist in the music playing, a flamenco guitar woven around the rather calm beat, adding an exciting rhythm to the traditional melody.

My smile widens when I see Vivian and Dominique making their way toward me, both mirroring my contentment. Vivian in a floor-length strapless blazing red gown encircles her arm around my waist and squeezes me tight against her with the softest of grins. Dominique, ever dapper in a timeless, sophisticated black shift dress beams at me and stands by my other side. Our expressions soften and our eyes become shiny on cue as we turn our attention to the heavy, parted doors behind us.

Alma radiates a smile at the two little girls with glittery purple ribbons in their shiny curls that throw flowers out of the white basket at her feet. She is a stunning sight with her mocha skin shimmering against the snowdrift of lace hugging her curves, lingering behind her. A dress that has been in her family for over four generations, each bride in her turn adding her own personal touch. Alma's was the delicate champagne lining to the splendor design of lace and tulle. I follow her with my gaze as she makes her way toward her husband-to-be who looks back at her in utter reverence. I chance a glimpse Sebastian's way and I'm momentarily startled by the stare he has on me, by how similar it is to the one the groom has on his bride.

"I'll be right back," I tell my friends who reward me with knowing smiles following my stare that ends on Sebastian.

"Hola," Sebastian whispers next to my ear, leaving a soft kiss on my temple. I take his arms and wrap them around me, dissolving into the serene sensation that is to be held by him. I lean with my back deeper into his hug, pressing against his chest. I tilt my head back, resting my cheek on his chest, looking up at him. He dips his face to gift me with a soulful creamy brown look. I inch up, he leans closer, and we meet in the middle for a lingered supple kiss.

"Promise to take me somewhere quiet for a glass of wine later?" I quietly ask, watching Alma's eyes gloss as she listens to the priest as he asks her if she'll take the man standing next to her to be her lawfully wedded husband.

"I do," Sebastian whispers back. I crane my neck to look at him over my shoulder once more. He grins at me. "How about I promise to take you somewhere better later?"

"Deal. But it should be a quiet place. After tonight, I'm not sure I'll be up for anything too energetic."

"We'll see about that."

He holds me tighter against him. We stay like this till the groom is requested to kiss his bride. When the grand kiss seals the deal, my gaze trails to Stephy who's standing alongside Embar in mauve bridesmaids gowns, matching perfectly except for the fact that Embar is grinning and Stephy is wiping tears with the back of her hands, donning the dreamiest expression. When she senses my stare on her, she shrugs with a timid grin. I blow her a kiss and return her smile.

"I'll see you later," I say, and rise to stand on the heels of my feet to reach Sebastian's lips.

"Don't work too hard," he says to my mouth before we part.

Me, to continue supervising the event, check on the staff, see that everyone is in sync with the agenda, and talk to my partners, and Sebastian to nurse a glass of wine at the bar.

Before we know it, the night is over and so is our first significant catering gig. I meet up with Vivian and Dominique in the makeshift kitchen, an extension to the huge tent the reception was held at.

"To many more." Dominique raises a bubbling flute at us.

"Ojalá." Vivian snatches Dominique's glass and downs the greater part of the golden liquid in one swallow. "Salud!"

"Let's go say good-bye to the bride," I say.

Vivian, Dominique, Embar, Stephy, and I huddle around Alma, wishing her a perfect honeymoon between smooches and hugs, and one teary-eyed Stephy.

Talking to Vivian, I almost miss the bouquet Alma throws behind her back till it nearly crashes into my face. I send my hand up and give it a little sideways smack, sending it right into Stephy's waiting hands. I wink at her and she nods with the hugest grin.

Vivian, Dominique, and I remain on the front lawn, discussing last tasks before we can all call it a night. My attention is drawn to Stephy, who's standing a few steps away, goofily smirking at her phone. Her smirk expands as she rapidly, with much animation, types on the screen.

I leave my partners who are now deeply absorbed in a conversation about a potential client scheduled to meet with Dominique come Monday.

"Hey, what's up with the secretive smile. A new boy?" I tease Stephy, reaching her.

"Flirtexting with Kai." Rose hue tints her plump cheeks as soon as the last syllable leaves her glossed lips.

"My Kai?" I shoot in mild puzzlement.

She bites her smile, her own expression slightly muddled though she can't decide what to think. "My Kai," she chirps. Her smirk returns full-on when an incoming message chime comes from the device in her hand. I shake my head with a thin smile, making a mental note to investigate the matter further when either suspects are less engaged with "flirtexting."

"Okay, so, you're off for tonight," Vivian declares upon my return.

"Oui. Go, go, go." Dominique nods a few too many times, somewhat offensively, seeming way too eager to get rid of me.

"Wow, I feel welcomed," I scoff. "What do you mean? There are still too many things to do."

"Not for you." Vivian grins at me and Dominique tips her chin, gesturing to somewhere behind me.

I turn around to Sebastian, who takes my hand in his. "Let's go to that place I promised you earlier."

I turn to my friends once more and wince. They both appear like they are about to shoo me away. "Are you sure?"

Dominique rolls her eyes. "Can you just let it go, woman?"

Sebastian snorts a laugh that Vivian joins.

"Okay, got it. I'm going."

"How about that little rooftop bar near Passeig de Gràcia? The one that serves those amazing pimientos de padron?" I suggest as we make our way toward the main exit of the church.

"How about Paris?" Sebastian asks, and I freeze in my spot.

I blink at him and blink again. "Whoa? Paris?" I swallow over my confusion.

"Yeah."

I turn to look over my shoulder toward the giggles coming from behind us. Vivian gives me a thumbs-up and Dominique sends me a gigantic smile. "Happy birthday," they chorus.

"My birthday isn't for a few more days," I murmur, turning back to Sabastian.

He shrugs. "You once mentioned that you wanted to visit Paris with me. So yeah, see it as an early birthday present."

I wish I could capture the smile he has on right now because it's so adorable, so powerful, I can feel it permeating into my belly.

I jump at him and pepper him with kisses, making him release a staccato of chuckles. "What, like we're leaving right now?"

He raises his eyebrows with a thin smile and nods.

Epilogue
"Pictures of You"
The Cure

I blink one eye open. I flicker the second and flutter them both a couple of times more, adjusting my vision to the softly lit room. A few bright morning rays of sun waft through the velvety, burgundy curtains, coloring the room in a subtle pale rose hue. My eyes encounter the wooden coffered ceiling, and I smile, feeling wholeheartedly blissful. I crane my neck, pressing my cheek into the pillow, and drink in the man lying next to me who's steadily breathing, sound asleep. Sebastian is prone on the bed, his arms, toned and tanned, hugging the plump white pillows. His dark lashes caressing his sharp cheekbones. His full lips slightly parted, wordlessly chanting an incantation, luring me to taste them. The blanket is covering him up to his waist, allowing me a close view of his wide back and irresistible to touch mocha skin. A cluster of dark, silky hair is hiding his thick brow. I send my hand to brush it away gently. With feathery touches, I trace his lightly bristled cheek, taking a full of gratification, profound inhale.

"I love you," I whisper. I haven't used this sentence too often throughout my life, but whenever I did, I unreservedly meant it. And yet, I don't think that these three little words have ever had such an ample meaning for me. Quietly, I climb out of bed, taking extra care to keep it silent. I slide into my dress that has been hanging on a textured, golden picture frame, since last night. Courtesy of a very late, urgent, borderline aggressive, gotta-try-every-surface-of-the-suite boisterous sex. I adjust the painting back in place and reach for my phone, tucking it into the front pocket of Sebastian blazer I shrugged around me.

It's unclear what prompted me to wake up this early. But I don't really mind, it's worth it though because I get to see the city waking up and it's a unique feat to experience. A couple of stores away from where our hotel is located, a passage from The Avenue des Champs-Élysées, commonly described as the world's most beautiful avenue, I come across a corner old boulangerie, a French equivalent to Carbs Paradise. I let the lady in the salmon pink suit and the sophisticated up do putter around, open her store for the day and take a seat to wait on a nearby bench. Perfect time to call Kai.

"Hey, aren't you asleep?" I say as soon as he answers my call.

"Why are you calling if you thought I was asleep?"

"Because I can." I smile at the brief chuckle coming from the other end, a sound that always makes my lips twitch. The sound of Kai's voice to me is like wearing an old snuggly tee. Whenever I hear it, I'm bathed with comfort. "What are you doing up so late?" It should be around one am in his time zone.

"Working. Airbrushing the shit out of these photos I took as a favor to a friend of my mom's."

"Momma's pimpin' you?"

He chuckles. "Don't ask. A fucking bar mitzvah."

I break out in laughter. I can just imagine Kai at such an event. I bet he passed the night with his camera in one hand and an ever filling glass of scotch in the other. I can't see how he would have survived it any other way.

"And now you're making them look nice?"

"Let's just say nature isn't always kind."

"I love it when you're so thoughtful."

"Okay, we're done with me. What are you up to?"

"I'm in Paris." I swear my eyes just dreamingly closed on their own.

"No shit."

"An early birthday present from Sebastian."

"Dude's good. I need to up my game."

We both let out a light chuckle. It's easier laughing it off now, after the extensive and stern conversation Kay and I had when I made the decision to stay in Spain. His offer to "consummate" our pact and the seriousness of my relationship with Sebastian were two of the main subjects we dissected. A conversation in which Kai apologized, once more, for the way he acted in Spain. For being selfish rather than considering the implications of our friendship.

"Speaking of games, what kind of game are you playing with Stephy?"

There's a moment of silent. "We sort of hit it off whenever I visited you. We exchanged numbers and kept in touch. She is sweet, Liv."

"Mmmhmm."

"Incredibly sweet."

"Agree."

"I think I'll have to visit you again, soon."

"I think you should. Well, I have a date with my man and French pastry so I should probably go. Ta-ta."

By the time I end my call with Kai, salmon pink suit lady has officially opened the bakery. Though, really, calling this place plainly a bakery is pure blasphemy. It's more akin to the Mecca of baked goods. I'm welcomed by the fragrant aroma of freshly baked bread, a hint of rich cocoa, the light sweetness of sugar, zesty lemon and powdery, spicy cinnamon, as soon as I step in. Baguettes, glazed pastries, and mouth-watering croissants. My salivary gland is working overtime. I leave the little food utopia armed with a couple of pain au chocolat, a chocolate-filled puffed pastry, in one hand and two cups of café au lait in a carry tray in the other.

Sebastian is still peacefully asleep when I return to our room. I peel my clothes off down to my panties and put on one of Sebastian's undershirts.

"Buenas," a husky murmur comes from the bed. I turn around to a crooked smile and a squinting eye.

"Morning." I take a few steps toward the bed, setting the amazingly smelling loot I got on the little sidetable. Sebastian's hand snakes from under the cover and curls around my wrist.

"Come to bed."

God, his morning voice, all hoarse and coated by that accent. My salivary gland is over timing once more, only this time it has nothing to do with food.

I lift a finger, signaling "a moment please," and haste to the bathroom.

311

Sebastian is slouched high on a couple of pillows upon my return. Nearing the bed, I lift one leg, sinking my knee to one side of his pelvis. I bring my other leg to rest in the same position next to the other side of his hipbone. Gently, I lower my rear till I'm straddling him. Sabastian watches me attentively, his lip tipped to the side. I bring my index finger forward, the one I've smeared with a dab of toothpaste.

"Open up, handsome," I say in a ludicrous "sexy" voice and bring my finger near his mouth. Sebastian opens up over a grin and I rub my finger against his warm tongue. He chuckles and lightly bites my finger as I try to retrieve it.

"Now, where were we?" I dive with my mouth toward his. He meets me halfway, raising his upper body for our mouths to meet quicker. His hand finds the nape of my neck, his fingers combing my hair. I cross my legs around him, hugging his waist, my hands tracing up and downs his biceps.

As we leisurely ease back, I hand him one of the coffees. Sebastian shifts backward to lean on the headboard, carrying me along with him.

"Thank you for the best birthday present ever," I say, taking a sip from my paper cup. His response is a warm smile. He asks me if I spoke to my mom yet while we munch on the heavenly pastry and drink coffee.

"Yes, and it was a treat, just like I thought it would be." I've been pushing aside that phone call for a while. Around a week ago, I decided that the whole situation was absurd and finally called her with the news I knew she wouldn't easily gulp down. "I guess I have this innate talent for devoting myself to being something other than who I am, or doing things I don't want to do just so she will be pleased with me. And I told her so, together with the news that I won't be coming back." I snort in contempt. "She said it's my life I'm playing with, and since I'm not clever enough to take good advice, there's nothing much she could really do."

Sebastian shakes his head, his lips in a flat line.

"To make an annoyingly long and equally irritating long story short, I basically told her that as much as I love her, I don't really care what she thinks. So, yeah, she was ecstatic." Needless to say, that call didn't end with warm wishes of good luck or any sort of pleasantries, for that matter.

"Speaking of mothers who adore me, did your mom buy us the tickets here?"

Sebastian's eyes twitch at the corners and trail up to mine while his teeth sink into the pain au chocolat. He chews on the contents of his mouth with a smile under my animated gaze.

"She actually thought it was a great idea to take you here for your birthday." He wipes his grinning mouth with the back of his hand. I raise an eyebrow. "When I told her that you aren't going back home, after all, I think she realized there's actually a future for the two of us and she was glad. In fact, she was genuinely happy for me."

For a span of a moment, I process what he said and a smile blooms on my lips. "She actually gave me something to give you, but I'm not sure where it is now."

"She sent me a present?"

He tilts his head from side to side, considering my question.

"You could say that."

"What is it?"

Sebastian flips us over so I'm lying on the bed and he's on top of me.

"Tell me," I persist.

His lips feather the skin of my neck, reaching higher to my jaw, a little higher, reaching my lips. Unceremoniously, his tongue is plunged into my mouth, tasting divinely of chocolate and him. I melt into his kiss, and everything else forgotten.

The rest of the day passes lazily with naps, a late, light lunch due to extensive time spent in bed that had nothing to do with resting, and an easy walk along the river Seine.

Night has taken over the city and the air becomes chilly as we make our way back to the hotel after a perfect dinner in a small traditional restaurant. Sebastian takes off his jacket and shawls it around my shoulders as we walk in pleasant silence, admiring the beauty that is the Champs Elysees at night, with its old architecture and massive buildings beautifully illuminated with tiny lights.

Sebastian's arm embraces my waist, and he leans in to leave a soft kiss on my hair. "It's so incredibly beautiful here," I say.

He nods. "You know that you have this expression when you're at awe, or muddled, that I'm crazy about."

I scrunch my face in query, looking at him. "What expression?"

"Sort of like the one you are wearing right now, but not quite."

I cock my head with a faint smile.

"Come, I have an idea how to show you."

"What?" I ask through a giggle, letting him tug me after him, trying to figure out where he is taking us.

I giggle some more when we stop next to an old photo booth. "I didn't know these even existed anymore."

"Well, they do." His grin echoes mine. He gestures for me to get in with an exaggerated curtsy, and I obey, my smile intact. Sebastian's wide frame almost overflows the confined space. He takes a seat on the low stool and pulls me to sit sideways on his thighs.

"Hola." He smiles at me and gives me a quick kiss. He produces a couple of coins from his pocket and inserts them into the machine.

"So, about that expression of yours." He kisses me again over a unified smile as the first click sound indicates a photo has been taken. He hugs me, pressing his cheek against mine and says with humored lining, "Smile at the camera." And another click is heard.

I make a goofy face, looking ahead when all of a sudden he says, "Marry me." I'm sure he's managed to get the expression he was looking for, as in the next couple of shots the camera captures me utterly flabbergasted. When I finally regain my wits, I turn to look at him, my jaw still dropped and my eyes still wide open.

"Did you just?" I say and don't even let him answer. "Good one, you got me. Haha." I watch him carefully. "It was a joke, right?"

He returns my stare and twists his mouth, moving it from side to side. "Let me see, you are much older than me, and sometimes you are sort of too nitpicky and uptight, yeah, let's not forget uptight, and it took you almost forever to actually let me in, *and* you always have to taste my food. Umm, you know what, yeah;

maybe it wasn't such a great idea after all. Forget it. Joke. It was a joke."

Okay, now I'm even more shocked and a tad upset. Maybe hurt would be a more accurate way to describe how I feel. And mad. I'm also mad. Yeah, pretty damn ticked actually.

His lips tip up at my riled expression, and he chuckles. He looks down at the tiny square floor of the booth and then at me.

"Can you please stand up on the stool for me?"

I'm too stunned even to argue, and while I'm absorbed in composing the mother of all tirades, I do as told. When my anger is about to catch up with my vocal cords, he sends his arms around my thighs and tilts his head up to look at me. I look down at him and he returns my blazed gaze with a warm one.

"So, since I can't do the whole getting on one knee thing in this damn narrow place, this will do." I move my hands to his shoulders for support because the combination of the flimsy stool I'm standing on and the fact that I'm starting to lightly shake is not the greatest combination. "You okay?" he asks. "I was just messing with you, Liv."

I'm not sure I am okay because my heartbeat is a mile a minute as I wait for him to go on, but I still nod.

After a silent beat, looking at me with soulful eyes, Sebastian asks. "Liv, would you marry me?"

I can feel my features wavering from joy to overwhelming emotion and back to happiness. For an extent of a loaded moment, every possible positive emotion runs through me.

"Of course." It's a weak whisper because it's the only sound I can produce given my throat is swelled. Sebastian grabs me by my hips and helps me down, right into his arms. Right into his embrace. Right onto his mouth. I sense him searching his pocket while we continue to kiss tenderly. He slowly breaks off our kiss, tilting back to look at me.

He takes my hand in his and slowly slides an antique looking, elegant ring with a blue sapphire, studded with a halo of diamonds on my finger. Mesmerized, I look at the ring now decorating my hand and bring my eyes to his.

"It's so beautiful! I love it."

"It belonged to my grandmother. Remember that thing my mom gave me to give you?"

"I love you beyond words." I throw my arms around him, pressing my face to his noticeably beating heart, happier than I've ever been in my life.

Long moments have passed when I finally slowly ease my lips back from my fiancé. Sebastian reaches his hand to the machine in front of us to fish out the photo strip with two fingers. He gives it a peek and grins. Pressed snuggly into the side of his biceps, I lower my head to have a glance.

"This expression," he says, and our smiles expand.

It feels like my journey to find happiness has finally come to an end at this very instant. Lastly, I understand the true secret of being genuinely content as I look into the eyes of the man I'm ready to spend the rest of my life with. It's about not following the path. It's about drawing your own map, even if it's not the easiest way to reach your destination. Because then at least you own it and it's entirely yours. And you need to remember to do it while accepting and loving yourself. Loving yourself *with* that couple of extra pounds and the things you sometimes utter with so little thought. With all the imperfections that make you who you are because, above all else, you can't leave your true self behind. Yes, in the end, it's about experiencing it all and having that special someone to share it with. The one who makes you feel at home no matter where you are. Because a real home is not a dot on the globe or four walls and a roof.

Home is where your heart chooses to be.

Ah! Let's see you one up this pearl of wisdom, Dr. Smartass!

Note from the Author

Dear Reader,

Thank you *so much* for taking the time to read LEAVING ME BEHIND.

Leaving Me Behind is the first full length novel I've ever written. It's also the first book I've ever rewritten. It's the first book that has some of my own life's experiences from living as an expat for the greater part of my life, laced in the story.

Besides being "my first," this is also the first book I was about to give up on. Yes, I was minutes away from letting it rest in peace, buried in a folder for ever after. But I'm glad I didn't and hope you feel the same way! ☺

So, if you have any extra time, it would be great, REALLY GREAT, if you leave a review where you bought it. ;-)

Also, I more than love hearing from my readers, honestly, it's the best part of the whole writing process. So, send me an email at: author.sehrlich@gmail.com or chat with me on Facebook.

Thank you for allowing me to share my stories with you, and I hope to be re-invited to your bookshelf with my next releases.

Again, THANK YOU!

Loads of x's & o's,

Sigal

Acknowledgments

LEAVING ME BEHIND is the first full length novel I've ever written. It's also the first book I've ever rewritten. It's the first book that has some of my own life's experiences from living as an expat for the greater part of my life, laced in the story.

Besides being "my first," this is also the first book I was about to give up on. Yes, I was minutes away from letting it rest in peace, buried in a folder for ever after. But I'm glad I didn't. Eventually writing it turned out an entertaining, introspective and beautiful journey.

It's a book about following your dreams and learning that the *road*, *hope* and *aspiration* are a great part of the ride, if not the actual reward. It's a book about finding yourself, true friendships, and last but definitely not least, unexpected love.

For me, just like Liv, being an expat, raised more than once, the big questions: where is home, and what does it stand for?

And just like Liv realizes that home is not a location on the globe, or four walls and a roof, but where your heart chooses to be - for me, no matter where I actually am, the US, Europe or the Middle East, *home has always been and will be* where my three nutty kiddos and my (definitely) better half are.

Some gigantic, heartfelt thank yous for those who helped, encouraged, and shared with me the beautiful experience of writing this book.

Beth, Beth, Beth… I think thank you doesn't even begin to cover how grateful I am to you. *Thank you for making this book happen!* Thank you for listening, reading, editing, laughing, shedding a tear (or two) and mostly, loving the story and characters as much as I do.

My Betas, Teele, Hila, Ravit, Beth and Nicole. Big, fat, thanks!

Nicole Hornbaker, for your magnificent work and your priceless suggestions. I can't imagine writing a book without you somehow involved.

Jenny, for all the hard work and professionalism. Jenny, I think this is the beginning of a beautiful friendship.

Ravit, for your time and dedication, the laughter, sarcasm, ideas, and suggestions. It's always a blast working with you on the final TLC touches of a book. I'm beyond thankful for all your help.

Anais Chevalier, for helping with the French translations. Merci!

Pilar Paz, Muchas gracias por la ayuda con el Español

Capy and Sylvie, well, for existing.

Gal, as always, for making this thrilling journey called life as great.

My kiddos, for being as perfect as you are and still loving me unconditionally even with less mommy-time.

My cyber BFF, my favorite author, my dear, dear friend Olivia Luck, for being you.

For Artie, just because!

BLOGGERS, truly incredible bloggers. I'm forever grateful and humbled by your continuous support. You are simply the best.

Special gigantic gratitude to some special ladies: Julie B., Sharon T., Bianca T., Kelly S., Lies, Carmie, the sweet, sweet Tatia, and the lovely ladies at *Love Between the Sheets*.

And last but not least, my readers. Since Layers was released I've been constantly overwhelmed by your response. You guys are truly amazing and I could have not asked for better readers.

Thank you! Thank you, and then some. Thank you for reviewing, messaging, emailing, loving, liking, spreading the word. You rock big time!

Also by Sigal Ehrlich

Layers

Inner Core

Retrace

About the Author

By teen age, Sigal already lived in three different continents where she was lucky enough to experience and visit varied places, meet unique people, which only helped fuel her overly developed imagination. Currently, Sigal calls Estonia home where she lives with her husband and three kids.

Not exactly sure where they will end up next ...

Sigal would love to hear from you, please visit her on her website, Twitter, and Facebook.

http://www.sigalehrlich.com/
@Sigal_Ehrlich
https://www.facebook.com/sigalehrlich.author
http://www.pinterest.com/authorsehrlich/
auhtor.sehrlich@gmail.com

www.ingramcontent.com/pod-product-compliance
Lightning Source LLC
Chambersburg PA
CBHW020217260626
47156CB00002B/428